PRAISE FOR DONNA GRANT'S
BEST-SELLING ROMANCE NOVELS

"Grant's ability to quickly convey complicated backstory makes this jam-packed love story accessible even to new or periodic readers." - *Publisher's Weekly*

"Donna Grant has given the paranormal genre a burst of fresh air…" – *San Francisco Book Review*

"The premise is dramatic and heartbreaking; the characters are colorful and engaging; the romance is spirited and seductive." – *The Reading Cafe*

"The central romance, fueled by a hostage drama, plays out in glorious detail against a backdrop of multiple ongoing issues in the "Dark Kings" books. This seemingly penultimate installment creates a nice segue to a climactic end." – *Library Journal*

"…intense romance amid the growing war between the Dragons and the Dark Fae is scorching hot." – *Booklist*

A Dragon's Tale (Whisky and Wishes: *A Holiday Novella*,

Heart of Gold: *A Valentine's Novella*, & Of Fire and Flame)

My Fiery Valentine ~ The Dragon King Coloring Book

Dragon King Special Edition Character Coloring Book: Rhi

DARK WARRIORS SERIES

Midnight's Master ~ Midnight's Lover ~ Midnight's Seduction

Midnight's Warrior ~ Midnight's Kiss ~ Midnight's Captive

Midnight's Temptation ~ Midnight's Promise

Midnight's Surrender

CHIASSON SERIES

Wild Fever ~ Wild Dream ~ Wild Need

Wild Flame ~ Wild Rapture

LARUE SERIES

Moon Kissed ~ Moon Thrall ~ Moon Struck ~ Moon Bound

WICKED TREASURES

Seized by Passion ~ Enticed by Ecstasy ~ Captured by Desire

Books 1-3: Wicked Treasures Box Set

HISTORICAL PARANORMAL

THE KINDRED SERIES

Everkin ~ Eversong ~ Everwylde ~ Everbound

Evernight ~ Everspell

KINDRED: THE FATED SERIES

Rage

DARK SWORD SERIES

Dangerous Highlander ~ Forbidden Highlander

Wicked Highlander ~ Untamed Highlander

Shadow Highlander ~ Darkest Highlander

ROGUES OF SCOTLAND SERIES

The Craving ~ The Hunger ~ The Tempted ~ The Seduced

Books 1-4: Rogues of Scotland Box Set

THE SHIELDS SERIES

A Dark Guardian ~ A Kind of Magic ~ A Dark Seduction

A Forbidden Temptation ~ A Warrior's Heart

Mystic Trinity (a series connecting novel)

DRUIDS GLEN SERIES

Highland Mist ~ Highland Nights ~ Highland Dawn

Highland Fires ~ Highland Magic

Mystic Trinity (a series connecting novel)

SISTERS OF MAGIC TRILOGY

Shadow Magic ~ Echoes of Magic ~ Dangerous Magic

Books 1-3: Sisters of Magic Box Set

THE ROYAL CHRONICLES NOVELLA SERIES

Prince of Desire ~ Prince of Seduction

Prince of Love ~ Prince of Passion

Books 1-4: The Royal Chronicles Box Set

Mystic Trinity (a series connecting novel)

DARK BEGINNINGS: A FIRST IN SERIES BOXSET

Chiasson Series, Book 1: Wild Fever

LaRue Series, Book 1: Moon Kissed

The Royal Chronicles Series, Book 1: Prince of Desire

~

MILITARY ROMANCE / ROMANTIC SUSPENSE

SONS OF TEXAS SERIES

The Hero ~ The Protector ~ The Legend

The Defender ~ The Guardian

COWBOY / CONTEMPORARY

HEART OF TEXAS SERIES

The Christmas Cowboy Hero ~ Cowboy, Cross My Heart

My Favorite Cowboy ~ A Cowboy Like You

Looking for a Cowboy ~ A Cowboy Kind of Love

~

STAND ALONE BOOKS

That Cowboy of Mine

Home for a Cowboy Christmas

Mutual Desire

Forever Mine

Savage Moon

~

Check out Donna Grant's Online Store at

www.DonnaGrant.com/shop

for autographed books, character themed goodies, and more!

DARK ALPHA'S COMMAND

REAPERS, BOOK 15

DONNA GRANT

DEAR READER

The time has come for Balladyn's book. For a character who was never supposed to have lasted more than a couple of books—much less been redeemed—he's certainly made his mark on me and so many other readers. He's taken me to some dark places, but he's also shown me things that made me soon realize there was so much more to Balladyn than I first thought.

It's not the first time I've redeemed a character. Honestly, it's never my intention. It just sort of happens. It's an amazing process, because I'm always as shocked as you, the reader. Just when I thought I knew how Balladyn's story would end, he surprised me again. I'm coming to expect it from him. And I'll freely admit that he's become one of my all-time favorite characters to write.

This book. Well, it was *agonizing* to write. Even more so when I read through it to do my corrections. And I won't even discuss the edits. This book was…difficult. Yet, now as I sit before the finished product, anxiously waiting for it to reach you, I can't help but smile. There's nothing about Balladyn that has been easy, and he proved that with his book. I probably should've seen it coming, but I didn't.

It still boggles my mind that what began as a single series back in 2008 has morphed into five series that encompass the Dark World. I look back at starting from the *Dark Sword* series to the *Dark Warriors* to the *Dark Kings*, then the *Reapers*, and onto the *Dragon Kings* as well as upcoming the *Skye Druids* series.

For those who have read the *Reapers*, you'll know that the series crosses over into the *Dark Kings/Dragon Kings* often, and vice versa. Because all these series are part of the overall Dark World, it makes sense that there is cross over. Dark Alpha's Command, while being a *Reaper* book, is actually the start of the spin-off series, the *Skye Druids*.

I've had a love of Druids for a long time. So much so that I tend to add them in whatever series I'm working on. The MacLeod Druids first show up in the *Dark Sword* and *Dark Warriors* series, and I'm happy to report that if you've read those books, you'll see some familiar names pop up in DAC. Consequently, if you've not read the *Dark Sword/Dark Warriors* series, then you'll get to meet them in this book, and you can go back to their series to find out about each couple and the villains they vanquished.

To help with those whose eyes are crossing (believe me, I know! I write these books, and I *still* get confused sometimes), let me break it down for you by series:

Dark Sword – 6 books set in Medieval Scotland.

Dark Warriors – 8 book/1 novella set in modern-day Scotland (a continuation of the DS series). Same characters, just time traveled to modern times.

Dark Kings – 18 books/10 novellas/6 short stories/2 coloring books set in modern-day Scotland. Also known as the Dragon Kings.

Reapers – 15 books/1 short story set in modern-day Ireland and Scotland.

Dragon Kings – Spinoff of the Dark Kings. 2 book/2 novellas so far. Set in a fantasy world named Zora.

Skye Druids – Spinoff of the Reapers. Set on the Isle of Skye. First book, **IRON EMBER**, releases October 2022.

As always, I'm beyond honored that you've taken this journey with me. Whether this is your first book of mine to read, or your hundredth, I'm forever grateful to share my stories with you.

xoxox,
DG

CHAPTER ONE

Death's Realm

Balladyn's eyes snapped open, his heart racing as he gasped for breath. The yawning, opaque terror occurred abruptly, like a hard punch to the gut. Only one thought went through his head: *find it.*

Without hesitation, he teleported to the Fae doorway. Just before he stepped through, he remembered his vow to Death. Balladyn clenched his jaw at the physical pain that gripped him when he halted. He needed to find Erith and tell her what was happening. But the thought of wasting that time when he could be searching for whatever called to him made him want to bellow with annoyance.

He was being pulled in two.

"Balladyn."

Erith's calm voice reached him. He turned his head to the goddess and stared into her lavender eyes.

She looked him over before lifting her chin, a small frown puckering her forehead. "What is it?"

"I…don't…know," he managed to get out. The alarm and distress were so boundless he could barely speak. He braced his hands on either side of the doorway. It was the only way to stop himself from just walking through—and hopefully ending the torment that had him in its merciless grip.

Erith nodded to someone on Balladyn's other side. He didn't bother to look. It was most likely her consort, Cael. Balladyn dropped his chin to his chest. He had to go. He *needed* to leave.

Right that instant. If he didn't…

"You want to leave."

It wasn't a question. "I have to," he ground out. His body shook as he fought to remain where he was. Every second was excruciating. If he left, the agony would end. He didn't know how he knew that, only that the knowledge was there.

"Tell me what's happening."

He squeezed his eyes shut. The words stuck in his throat as the pain intensified. The compulsion to find whatever called to him across the realms was too great to resist. He parted his lips, wanting to tell Erith what he felt, but he couldn't. Balladyn pushed away from the doorway and started to walk through it.

"Wait," Death commanded in a sharp tone.

Her order froze him immediately. The ensuing deluge of despair made him throw back his head and bellow. He had to get…*fek*. He had no idea where he needed to go, only that he had to go. Immediately.

"Follow him. Don't let him out of your sight," he heard Erith say. Then, "Go, Balladyn."

The instant she released him, he was through the doorway. He let whatever pulled him determine his course. He was mildly startled to find himself not just on Earth but in Belfast. He paused long enough to orient himself in the narrow, old-town street. The night was cold and rainy. Lights strung over the road and suspended from each building lit the area and reflected in the puddles on the ground as locals and tourists rushed to get out of the rain.

Balladyn didn't look behind him to see who followed. All that mattered was locating who or what had reached through time and space to him. His head snapped to the right when he felt the sharp tug again. He strode down the street until he came to a narrow alley.

He heard nothing over the steady beat of the rain. When he turned to go down the lane, he felt a hand on his shoulder.

"This could be a trap," Eoghan cautioned.

Balladyn looked into the molten, silver eyes of the Reaper who led their team. "I have to."

Eoghan released him and nodded, letting Balladyn know without words that his team was there and would watch his back.

Balladyn blinked the rain from his eyes and started walking. With every step, something urged him to hurry. He was running by the time he reached the end where it opened to a small area. He slid to a stop and let his gaze scan the space. It was dark and quiet. Nothing stirred. Then he smelled it—blood.

The sound of a slight cough reached him. His head swung to the side, and he made out the shape of someone on the ground. Balladyn rushed over. The instant he knelt and saw the red hair, his breath caught. He found himself staring into the beautiful face of Rhona, the head of the Skye Druids.

"What the hell?" Bradach asked in a shocked whisper.

Balladyn glanced down at Rhona's body and found her hands clutching her abdomen, blood running quickly through her fingers. Her heartbeat was faint, her breathing shallow. She wouldn't live much longer. Certainly not long enough for him to get her anywhere that someone could help her.

Another bellow rose within him. He didn't know what Rhona was doing in Ireland or what had happened to her, but he couldn't let her die. Not like this.

"Rhona? Open your eyes," he begged. "Look at me."

But she didn't move. Suddenly, he remembered reading about some ancient magic in one of the books in his library. Without hesitation, the words he had read filled his mind. The magic sprang forth and wrapped around Rhona.

"What the hell did you just do?" Ruarc demanded.

Balladyn lifted Rhona in his arms. "I have a library of books. I made use of some ancient knowledge in one. This won't last long. She's lost too much blood. We have to get her to safety."

"She could be a trap for us. I hate to say it, but the Six could've learned of our connection to Skye through Sorcha and me," Cathal said.

Rordan grunted. "Not only is Rhona Sorcha's cousin, but she's also the leader of the Druids."

"We'll find our answers later," Eoghan said. "Cathal, fill Erith in on everything and return with Sorcha. Dubhan and Bradach, you two take a look around. See if you can spot any of the Fae Others, the Six, or their soldiers. The rest of us are going to Skye."

Balladyn didn't wait for Eoghan to finish speaking before teleporting inside Rhona's cottage. It was dark inside, but he saw well enough to make his way down the hall to her bedroom. He gently laid her on the bed. When he stepped back and saw the blood on his arms, his heart clutched painfully.

"What now?" Rordan asked.

Balladyn turned his head to Eoghan. "We need Druids."

"Can we trust them?" Ruarc questioned.

Eoghan blew out a breath as he flipped on the light in the room. "We don't have a choice. Rhona needs their healing."

No sooner had he spoken the words than Cathal arrived with Sorcha. Tears welled in her eyes the minute the Druid spotted Rhona on the bed. "I'll get the others," Sorcha said and turned to her mate.

The urgency driving Balladyn had stopped when he found Rhona. He didn't know if she had called to him or if it had been something else. As far as he knew, no one could penetrate time and space to reach a Fae other than Death. Not even someone as powerful as Rhi could do that. So how had the message reached him?

"The Druids aren't going to be happy to see all of us," Eoghan pointed out. "We need to remain veiled."

Ruarc grimaced. "Should we even stay?"

"I'm not leaving her," Balladyn stated.

Eoghan quickly said, "None of us is. We need to know what happened."

They could only get answers through Rhona, and only if the Druid lived. Balladyn kept his gaze on her hands. There was more blood than he'd initially realized. It soaked her wet clothes. The magic he used had paused it, but he had no idea how long that would last. The Druids needed to get there. Soon.

They heard approaching cars. Balladyn regretfully moved away from the bed and veiled himself. He never took his eyes off Rhona as he backed himself against the wall just as the Druids rushed into the room with Sorcha.

Disbelief registered on all their faces, but they held their tongues and took their places around the bed. They held their hands over Rhona's body just as the blood started to pour through her fingers once more. The Druids began to chant. Balladyn's chest squeezed with an iron-vise grip as he silently urged them to go faster. He would've offered his magic if he thought it would have done any good.

Rhona's flame-red hair lay wet and limp against the dark blue sheets, and the moisture from her soaked clothes seeped into the bed linens. Her skin remained pale, the kind of sunken pastiness that preceded death. He fisted his hands, feeling another bellow rising. Balladyn had no idea what was wrong with him. It had been a long time since he had lost control of his emotions as he had earlier with Death.

The Druid leader might not be a huge fan of the Fae, but she had recently helped the Reapers. What could she have gotten herself mixed up in that'd left her dying alone on a street in Ireland? The more he thought about it, the more he had to know the answer. One way or another, he would find out everything.

Tense minutes passed in unbearable slowness before Balladyn saw color begin to return to Rhona's face. He didn't breathe easy until the Druids slowed their chanting and then finally stopped. He eyed the group of five, noting the sweat on their faces, their ragged breaths, and the exhaustion in their expressions. Saving Rhona had taken a lot of healing magic.

"What the bloody hell is going on?"

Balladyn slid his gaze to the man who had spoken, his Scot's brogue thick. His dark blond hair was cut short. He was of average height with a stocky body and a fuzzy beard that looked like an animal living on his face. He directed his close-set brown eyes at Sorcha.

"You know as much as I do, Evan," she replied.

He snorted. "Somehow, I doubt that."

Cathal, who had remained by his mate's side since he had gone with her to gather the Druids, glared at Evan. "She's not lying."

"Enough," said an older woman, her gaze directed at Evan. "Kerry, Lyra, and I will get Rhona cleaned up. When we're finished and rested, we can talk."

Sorcha nodded. "I'll help you."

Balladyn looked at Eoghan and shook his head, letting Eoghan know that he wasn't leaving Rhona for a second.

Eoghan flattened his lips but issued a brief nod before motioning for the other veiled Reapers to leave the room. They teleported out quickly after. Balladyn watched Cathal lean down and whisper something to Sorcha before Cathal's gaze briefly met his. Cathal then turned on his heel and walked out.

"Thank you, Violet," Sorcha said as she walked to the woman.

Violet didn't smile. She had her gray hair trimmed in a short bob that ended right below her ears. Locking her blue eyes on Rhona, she twisted her hands nervously. Despite the lines on her face, Balladyn could still see hints of the beauty she had once been.

"That magic was…" Lyra couldn't finish. She shook her head of black curls currently pulled away from her face by a scarf. Deep brown eyes lifted to look between Sorcha and Violet. Her dark skin still wore a sheen of sweat. "I didn't think we would be able to heal the wounds."

"There were so many of them," Kerry whispered and gently touched Rhona's cheek. She shifted her full-figured body, her short, thin brown hair hanging limp around her full face.

Anger churned within Balladyn. *Who* had done this to Rhona? And why?

"We healed her," Sorcha said.

Though they didn't say it, Balladyn saw that they believed they had come very close to losing Rhona. His hesitation in leaving Death's realm when he'd first felt the pull had nearly resulted in her death. If he had waited even another few seconds, she would likely be dead. That thought made him want to destroy something.

Violet shook herself. "Come. Let's get Rhona changed and cleaned. She doesn't need to see any of this when she wakes."

While the four of them removed Rhona's clothes and wiped away the blood, he let his mind wander back to the alley where he had found her. Balladyn went over everything in his mind's eye, trying to see if he had missed someone or something. When he looked at the bed again, Rhona was dressed in a black shirt and lying beneath fresh sheets. Kerry was the first to leave the room. Violet and Lyra both touched Sorcha's shoulder before they, too, filed out.

The half-Fae, half-Druid stared at the bed as she said, "Thank you for finding her, Balladyn."

He lowered his veil and bowed his head to her.

Tears fell down her face when she turned to him. "How did you know where she was?"

"I have no answer. I've never felt anything like it before."

She nodded slowly. "The Druids will want to know."

"Eoghan or Cathal can tell them everything. They and a few others were with me. I'm not leaving Rhona's side."

Sorcha tucked an auburn curl behind her ear and smiled before she left.

Balladyn swung his gaze back to Rhona. How had he known that she was hurt? Was she the one who had called to him? Skye Druids were the most powerful of all Druids on the realm, but he hadn't known she had that ability.

If it had been her.

But who else could it have been?

CHAPTER TWO

The sickening feeling of the knives entering her body made Rhona want to scream in pain and fury. She had walked into an ambush.

By her own kind.

The very thought made retribution burn hotly inside her. Her killers had known what they were doing. They hadn't just struck with blades—they had also used magic. The spell had been dark and foul, with words she had never heard uttered before, but she'd had enough wherewithal even through the agony to try and block it. Unfortunately, she hadn't been successful. Not completely. Enough of their spell had gotten through.

But not all of it.

That was the only reason she was still alive. When they left her for dead, she managed to roll onto her side and then attempted to crawl somewhere she could be found and, hopefully, saved. Of course, she might have only prolonged her death. Had the spell worked, she would have likely breathed her last before her assailants left.

Tears filled her eyes and fell down her cheeks to mix with the rain. Pain unlike anything she had experienced before consumed her, devoured her. There wasn't a single place on her body that didn't scream in anguish. The feel of her warm, thick blood rushing from her wounds and through her fingers was another reminder that her life drained away with every beat of her heart.

She fought hard to stay alive, even though she knew it was next to impossible that she would return to Skye and warn the Druids of what was coming. She screamed, but it never escaped her lips, only echoed through her head. The spell. What had they done to her?

Trepidation and anger roiled in her belly as she screamed again. Over and over, she yelled. For her stupidity in walking into a trap, for not being more aware, for not getting her magic up in time, for…failing.

The rain beat upon her body in a steady tempo. She wondered how far she had gotten while crawling. Was she close to anyone? She couldn't hear anything over the rain. When she tried to move again, the agony that tore through her left her wheezing. She stilled, knowing she was going to die alone in a dirty alley.

Rhona didn't know how long she sat there before she realized that it wasn't the rain she heard at all but rather distant drums. The Ancients. She had been a small child the first and only time she had heard them. Did they come for all Druids when they died? Would she find her place among them? Did she even belong?

The drums grew louder, and along with them came soft chanting that she couldn't understand. She strained, trying to hear what the Ancients said.

"Rhona? Open your eyes. Look at me."

The deep voice calmed her instantly. It wasn't an Ancient. It was someone close. She knew it, but she couldn't place who it belonged to, and trying was energy she couldn't expend. Everything went to staying alive.

Something washed over her, easing her pain. She wanted to open her eyes and see who it was, to answer him. However, she could do nothing but release her screams in her head. There was so much she needed to say. She had to warn her brethren on Skye. They needed to know what was coming.

"I'm not leaving her."

That voice again. Some of the fear that had gripped her so

tightly loosened. She didn't know if the voice was a figment of her imagination or if the man was really there. He had a nice Irish accent. A face began to form in her mind. Just as it was coming into focus, pain lashed through her once more, and the vision vanished like smoke.

Rhona fought for as long as she could, but she was quickly losing energy. She felt the black fingers of death reaching for her. She hadn't been the Druids' leader for long, and she had done a horrible job. How had she allowed herself to be ambushed? Now, she was going to die without being able to warn those on Skye. What had Corann been thinking in choosing her as his replacement?

She let out a final scream of dread, frustration, and resentment. Rhona wanted to hear the man's voice one last time before the darkness took her for good. She listened, hoping he would say something else, but she was alone.

Like always.

When death's grip took hold, she didn't fight it. Maybe she would find peace in the afterlife. Just as she was giving up, a wash of magic wrapped around her. Then she began to hear the drums again. When had they stopped? Oh, yes, with the voice.

She started to feel heavy. Though she wanted to remain aware, she began drifting as if on a softly moving river. It was as if she were basking in the warm sun as the light enveloped her. The pain that had racked her eased with each exhale before she found herself being pulled under by a healing sleep.

Rhona's eyes snapped open. Had it all been a nightmare? She stared at the ceiling of her bedroom. There was no rain, no darkness or killers waiting. She tugged her arms from beneath the covers and looked at her hands, seeing they were clean of the blood that had rushed through her fingers. Tears welled in her eyes. She could move freely again. Nothing hindered her. How she wished everything she remembered had been a nightmare, but she knew it wasn't.

She gazed around the room, looking for anyone who might be with her, but she was alone. She threw back the covers and swung her legs over the side of the bed. Her knees were unstable when she got to her feet. She carefully walked to the mirror hanging on the back of her door and braced one hand on the wood to steady herself. The clothes she had worn were gone, replaced by some lounge clothes from her drawers.

She took in her abdomen in the mirror. She could still feel the blades as they punctured her skin and sank into muscle, bone, and organs. Her hand shook as she carefully lifted the hem of her shirt. The wounds were healed, though the puckered skin around them was still pink. She squeezed her eyes closed as she recalled the pain.

She released her shirt and used the mirror to look at the corner behind her. Someone was there. Someone she knew. She waited to feel panic or alarm, but found only calm.

"Show yourself," she demanded.

For a heartbeat, nothing happened. Then a Fae lowered their veil. But it wasn't just any Fae, it was a Reaper. And one she knew.

She met Balladyn's red eyes in the mirror. He had the top half of his long, black and silver hair pulled away from his face. Like all Fae, he was heart-stoppingly gorgeous but had an air about him that was different than the rest. Something that set him apart from any other. She gazed at his strong jaw and chin. He had thick-lashed eyes and lips that were full and should look feminine but didn't. He was a man that would make anyone do a double-take. Add his tall form with defined sinew that wasn't too large, and the complete package would take anyone's breath away.

Including hers.

He said nothing, but he didn't need to. She knew in that moment that he was the one who had found her. It was his voice that she had heard, the one that had given her peace.

"You shouldn't know I'm here," he finally said.

She ignored his frown and pushed away from the door to face him. Bloody hell, she was weak. "You found me."

"Aye."

"How?"

"I was hoping you could tell me."

Now it was her turn to frown. "What do you mean? I couldn't speak."

He drew in a deep breath that caused his shoulders to lift in his charcoal shirt. "I felt something that drew me to you."

She looked away, trying to think how that was possible.

"It'll take time, but you'll forget about what happened."

Rhona jerked her gaze back to him. When he nodded at her, she realized that she had been rubbing her stomach over the healing wounds. She immediately dropped her arm. "I don't think I'll ever forget the feeling of the blades being shoved into me."

"You'll never forget that. Or the pain that accompanied it. But, eventually, the scene replaying in your head will get fuzzier. It'll become harder for you to pull up details."

She had always found Balladyn interesting, even when she didn't want to. His latest statement made him more so. "You were ambushed?"

"I was betrayed." He paused and swallowed. "The Druids' healing magic brought you back from the brink of death. Your wounds look good. You may not even have scars."

At least not ones anyone could see. But they would always be there. She stared into his red eyes.

"Everyone is waiting to talk to you."

She shook her head. "I'm not ready."

"You can only put them off for so long," he cautioned.

Rhona couldn't seem to look away from him. How odd that she used to make fun of the Irish and their accent. Now, she couldn't seem to get enough of his voice. "You stayed with me, didn't you?"

He hesitated before nodding once.

She'd thought she was finished with tears, but her eyes burned with them again. She tried to blink them back. "Thank you."

"What happened?"

One tear dropped to her cheek. She swiped it away, but another took its place. Then another. She put her back against the wall and slid to the floor. She knew she needed to tell everyone what'd happened, but it kept replaying in her head on repeat. The horror, the terror taking hold over and over.

Balladyn was suddenly squatting before her. He didn't touch her, but she wished he would. She needed something to ground her, but she didn't have the courage to reach out to him.

"You're safe now," he said.

She sniffed and wiped her nose with the back of her hand. "I'll never be safe again."

"Tell me who it was. I'll find them."

Rhona blinked at the fury in his words and the spark of vengeance in his eyes. That only made the tears come faster. No one had ever said anything like that to her before. "Why?"

"Because you called to me through time and space."

"I didn't mean to bring you into this."

He touched her face with the back of his fingers and gently swiped at a tear. "I'm not sorry for that."

The door opened, breaking into their conversation. Rhona looked up to find Sorcha. Her cousin's face crumpled as she dropped to her knees and wrapped her arms around her. Rhona returned the embrace while she watched Balladyn teleport back to his corner.

"How are you feeling?" Sorcha asked as she leaned back.

Rhona forced a smile. "Better. Thank you for your help."

"We've been worried sick. You slept for such a long time. Hours and hours. Most everyone left. Violet and Lyra remained, though. Are you ready to talk?"

"No," she answered honestly. Then she licked her lips. "But I will. All of you need to hear this."

Sorcha glanced at Balladyn. "Everyone knows Cathal is here, but not the others."

"Of course, your mate would be with you. It's to be expected. No one needs to know about anyone else."

Sorcha climbed to her feet and held out her hand. The time for Rhona to hide in her room and cry was over. She grasped her cousin's hand, and Sorcha pulled her up. Rhona looked at Balladyn.

"I'm not going anywhere," he whispered.

The relief she felt at his words staggered her. She couldn't explain why she, a powerful Druid in her own right, felt safe with him near. She flashed him the first genuine smile she'd been able to conjure since she had woken.

"You need to be veiled," Sorcha told him.

Rhona squared her shoulders and mentally shielded herself from the onslaught of emotions that would come her way when she spoke of what'd happened. She found her slippers and her favorite cream cardigan before walking from the room.

CHAPTER THREE

Balladyn steadied himself before teleporting, veiled, into the main area of the cottage. Fire danced in the hearth, the logs popping occasionally. A couple of candlesticks and pictures adorned the mantel. A cinnamon candle had been lit, and the scent softly floated through the rooms. A dark gray sofa sat beneath a window across from the fireplace, a black-and-green-tartan throw draped over one side and matching pillows placed artfully on the cushions. A well-worn, brown leather reading chair sat to one side. There was a glass coffee table and a smaller side table between the chair and sofa, where Balladyn spotted a pair of reading glasses sitting atop a book. A dark green shag rug filled the space.

The cozy warmth of the fire and the décor gave the place a comforting ambiance that Balladyn liked. He wanted to tell Rhona, but the two Druids were in the room, with more to arrive soon.

Balladyn watched both Violet and Lyra embrace Rhona, their affection for their leader evident. Still, he observed them closely. After all, she had said it had been an ambush. That didn't mean it had anything to do with the Druids on Skye, but until he had more information, everyone was a suspect.

"You gave us a fright," Violet said as she took Rhona's hands and smiled.

Sorcha walked in from the kitchen, carrying a tray filled with cups and a teapot. She set it on the coffee table and poured some into a mug, adding honey before handing it to Rhona. "This will help."

"Thanks," Rhona murmured and slowly lowered herself on one side of the sofa.

Balladyn let his gaze move over her oval face, taking in the delicate features and the smattering of freckles across her nose and under her eyes. He especially liked how a thick red lock fell across one cheek. Her large, expressive eyes were a beautiful, vibrant shade of green that stopped him in his tracks every time she focused on him. And her lips…he couldn't look at them without imagining what she would taste like.

She was trim but had curves that she didn't mind showing. Despite what she had just endured, she held herself regally, hiding any vulnerability. There was strength inside her that he didn't think she realized yet. She was being tested, though. He suspected that everyone would find out just what type of Druid she was.

And he hoped he was there to see it.

Balladyn glanced away from her as Dubhan and Bradach arrived, yet his gaze returned to the Druid quickly. Rhona was a beautiful woman. He had acknowledged that from the first time he had seen her, but something had changed within him. It had to be because he had found her in Belfast. Now that she was healed, he couldn't take his eyes from her.

Rhona brought the mug to her lips and took a sip as her gaze lifted in his direction.

Balladyn frowned. That was the second time she had known where he was. There was no way she should have been able to see him while veiled. Could she see him or just sense him? Was it him alone, or could she do that with any Reaper?

He happened to glance to the side and noticed Eoghan scowling at him. Balladyn looked away. No doubt Eoghan had noticed where

Rhona's gaze had gone. Eoghan would have his answers as soon as Balladyn did.

The room's energy was subdued as they waited for the arrival of the other three members who had healed her. The Druids no longer outnumbered the residents on Skye. Less than half of those who called Skye home were Druids. Rhona was their leader, chosen by the former head of the Skye Druids, Corann. Five deputies were also chosen to carry information from the head of the group to the rest of the Druids.

A knock sounded on the door. Cathal opened it, and the same three Druids from earlier filed into the cottage—two men and the buxom, older woman named Kerry. They greeted Rhona with smiles and what appeared to be genuine warmth. Balladyn hoped for her sake that no one close to her was the one who'd betrayed her —though that was generally how it went.

The Reapers had to quickly teleport out of the way when the three others found places to sit or stand in the cramped living area. The Reapers' veils might keep them hidden from sight, but if anyone bumped into them, they would feel it. The Reapers couldn't speak, or they would be heard. But they could see each other, and that was something that no other Fae could do.

Evan cleared his throat as he declined a cup of tea. "We're all delighted to see you up and about, Rhona, but I think it's time you shared what happened."

Balladyn wanted to hit him. They had seen her wounds. They knew how close to death she had come, but the wanker wasn't giving her any slack.

"Evan," Lyra snapped, her anger as palpable as Balladyn's.

Rhona lifted a hand to quiet everyone. "It's all right, Lyra. Besides, Evan is right. If I wasn't ready to talk, I wouldn't have called all of you here."

Sorcha sat beside her cousin, her eyes moving from Druid to Druid. She seemed to be searching for anything that would alert her that one of them meant to do Rhona harm. Balladyn wondered how the five Druids would feel if they knew that Reapers were sizing them up along with Sorcha.

Rhona's hand shook slightly as she set aside her cup of tea. She clasped her hands in her lap. "As some of you are aware, I was invited to Ireland with the other Druid leaders."

"To discuss the creation of our group of Others, correct?" Kerry asked.

Rhona's gaze swung to the Druid. "That was part of the reason, aye."

"What was said?" Evan asked excitedly. "We know there are groups of Druid Others."

The more he spoke, the more Balladyn wanted to toss him out of the cottage.

"For the love of all that's magical," the second man snapped. He had a portly belly and glared at Evan. "If all of you would shut your mouths, we might get some answers."

Violet nodded in agreement. "Thank you, Roy. I was about to say that."

Rhona looked at him again. Balladyn wanted to reassure her, but he kept quiet. She then took a deep breath and spoke. "It was dark when I arrived at the destination. And quiet. I knew that something was off, but I was immediately surrounded as I brought up my magic to shield myself. I can't tell you how many there were. I lost count of how many times they plunged the knives into my body. They weren't content with physical weapons either. They didn't want me just to die. They wanted me to die *painfully*. They used a spell to paralyze me. What magic I was able to get up allowed me to block a wee bit of it so I could move some, but even then, I knew I was going to die in that alley."

"That's when I happened to stumble upon her," Cathal said to the room. "I brought her here, and you know the rest."

Balladyn was happy to have the Druids think it had been happenstance that Rhona had been found. Especially since he had no explanation for how he'd known she needed help. If she hadn't been able to use her voice, then she hadn't called to him. That meant he was no closer to understanding how he had been able to find her or even know she was in danger.

"Why would anyone want to kill you?" Lyra asked Rhona in the silence that followed.

Evan's forehead creased with a deep frown. "Are you sure it was Druids? You were in Ireland. It could have been the Fae."

Rhona scooted back on the sofa after grabbing her tea. "As I said, it was dark. I couldn't see anyone. Not the number of people, not their faces, and not if they were Druids I knew. But I heard the spell. It was Druids."

"What does this mean for us?" Kerry asked.

Rhona took a drink of the tea and then shrugged. "That someone wants me dead."

"It has been decades since anyone came after a Skye Druid," Roy said gruffly.

Violet pursed her lips. "What troubles me is the spell. They didn't have to use that. Rhona would've been incapacitated without it."

Rhona stared into her teacup. No doubt she was reliving the incident. Every Reaper in the room could sympathize with her. She would have a long road of healing ahead of her, but first, they needed to find out who'd attacked her.

Balladyn watched the Druids closely. Rhona might have left off saying that it could have been someone on Skye, but the implications were there. And it left Balladyn deeply unsettled.

The Druids began talking amongst themselves, with Cathal and Sorcha joining in. The only one not speaking was Rhona. She took in every word, though. She opened her mouth as if to say something a couple of times but seemed to change her mind at the last minute. Balladyn wanted to know what she was thinking. To be fair, though, she was processing a lot. He wasn't sure he could've sat there so calmly after just experiencing an attempt on his life.

One that had come damn close to being fulfilled.

"All of this stays here," Rhona said loudly, drawing everyone's attention. The room went quiet as all eyes turned to her. She swallowed and looked at each Druid. "If someone from Skye betrayed me, I don't want to alert them by anyone sharing what I've told you."

Violet leaned forward in her seat, concern evident in her blue eyes. "You can't possibly think it was one of us."

"I don't know *what* to think. Which is why I'm telling you not to share. I only told you five because you were called to heal me."

Evan shook his head as he dropped his arms to his sides. "If we hadna been here, you wouldna have told us anything, would you?"

"Would *you* in my place?" Rhona snapped, showing her anger for the first time. "If someone ambushed you, thrust blades into your body multiple times, used a spell so you couldn't move, and then left you for dead, would you go around telling everyone? Or would you wait and attempt to uncover who was involved? I'm opting for the latter."

Kerry pushed up from her chair and nodded. "That's completely understandable. I won't say anything to anyone. Please, let me know if I can help you with sorting out these vile people."

"I second her words," Violet said as she got to her feet.

Roy grunted and crossed his arms over his chest as he nodded from his place by the wall.

"You know I'm with you," Lyra added.

Evan flattened his lips. "I'm one of your deputies. Our home is sacred. I'm no' going to stand for anyone attacking one of us."

Balladyn wasn't sure he believed any of them. If a Skye Druid had betrayed Rhona, it was likely someone in the room now.

Rhona bowed her head. "Thank you all."

"We'll leave you to rest," Kerry said and made for the door.

It wasn't until the last of the Druids had departed that the Reapers lowered their veils. Rhona sank back against the cushions and let her fear and anxiety show.

"I'm so angry. I want to do something, but I don't know where to start," Sorcha said.

Eoghan took the chair and leaned his forearms on his knees as he looked at Rhona. "I can't help but think that the Fae Others are involved somehow."

"I have nothing to argue against that." Rhona propped her elbow on the arm of the couch and rubbed her forehead. "I was there to discuss Druids organizing their own group of Others."

Cathal asked, "Did you really see nothing?"

"Nothing," Rhona admitted.

Sorcha sighed loudly. "Then it could have been anyone."

"Not just anyone," Balladyn said. "Someone specifically wanted Rhona out of the way. We need to find those who have a motive."

Rhona snorted as she looked his way. "That's any Druid on Skye who might want my position."

"Corann held your position for a long time. Did anyone come after him?" Rordan asked.

Rhona shrugged, shaking her head. "Not that I'm aware of. But times have changed. Some Druids on Skye are adamant that we need a group of Others."

"That is worrying," Bradach stated.

Torin raised his brows and nodded. "We're doing everything we can to fight the Fae Others before they can take control. Why in the world would the Druids want to follow them?"

"Power," Sorcha and Rhona said in unison.

Rhona shrugged. "It's always about power."

Balladyn leaned a shoulder against the wall. "Who gets to decide who becomes part of the six who lead?"

"Good question." Rhona squeezed her eyes closed for a moment. "It doesn't seem to matter to some Druids when they hear about what the original Others did. They also don't appear to care that it means working with *droughs*."

Sorcha got to her feet and paced. "After all the battles waged to fight the *droughs* through the centuries, now Druids want to unite and work *with* them? I can't imagine any of this running smoothly."

"It won't," Eoghan replied. "What happened with the Fae Others will happen with every group."

Ruarc blew out a breath. "The Six, specifically Lena, wants to rule the Fae and wipe the Earth of humans. If she got wind that Druids were following them in forming groups of Others, she might have attempted to put a stop to it."

"She would send the soldiers, though," Dubhan pointed out. "I don't see them waiting in the dark to ambush Rhona."

Cathal shook his head. "Rhona said it was Druids, so the Fae Others aren't relevant to this."

Sorcha threw up her hands before letting them slap against her thighs. "Then what do we do? Wait for another attempt on Rhona's life."

"This falls to me," Rhona said. "The Druids are my responsibility."

Sorcha gave her a flat look. "There's no way you're doing this alone. I'm staying to help."

Balladyn met Rhona's green gaze. He was staying, too. He didn't care what Eoghan or Death had to say about it.

CHAPTER FOUR

It was on the tip of Rhona's tongue to ask Balladyn to stay. Yet she knew she couldn't. He was a Reaper with duties far from Skye.

Eoghan straightened in his seat. "I had Bradach and Dubhan look around where we found you, Rhona."

She looked down at her lap. All she wanted to do was forget what had happened. Unfortunately, that would never happen. And if she didn't want a repeat, she needed to get her shite together and face it. Even if all she really wanted to do was hide in her room and hope the world forgot her.

"We followed the trail of your blood to the building," Bradach said.

Rhona forced herself to look into the Reaper's silver eyes. She wondered at times why they allowed her to know about them. Of course, she was only human. She had no dealings with the Fae, other than the Reapers—no Skye Druid did.

At least, not anymore.

Dubhan ran a hand through his longish, black and silver hair. "You got farther from the building than I expected. No one was inside, however."

"More's the pity," Sorcha stated angrily.

Rhona glanced at her cousin. "They believed I would die. Why stick around?"

Eoghan caught her attention. "How did you call for Balladyn?"

"I didn't." Rhona had expected this question, and she knew that none of them would be happy with her answer. But it was the only one she had.

Eoghan's head swiveled to Balladyn. "How did you know she was in trouble?"

"I didn't. I felt an uncontrollable pull toward something, and I had no choice but to follow it. I didn't know it was a person I needed to locate," he replied.

Rhona glanced at Balladyn and found his crimson gaze on her. She didn't know what to make of him finding her. She hadn't called his name. She hadn't called *anyone's* name because she hadn't been able to. She hadn't even thought his name.

Eoghan blew out a long breath. "Something has bound the two of you."

"Does it matter?" Balladyn asked. "She was in trouble, and I found her. Rhona is back where she belongs."

Torin grunted. "Aren't you the least bit curious how you knew to find her?"

"I am, but there are more pressing matters," Balladyn stated.

Rhona swallowed and set aside her now-cold tea. "I want to thank all of you for saving me."

"That was Balladyn," Cathal said.

Rhona found herself gazing into Balladyn's red eyes once more. "I owe you a debt of gratitude and thanks I'll never be able to repay."

"Stay alive. That will suffice," he answered.

Eoghan got to his feet. "We're not leaving Skye until we know for certain that Lena and the Six aren't involved. She could well have learned about our connection to Skye and the Druids because of Sorcha."

Rhona frowned. "How did this Lena learn of the Reapers to begin with?"

"One of the original Others who disappeared. No one tracked

him down because they didn't think Brian was a threat. Obviously, all of us were wrong about the coward," Eoghan replied. He bowed his head to Rhona. "Cathal will stay visible. That way, none of the Druids will think twice about sensing a Fae on Skye. The rest of us will remain veiled while we're around."

Rhona liked the idea of Balladyn being in her cottage, but she wasn't keen on the rest of them moving about her house like ghosts she couldn't see. "Inside?"

"We'll leave you to your privacy," Eoghan said with a knowing grin.

In the next instant, they were gone. All except for Balladyn, Cathal, and Sorcha. Her cousin cleared her throat and took Cathal's hand. "We can stay if you want company."

"I'm surrounded by Reapers. I'll be fine." Rhona forced a smile that she didn't feel.

Cathal pulled Sorcha up beside him. "We'll find those responsible."

Then it was just her and Balladyn. Rhona slid her feet to the floor and into her slippers to warm her toes. "You don't have to stay. I'll be fine."

"You're far from fine. The others might not see how your hands shake or that you're fighting against breaking down as what happened replays in your head. But I do."

"No one can help me."

He lifted one shoulder in a half-shrug. "Perhaps not, but I don't recommend being alone right now."

"Were you alone after you were betrayed?"

His red eyes glanced away. "For a short while. My situation was different than yours."

"You were betrayed and stabbed. How can that be any different?"

"I died."

Her lips fell open in shock. He'd said that he had died, but he was very much alive in front of her now. "I don't understand."

"Every Reaper was betrayed and killed."

"All of you?" she asked in astonishment.

Balladyn slowly nodded. "Call it a prerequisite to Death choosing us to serve her."

"So, she brought you back?"

"She held our souls and gave us the option to either serve her or die."

Rhona blinked. "Have any opted not to serve her?"

"I've never asked," he said with a hint of a smile on his lips. It died quickly, however. "My point is that, sometimes, it's better to have someone with you."

Her heart skipped a beat as she thought of him. With her. "And that's you?"

"If you want it to be."

"I do." She wanted no one else.

He bowed his head. "Then I'll stay until you say otherwise."

A burst of joy flared in her chest, knowing that he would be near and, therefore, allow the safety she felt with him to last longer. Rhona lowered her gaze to her lap. The instant she spied her hands, she recalled how they had been soaked with her blood. She hastily looked away. "When will I stop feeling my blood on my hands?"

"Faster than you expect, but not nearly soon enough."

"Thanks for the cryptic answer," she said with a smile. She thought about getting up and cleaning, but she just wasn't up for it. Instead, she used a spell to move the cups, teapot, and tray to the kitchen.

Balladyn didn't budge from his spot across the room.

"You can sit," she said.

He eyed the furniture and finally walked to lower himself into the leather chair that Eoghan had vacated.

Rhona grabbed the throw and pulled it over herself as she settled back on the couch, staring into the fire. "What do you think of my deputies?"

"Are you asking if I think one of them might have betrayed you?"

She looked his way and nodded.

His lips flattened for a heartbeat before he shrugged. "I don't like Evan's push for the formation of a Druid Other group here, but that doesn't mean he did it. Violet, Kerry, and Lyra seem like good people, but that doesn't mean they didn't do it. Roy is gruff, but you know where you stand with him."

"Each of the five holds their position as a deputy because of their magic."

"I don't doubt that. Are they liked among the other Druids?"

It was her turn to shrug. "Not everyone will be liked by all, but I can say that most everyone absolutely adores Lyra. She's a very giving individual. Violet has been a staple on Skye for many years and sought for her guidance. In truth, she should hold my position."

His brows snapped together. "Why do you say that?"

"Everyone thought she would get it if anything happened to Corann. Her standing in the community, her power, and her wisdom in general."

"How did you come to be the leader of the Skye Druids?"

Rhona fiddled with the fringe on the throw. "Corann chose me."

"And you disagree with that?"

"I do."

"He was a good man."

Her eyes widened. "You knew him?"

"Aye. How did he live for so many centuries?"

"That's something everyone wants to know. He was incredibly secretive."

"My guess is he had a good reason."

She turned her attention back to the fire. "I'm beginning to see that."

"The Fae and Skye Druids used to have a strong bond."

"*Used* to. Usaeil ruined it."

"You could change that."

Rhona slid her gaze to him. "I'm fighting to stay in the position I'm not even sure I deserve, and you want me to open Skye up to the Fae again? The rest of the Druids don't even know that all of you are Reapers. I can't imagine that going over well."

He shrugged. "There was a reason the Druids and Fae were once allies."

"And what was that?"

"The Fae entrusted you with the knowledge that we were on this realm. We shared our weapons and magic, expanding the Druids' knowledge."

Corann had told her the same thing once. She was about to ask why they needed the Fae now when it dawned on her what he was doing. "You're trying to get my mind on something other than the attempt on my life."

"Is it working?" he asked as his lips curved into a smile.

Her heart skipped another beat. Damn, he was gorgeous when he smiled. She wondered what it would feel like for someone like him to love someone like her. "Maybe."

CHAPTER FIVE

Death's Realm

Erith paced the top of the white tower, her gaze going again and again to the Fae doorway Balladyn and the second team of Reapers had walked through.

"At least we know why Balladyn wanted to leave."

She paused at the sound of Cael's voice. Erith walked to the window and gazed out. "I think *wanted* is too mild a term. He would've gone regardless. Something was dragging him away."

Cael walked up behind her and put his hands on her arms. "We can go to Skye, check on Rhona and the Druids, and get all the answers you want."

"*I* want?" she asked with a snort and leaned to the side to look at him. "You want them, as well."

He flashed her a seductive grin. "I do."

Erith turned in his arms and looked into his purple eyes. "I don't have a good feeling about any of this. Not Balladyn hearing something across realms, not the battle he was losing against following it, and especially not the power he exhibited with that bellow."

"Aye," Cael replied with a twist of his lips. "I've been thinking about that since it happened. Balladyn didn't seem to even realize that the wind had picked up or that lightning flashed around him."

"He's always been powerful, but this is…something else."

"If it's enough to worry you, then tell me what needs to be done."

She sighed. "That's just it. I don't know."

Cael glanced behind her. "Eoghan's back."

In an instant, she was outside the tower with Cael beside her. Eoghan was the first to emerge from the woods. When his liquid-silver eyes met hers, she knew that things hadn't gotten any better.

"I have few answers," Eoghan said and ran a hand down his face. "I'm more confused than I was before we left."

Cael crossed his arms over his chest. "Did Balladyn exhibit any more of that power?"

"Nay. But it was close. There's something different about him."

Erith glanced at the ground. "I knew it."

"How did Balladyn hear Rhona's call?" Cael asked.

Eoghan shrugged. "That's just it. She says she didn't call for him."

"Start from the beginning," Erith commanded. She listened as Eoghan repeated the story Rhona had shared, along with everything he and the Reapers had witnessed.

Cael's frown deepened. "Wait. Did you say that Balladyn used magic you've never heard of?"

"He said it came from one of the books in his library," Eoghan explained.

Erith nodded. "It could have. He's a collector. His collection is more impressive than even mine."

Cael's head turned to her. "Aren't you worried about the new magic he used on Rhona? Could that be what caused the lightning and wind?"

"I'm not. The magic Eoghan spoke of was used solely to slow or halt Rhona's blood loss. That's probably the only thing that saved her," Erith answered.

Eoghan looked from Erith to Cael and nodded. "It is."

"If Rhona didn't call for Balladyn, what I really want to know is how he knew that she was hurt," Cael said.

To calm the rising storm of worry gathering within her, Erith watched a bumblebee flit from flower to flower. "This has to do with the Six."

"You don't think Lena has taken over?" Eoghan asked.

Cael dropped his arms to his sides and grunted. "We'd know if she did. It's coming, though."

"I was hoping they would implode from within," Eoghan replied with a sidelong look.

Erith swung her gaze to Eoghan. "Stay on Skye. Watch everything. You made the right call to remain veiled. The Druids don't need to know that all of you are there. If anyone comes for Rhona again, and I suspect they will as soon as they discover she survived, take them."

"Take them?" Cael repeated.

She looked at him and grinned. "How else are we to get the answers we seek?"

"It's not our usual way, but perhaps it's time for a change," Eoghan said. He paused before asking, "What if Balladyn displays more of the power?"

This is where Erith wasn't as sure of the outcome. "I don't know. When Usaeil betrayed him the first time and left him injured on that battlefield for the Dark King to find and kill, I waited to make Balladyn a Reaper. Taraeth went back on his word to Usaeil and threw Balladyn in the dungeon instead with the Chains of Mordare."

"Crafted by a Dark. And the chains drain the magic of any Fae who wears them," Eoghan said in distaste.

Erith shoved some hair out of her face that the wind had lifted. "Balladyn fought far longer than anyone ever has. The chains didn't just drain his magic, it turned him Dark. Balladyn's anger at being taken and imprisoned fed the chains."

Surprise flickered across Cael's face. "Are you saying that you think the chains might have…altered him?"

"I'm saying that the Chains of Mordare were a formidable

weapon used to break many Fae. Used against someone like Balladyn? I think anything is possible. For all we know, he could've weakened them enough for Rhi to break them when they were used on her."

Eoghan's brow wrinkled. "Balladyn was the one who *put* them on Rhi. I don't think he would've done that if he thought that she could break them."

"He wouldn't have known." Cael's brows rose briefly. "Every Reaper knew of Balladyn's prowess on the battlefield. That, combined with his potent magic, made him a great ally."

"Twice betrayed, became King of the Dark, murdered, and is now a Reaper trying to find his way. He hasn't had an easy go of it," Eoghan said.

Erith smiled sadly. "None of you has."

"Not until we became Reapers," Cael replied.

Eoghan squeezed the bridge of his nose with his thumb and forefinger. "First, Aisling leaves to find Xaneth, and now Balladyn can sense something across the realms and is revealing new power. We're better when we're all together. Call Aisling to return. We could use her."

"Aisling is where she needs to be." Though Erith wasn't one to explain herself, this was different. "Xaneth's capacity to somehow find the Fae Others will be key in us bringing them down. I know it, and in order for that to happen, Xaneth needs to trust again."

Eoghan stared at her for a long minute. "I'll be the first to admit that Aisling could probably beat every last one of us in a fight, but that's putting a lot on her shoulders. Does she know what you've sent her to do?"

"She came to me, remember? She was the one who wanted to go after Xaneth."

"And if Xaneth harms her?" Eoghan asked.

Cael shook his head. "He won't."

"That's assuming Xaneth remembers the Fae he was before Usaeil tortured him," Eoghan snapped.

Erith caught Eoghan's gaze. "I know Aisling is one of your

Reapers. She's smart, and she trusts her instincts. I have complete faith in her, or I wouldn't have let her go alone. Trust in her."

"I know the pain of losing a fellow Reaper. I don't want to go through that again," Eoghan said.

Cael sighed. "None of us does, but you know as well as I do that while going against the Fae Others, it could happen to any of us."

Erith took a deep breath. "Right now, we're going to concentrate on what we can get a handle on, and that's Rhona."

"I still can't believe the Druids want to create their own group of Others," Cael murmured.

Eoghan lifted one shoulder. "Not all of them do, but the ones who want it are the loudest."

"Watch those," Erith told him.

Eoghan smiled, but it held no mirth. "Oh, we are. I've specifically got my eye on Evan. He's one of the deputies who helped to heal Rhona. He's very outspoken regarding what direction he believes the Druids should be going in."

"I don't understand it. Rhona and several Druids helped to take down Moreann, who led the Others. The Druids know what the Others tried—and failed—to do to the Dragon Kings," Cael said.

Erith felt herself pulled in different directions, and she knew that she had to stay focused on the Fae. But the Druids were now mixed into the thick of things with them, whether by chance or design. "We aren't the only ones who will have noticed the shift."

"You're talking about the Warriors and the Druids from MacLeod Castle," Cael said.

Eoghan's brows shot up. "Perhaps we should let them take over with this."

"Do you really think you can pull Balladyn away from Rhona after everything you've witnessed?" she asked.

Cael slid his gaze to her. "You can."

"That would spell disaster."

"He gave you his fealty."

Erith turned to Cael. "Nothing and no one should be able to communicate with any of us between realms. Anyone except me.

Think about that, my love. Something that strong, that *powerful*, got through to Balladyn. The influence he felt was so fervent that it was everything he could do to remain here. I might be a goddess, but even I'm not willing to hinder that link."

"When you put it like that, of course, you shouldn't," Cael admitted.

Eoghan said, "Balladyn is one of us. He might still be finding his way, but we won't let him down. We've got his back. And Rhona's. We'll get this handled."

"Take Fianna. You might need an extra Reaper," Erith suggested.

Eoghan nodded and called Fi's name. The minute Rordan's mate arrived, the two vanished into the thick flower garden that hid the doorway that led to other realms.

Only then did Erith looked at Cael.

He stepped closer and gently touched her cheek. "I don't like any of this."

"Neither do I, but this is the track we must traverse. I have no idea where it'll lead. Maybe to defeating the Fae Others. Perhaps in our defeat. I'll admit only to you that I'm scared. Too much is happening."

"You directed Eoghan to trust Aisling. Take your counsel and trust Balladyn."

"There's power in him he doesn't realize yet. I always knew it was there, but I couldn't begin to guess that it was as strong as it is."

Cael wrinkled his nose. "There may be more than you realize. How many times over the last months have you repeatedly told him that he's more than the celebrated Light warrior or the beloved Dark King that he was? Your words have made a difference. Him being here, with all of us, has made a difference. If I'm being honest, I'm more concerned about Aisling than Balladyn."

"Why are my Reapers being drawn away from me?" she asked, not liking the feeling in her gut.

"It's not because they don't want to be here. Both are answering a higher calling. Isn't that what you just informed me about Balladyn?" he asked with a slight smile.

She rolled her eyes and shoved him away. "Smartass."

He laughed and drew her to him. He grew serious as he said, "We'll survive this."

Erith smiled, her heart heavy with worry.

CHAPTER SIX

The more time Balladyn spent in Rhona's cottage, the more he liked being there. The space might be small, but it was filled. Everything inside the cottage was used and loved. He felt comfortable there, which surprised him. He wasn't comfortable anywhere.

At least he hadn't been in a long time.

He listened to the shower running, trying—and failing—not to envision Rhona naked. Balladyn kept reminding himself that the Druid needed protection and not his thoughts on stripping each layer of clothing from her body until she was bare before him.

"Fek me," he murmured and rose from the chair to walk around the room.

He went to the mantel and looked at the photos. One was of Rhona and Sorcha, along with Sorcha's younger sister when they were small children, playing at the beach. Their hair was wet, and sand speckled their smiling faces as their eyes squinted against the sun. The next photo was of Rhona with an older couple. By how similar Rhona looked to them, he suspected they were her parents.

Balladyn moved around the room, taking in the other pictures. Some had Rhona in them, but most didn't. He paused beside one in which Rhona stood with Corann, the previous leader of the Skye Druids, who had died taking down the Others.

"I think that's the only picture of him."

Balladyn startled and turned toward Rhona. She had her hair wrapped in a towel and wore jeans and a thick cream sweater. "It's a good picture."

"He was a good man."

"Aye."

She unwound the towel and draped it over the back of a chair in the kitchen. She began finger-combing her hair with measured strokes before pulling out a brush. The sight soothed Balladyn.

Rhona's bright green eyes met his. "You really don't know how long Corann lived?"

"I really don't."

"Was he human?"

Balladyn shrugged. "As far as I know."

"There has to be an explanation for how he lived so long."

"Someone other than me will have that answer."

Rhona's lips curved at the corners slightly. She said nothing as she grabbed her towel and walked away. He watched her, wondering how he was here. More importantly, he wanted to know who had called to him across the realms. *Something* had. But if it wasn't Rhona, it was connected to her somehow because the instant he'd found her, he'd no longer felt as if he were searching for something.

When he heard her turn on the blow-dryer, Balladyn looked out the window. The sky was gray and filled with angry-looking clouds that threatened rain at any moment. Wind swept across the island in fierce gusts as if daring anyone to venture outside.

He pulled his gaze from the yard when he heard Rhona approaching. To his shock, she walked to where her coat hung on a peg on the wall. "Going somewhere?"

"Yes, we are."

He quirked a brow and strode to her. "And where might that be?"

She faced him after zipping her coat. "There's someplace I need to go. It helps me think. Calms me." She hesitated for a moment. "I don't know why. And, honestly, it doesn't matter. But I feel safe when you're around, and I'd like for you to go with me."

"Of course." As if he would allow her to go anywhere by herself until he caught whoever had tried to kill her. He didn't let himself think about her comment on feeling safe with him. That was entirely too dangerous. He glanced outside again as she put on her scarf and grabbed some gloves. "You realize it's going to rain."

"It's winter on Skye. Wind and rain are guaranteed. Maybe even snow."

Snow made him think of his most recent holiday spent with the Reapers. It was a good memory in thousands of years of bad ones.

"You like snow?" she asked.

He shrugged. "I never thought much about it until recently. There was this…thing for the holiday."

"Thing?" she questioned with raised brows.

Balladyn grappled with finding the right words. "A holiday celebration in the mountains, put on by the mates. The Reapers decorated trees for them. The entire evening was a lovely event."

"It sounds special. I'm glad you had something like that."

He shifted, suddenly uncomfortable. It wasn't like him to open himself to others. "Where are we going?"

"My favorite place."

"Which is?"

She smiled. "The Fairy Pools, of course."

"Of course," he replied, a grin tugging at his lips. "Should I teleport us?"

"Yes, please."

He held out his hand.

A frown puckered her brow. "Don't you need a coat?"

Balladyn just smiled and waited for her to place her hand in his. The moment she did, he jumped them to the Fairy Pools and whispered Eoghan's name so the Reapers would know where they were. The wind buffeted around them in a particularly angry burst the instant they arrived. He steadied Rhona as he used magic to call a coat to him. The sound of her laughter when she saw it made him grin.

The weather kept tourists away, but he didn't think Rhona would've cared either way. She released his hand and began walking. She took the first crossing over the River Brittle with the steppingstones in the water and moved onto the gravel path that put the river to their right. He glanced around at the beautiful, rolling hills where the river cut through the land. Then he followed behind her on the well-worn path, his gaze on the rocky peaks of the Black Cuillin Mountains ahead. The mountains were a spectacular backdrop against an already beautiful sight.

As Rhona wound her way toward the Cuillins, Balladyn couldn't stop thinking about the few times he had visited Skye via the Fairy Pools. As a rule, the Fae preferred Ireland, but that was because the Dragon Kings didn't share Scotland with anyone—except humans and Druids.

Balladyn had never thought much about Scotland. Why should he? It was the Dragon Kings' home, after all. Nothing could be prettier than his Green Isle. But even he had to admit there was something special about Skye. Scotland might claim it, but ancient Celts from Ireland had settled upon its shores. Which meant that Skye's roots belonged to Ireland.

Maybe that's why he liked the island so much.

Rhona glanced over her shoulder at him. He met her gaze, noting that she had some color in her cheeks. It was most likely due to the wind and cold, but there was no mistaking that she looked better. With every step she took alongside the River Brittle, it was as if life poured back into her. Balladyn had heard how certain places could enhance Druid magic. Were the Fairy Pools such a place for Rhona?

Balladyn noticed an impressive boulder to his left that had remained after the ice had melted during the last ice age. There was history everywhere, and most humans had no idea. His thoughts shifted as they crossed the river once more, using more steppingstones. With all the rain, the river was high, making crossing difficult. Just as he was about to jump Rhona across, she easily navigated to the other side.

He followed her and moved up the natural rock steps to the first waterfall. This wasn't just the start of the Fairy Pools, it was also the highest of the falls with the deepest pool. Balladyn had swum there several times. He'd also jumped from the sides into the pool over thirty feet below.

After swimming with his memories, he looked up and noticed Ruarc and the other Reapers, all who remained veiled. Balladyn then searched for Rhona. She was well ahead of him. He could've teleported to her but decided against it. Instead, he continued along the path close to the river. The next pool with its clear, blue water was the one most humans used for swimming. It made a particularly stunning backdrop with its natural arch beneath the water.

Balladyn took his time moving from pool to pool. Some were calm and gentle, others rushing and wild, but they were all spectacular. Each one held something different for those who saw them.

When he finally caught up with Rhona, he found her sitting on a rock that extended out over a waterfall. He sat beside her, each of them lost in thought.

"You look relaxed."

Balladyn turned his head to her. "There's something about the sound of water over rock."

She smiled in return.

He shrugged and looked at the river. "I was remembering the times I used to come here."

"Did you visit often?"

"Only a handful. My duties usually had me elsewhere, but I enjoyed it the few times I did get to come. This place is amazing."

She sighed. "That it is. It's a tourist destination, which keeps it crowded year-round. At times, I wish no one knew about it, but it doesn't seem fair to keep something so beautiful to myself."

"There is a peace about this place that has nothing to do with the water and everything to do with magic."

"Yes."

He turned his head toward her at the sound of her soft reply. Their gazes met and held. He was sitting so close to her. If he moved his hand just a little, it would touch hers. He wanted to touch her, to press his body against hers. Desire ran strong and deep, making him forget the troubles that surrounded Rhona. All he saw, all he *wanted* was her.

Soft drops of rain fell from the sky sporadically, but neither of them moved. The wind whipped at her red locks, making them appear like flames against the gray sky. She was the most beautiful thing he had ever seen.

Her lips parted, and she asked, "Did something really pull you to me?"

"I've never felt anything like it before. It came out of nowhere, slamming into me. I knew nothing other than the fact that something wanted me somewhere."

"You didn't fight it?"

He glanced at the mountains behind her. "At first, I did. I had no choice. I follow Death's rules."

"But she let you go?"

"She did."

Rhona's shoulders lifted as she inhaled. "That feeling inside you led to me?"

"Aye."

"That's a wee bit disconcerting. I'm thankful, mind, but if I didn't do it, then what did?"

He propped one foot on the rock and rested an arm across his knee as he leaned on his other hand. Anything to keep himself from reaching for her. "Could you have used magic you weren't aware of?"

"I'm surprised I got any magic up at all before my attack. There wasn't time for a spell. I just called my power to me. Then I was immersed in pain. Since I couldn't speak and could barely move, I did the only thing I could and tried to crawl to someone. Eventually, I couldn't do even that. I simply lay there in the rain, feeling my blood seeping through my fingers."

A slight frown puckered her brow. He was instantly curious. "What is it?"

"I heard…drums."

"Drums? Was there a pub nearby with live music?"

She shook her head. "No. I heard the drums of the Ancients. Then I heard *them*."

"What did they say?" He held his breath, waiting to hear her response. The Ancients didn't talk to all Druids, so it was special when they did.

Rhona swallowed hard. "I thought they were welcoming me to them. I thought they were there because I was dying. But then I heard your voice. You don't think that they brought you to me, do you?" she asked skeptically.

"I've never heard of the Ancients speaking to anyone but a Druid."

She wrinkled her nose. "True."

"Whoever or whatever I felt brought not just the Fae but *Reapers* to your aid, and for a reason. The one thing I do know for certain is that you were meant to live."

CHAPTER SEVEN

Rhona lifted her face to the sky as the raindrops began falling faster. She shook her head and looked at Balladyn. "Some Druids can hear the wind. Others can talk to water and animals. And still more have so many other amazing abilities. I can't do any of that. I've tried it all. Nothing works for me. I have no idea what Corann was thinking when he chose me. I'm even more surprised that the Druids accepted me as their leader."

"Corann must have seen something you still haven't. He chose you because you're the best person to lead your people."

She wanted to believe Balladyn, but she couldn't. "I've done a bang-up job so far, haven't I?" She laughed ruefully. "We're more fractured than ever before, and I don't know how to fix it."

"Ask the Ancients."

That made her chuckle for real. "Do you know how many of us ask the Ancients for guidance? They rarely answer."

"It won't hurt to try, will it?"

She hated that he was so pragmatic about it. She was also irritated that she hadn't thought of it herself. The Ancients had spoken to her as she lay dying. She hadn't heard what they'd said, but she had known they were there.

"Fear is like a sickness. You need to cut it out before it infects everything."

Rhona looked into Balladyn's crimson eyes. "That's good advice. Difficult to do." She noticed that his eyes were lighter around the pupils. Not the deep, dark red as the rest of his irises. "Did you cut it out?"

"It's a never-ending battle," he said and looked away. "When you conquer one fear, another inevitably takes its place."

A shiver ran through her body from the cold, but she wasn't ready to leave the pools yet. "You don't act like a Dark Fae."

"That's because when we become Reapers, we keep our coloring, but we aren't the same as before. We're…more."

Obviously. Rhona had been mildly curious about the Reapers after Sorcha fell in love with Cathal. When the Reapers came to her not long ago and asked for help, Rhona had wanted to ask questions, but she'd bided her time. Now that she was alone with Balladyn, she discovered that she wanted to know every detail about him.

He had the look of a man who had been through a lot and wouldn't take shite from anyone. There was also a haunted air about him that hinted at the horrors from his past.

Suddenly, his head swiveled to her.

"Who are you?" she asked.

He briefly lowered his gaze to the ground. "Someone given a second chance."

"You say that as if you aren't sure you deserve it."

"Because I'm not."

"I disagree."

He released a breath. "You wouldn't if you knew about me."

There hadn't been any heat in his words, but she knew that he believed them with his whole heart. "Try me."

"I'd rather not," he replied.

She quirked a brow. "Is that fear talking?"

"*Touché*," he said with a chuckle.

Rhona shifted to face him. "The past is just the past. It created each of us, but who we are now, the actions we take, that's what's important."

"And you wonder why Corann chose you," Balladyn said with an easy smile.

She felt her cheeks heating at the compliment. "I'm going to cut my fear out of me. I'm going to embrace the role I have, no matter where that leads."

He stared at her in silence for a long time. Finally, his shoulders sagged as he came to some kind of decision. "I like you. I even like this place, and I usually hate anything to do with Scotland. Right now, you say I make you feel safe. I don't want that to change."

"Since you're being honest, I will be, as well. As a general rule, I don't like the Fae. But you're more than a Fae. You're a Reaper. I usually abhor the Irish accent. And I say *usually* because I like to hear you talk."

Balladyn swallowed and got to his feet. She stared at his outstretched hand, wanting to stay at the pools, even though the rain was increasing. The honesty and candor between them were refreshing. But there was also something…more. Desire. She wanted to see where that led.

In the end, she gave up and placed her hand in his. His fingers were warm as they closed around hers. In the next instant, darkness encircled her. Balladyn snapped his fingers, and a ball of light appeared above them. Rhona was surprised the light spread as far as it did, but it allowed her to see that she was in a cave.

"We're far below the pools," Balladyn explained. "This used to be where the Fae came before we met with the Druids at the pools."

"Corann told me there were caves once. He said they had been closed."

"We closed them to ensure that no Druid or human could find their way here. There was once a Fae doorway that led to the Light Castle, but that's been deactivated." Balladyn released her hand and walked to sit on a rock. He studied her once more. "The only thing I grew up knowing was that I wanted to fight the Dark. I joined the Light Army against my parents' wishes, but I knew it was what I was supposed to do. Everyone has a gift, and mine was battle, as odd as that sounds. There wasn't a weapon I couldn't use; magic I couldn't master. Half the time, I barely tried.

"The Dark and Light had been fighting for so many generations that I'm not sure anyone remembers the reasons now. Our civil war started to kill the planet. Still, we ignored it, each side believing they were about to win. Until we destroyed the realm and had no home. We found this one. As usual, the Dark created issues for the rest of us. The Dragon Kings wanted us gone for good. When we first came to Earth, the Light and Dark fought the Kings together. If we had trusted each other more, we might have made more headway, but there was too much animosity there. Soon, it became apparent that the Kings would win. Then, Usaeil ordered the Light to join them to beat back the Dark. Honestly, that was the only thing that saved us. Once the Dark were beaten, the Kings should've forced all of us to leave. They didn't. It's one of the few blatant mistakes they made. Yet we had a home again. With conditions, of course."

Rhona asked, "What kind of conditions?"

"We were never to leave Ireland, and the Fae were forbidden from interfering with humans."

She grinned. "We both know *that* didn't happen."

He didn't return her smile. "The Dark lured unsuspecting mortals to them and then feasted on their souls. The Light continued to fight them, but we never gained any ground. As I said, the Kings could've made us leave. I still don't understand why they didn't."

"Because they're good men."

Balladyn shrugged. "The Kings could *still* make us leave if they want. The Fae divided Ireland across the middle—the Light took the top half and the Dark the lower. Many Fae walk among humans every day all over the world, but most especially in Ireland. We still fight amongst each other, though steps have been taken to form a council of Fae instead of us remaining divided."

She nodded, her gaze never leaving his.

"I followed my heart when I joined the Light Army," he continued. "It was what I was meant to do. Before I knew it, I was in the Queen's Guard, which was a great honor. Only the best of the best were asked to join. Then, I became captain of the Queen's Guard. I had achieved everything I ever wanted."

"No wife? Children?" Rhona asked. She held her breath, hoping that no one held his heart.

~

Balladyn's thoughts shifted to Rhi at Rhona's question. He hadn't thought about her in weeks. He wasn't sure how or when he had realized that she wasn't the one for him, but it had happened. He was glad to see that Rhi was happy with Con. He still didn't care for the Dragon Kings, though.

"I'm sorry. I shouldn't have asked such a personal question."

He shook his head. "It isn't that. I was thinking. Remembering, really. There *was* someone once. She was in love with someone else, and when he broke her heart, I believed that I stood a chance. In the end, it wasn't meant to be."

"Her loss."

"It wouldn't have mattered. I lost everything soon after. Even if I would've won her, I would've lost her. That's when I was betrayed the first time. I was badly wounded during a battle with the Dark. I waited for her or any other Queen's Guard members to find me, but no one came. I kept trying to teleport out, but I couldn't. The next thing I knew, Taraeth, who was King of the Dark at the time, stood over me. I expected him to kill me. Instead, he took me to his dungeon. For the next several centuries, they tortured me with magical chains that sucked away my magic while also trying to turn me Dark. As you can see, the chains worked. Taraeth won.

"It didn't matter who I had been before that, I could never return to the Light, and I didn't want to. Rage ruled me. I wanted revenge on everyone I believed had failed me. The one I thought I loved? I captured her and put her in those same chains. They were supposed to be unbreakable, but she broke them. That's the type of man I am, Rhona. I wanted to ruin someone I claimed to love."

She smiled sadly. "You were hurting. You lashed out."

"That doesn't wipe away the facts. In the years I was Dark, I spent my time working my way up and earning Taraeth's trust. I saw firsthand how disbanded and out of control the Dark were. I'd like to say that was the reason I killed Taraeth and took the throne, but that would be a lie. The real reason was because Taraeth was weak, and I'd been biding my time until I saw my chance. Before I took the throne, I learned that he and Usaeil were on friendly terms when she came to visit him. The shock on her face when she saw me was something I'll never forget. You see, she was the one who had betrayed me and told Taraeth to kill me."

"For what reason?" Rhona asked, her brow puckered in a frown.

Balladyn chuckled wryly. "Because of Rhi."

"Rhi?" Rhona's shock was palpable. "As in Con's Rhi?"

"Aye."

Rhona's eyes widened as realization dawned. "She was the one you loved."

"We were never meant to be, but Usaeil was jealous of everything regarding Rhi. So, the queen lashed out at me. I turned my full attention to taking Usaeil down and showing the Light who she really was. That was when a Reaper approached me, asking for aid. I'd heard the stories that all Fae hear about the Reapers, but it was the ones I read that made me believe in them. Then, Fintan was suddenly talking to me. I never imagined myself working with the Reapers, but what he said made sense. I gathered the entire Dark force and joined the Reapers and the Dragon Kings to take down Usaeil."

The Druid's eyes crinkled at the corners. "I heard that was an awesome sight to behold. You did a good thing. You became a Reaper after?"

He nodded slowly.

"Wait." She frowned. "I thought you said that Reapers are all betrayed and killed."

"They are."

"Then…?"

Balladyn drew a deep breath and slowly released it. "I turned my back on Usaeil, and she buried her sword in me before I got a chance to kill her. Now, here I am."

"And the sadness I see in your eyes? Is it because you lost Rhi?"

"Nay," he said with a twist of his lips. "I was infatuated with her. Her brother was my best friend. We were always together. We got along great, so I just assumed we would end up together."

"Are you sad that you're no longer King of the Dark?"

That made him pause. No one had asked him that before. "In a way. I've never admitted that, even to myself. I knew the Dark could be great without tearing the Fae in two. I was working toward that. I've been told that I made good headway, but it all fell apart when I was killed."

"Then you must be mourning the Light that you were."

"Maybe."

She tilted her head to the side, her long, red hair falling over her shoulder. "Do you know what I see when I look at you?"

This was the part he'd dreaded. He'd told her the truth and hadn't sugarcoated anything. Would she be disgusted with him? Ask him to leave? Request another Reaper to guard her? All of it would be a punch to the gut, but he would honor her wishes, whatever they were.

"I see a good man who was dealt several hard blows, yet you found your footing each time and kept going."

Balladyn blinked. It took a moment for her words to sink in. When they did, he wondered if she understood exactly who he had been. "You do understand what a Fae does to become Dark, don't you?"

"I know you wore those chains for centuries. I can't imagine what kind of dark magic was used to break you down until you succumbed. What other choice did you have?"

"I've killed, Rhona." He wished he knew why he laid himself bare to her. The words were the most difficult things he had ever said. Yet she looked at him with utter trust. The kind he'd never thought to experience again. He shouldn't be telling her any of this, but he needed her to realize who he was. All of him.

Even the parts he wished he could bury and pretend didn't exist.

She shrugged as if it meant little. "You killed when you were in the Light Army."

"That was different."

"Was it? I've killed."

He snorted. "I highly doubt you did it outside of battle."

"Killing is killing. I still see the faces of those I've ended."

Balladyn stared across the way into her green eyes. He fought the urge, the primal instinct to go to her, to pull her to her feet and kiss her. How did she have the ability to effortlessly purge the shame and remorse he'd carried for what felt like an eternity?

She shoved her thick locks out of her face. "I sincerely doubt Death would have chosen you for a Reaper if she didn't see the good in you. Perhaps being a Reaper was your destiny all along. The only way to get there was to experience what you've gone through. Look where you are now."

"Aye," he murmured. But his thoughts weren't on his journey. No, he was thinking about Rhona. How he had been called to her. Maybe she was right. Perhaps everything that had happened had been meant to bring him to her. He'd saved her life, but he couldn't leave.

Because he knew that something else would be coming for her.

His skin prickled with awareness, of the feelings that were growing inside him. Things that he had no right to feel—much less act upon.

What he could do was protect her. The fact that Erith had chosen him as a Reaper spoke to his ability as a warrior. It was the one thing he excelled at. No one would harm Rhona. Balladyn would make sure of that at all costs.

CHAPTER EIGHT

Back at her cottage, Rhona couldn't stop thinking about Balladyn
and everything he had shared. She wasn't sure many in the universe
could have suffered as Balladyn had and still keep going.

The Reaper turned his head from staring out the window to pin
her with his crimson gaze. She wasn't embarrassed to be caught
ogling him. Gorgeous, compassionate, heroic, bold, mysterious, and
commanding. It was a feat for someone to have one of those traits,
yet Balladyn had them all and more.

"What?" she asked when a small frow furrowed his brow.

"I keep thinking about those who tried to kill you."

Right. Back to that. How could she have forgotten? But he was
right. They needed to know so she could prepare for the next attack.
Because there would be one. "You don't think it was Druids?"

"I know it wasn't the soldiers."

She hadn't seen the soldiers the Fae Others had created, and she
hoped she never would. "How do you know that?"

"Because they wouldn't have left until they knew you were
dead."

"Oh." What else could she say?

Balladyn walked from the window to where she stood in the

kitchen. He leaned against the counter. "The Six rarely do things themselves. That's why they created the soldiers, who move as fast as Reapers. The Six also gave them added magic."

"As Death did to you."

Balladyn nodded once.

"You don't think the Six would've sent any of their disciples after me, do you?"

"I'm not saying it isn't possible, but I can't see why they would when they have the soldiers."

She crossed to the kettle when it let out a whistle and took it off the stove. She turned off the burner and poured the hot water into two mugs for tea. "Which brings us back to the Druids."

"Are you suspicious of anyone here? Anyone you think might wish to harm you?"

Rhona glanced at him with a grin. "We're Druids. Any of them could take my life in an instant. But I can't think of anyone off the top of my head."

"What about Evan?"

Rhona shrugged as she set the kettle aside. She lifted the milk, silently asking Balladyn if he wanted any. At his nod, she put some into both of their mugs. "He thinks we should be headed in a new, contemporary direction. He, like many of the Druids on Skye, think we're stuck in the past."

"How many groups of Druids have created Others?"

"More than I'd like. What's worse is that the *mies* are welcoming the *droughs* into their fold by doing that. There's a reason the *droughs* were kicked out." She turned and handed Balladyn his cup of tea.

He held it, his brow puckering. "We allowed the two Druids from Earth who were involved with the original Others to go free because we believed they wouldn't cause any problems. We were wrong."

"You couldn't have known. None of us could have."

"We should have."

She twisted her lips. "We can't change that now. Obviously, they liked the power they had while in Moreann's crowd. I expect they're looking to find something similar."

"Do you think they can?"

"I'm not saying there aren't powerful Druids out there. Eilish for one. Not to mention those at MacLeod Castle. But excluding them, we're the most potent here on Skye. Mostly because we've kept the dilution of our Druid blood to a minimum. People can't help who they fall in love with, so there are always those without magic who marry into a family of Druids."

Balladyn took a drink of his tea. "Have you seen a decline in magic over the years on Skye?"

"Unfortunately. Take Corann for example. Though I have no idea what his true age was, he used to teach that every Druid on Skye was at least as powerful as he was or more. There isn't anyone here now who could even come close to wielding such magic."

"Not even you?"

She chuckled and shook her head. How she wished she had magic like Corann. "Not even close."

"I'm not so sure."

His words took her aback. "You've not seen me perform magic. How can you say that?"

"Just a feeling. Plus, I knew Corann. Not as well as you did, but the Druid was wise. He saw past the disguises everyone wore to make themselves look and feel better. He saw the person beneath. The one people try to keep hidden. He saw you, and he chose you as his replacement. That tells me there's much more to you than you realize."

Rhona briefly looked away. She wanted Balladyn's words to be true, but she wasn't sure they were. "I wish I had your confidence."

"Did you trust Corann?"

"Absolutely," she replied quickly.

Balladyn shrugged. "Then you shouldn't have any doubt."

"Corann wasn't infallible. He made mistakes."

"And you think you're one of those?"

Her stomach clenched at Balladyn's words. She had whispered them to herself so many times. This was the first time she had heard the words aloud, and it was even worse than when she said them in her head. What if Corann *had* been wrong? What if she didn't have what it took to lead the Skye Druids? What if…?

"It's a possibility," she murmured.

"Just like it's possible that he was right. Why are you determined to look to the worst side of this?"

"Because I don't want to be the reason the Druids on Skye fracture irrevocably."

He lifted the mug to his lips but paused before taking a drink. He eyed her over the rim. "Did you ever think it could be your uncertainty about your role that causes it?"

As if she needed something else to be anxious about. But she couldn't deny that Balladyn had a point. A very valid point. She had been second-guessing every move she'd made since Corann's death. That had made her bow to pressure from Evan and his supporters about forming a group of Others. Corann never would've done that. He would've told Evan and anyone else who felt that way to leave Skye. Why hadn't she done that? Because she'd been scared. That apprehension had prevented her from doing anything. And, like Balladyn said, it had manifested the current situation.

She didn't like the unease that roiled in her stomach. Yet there was a way to fix the recent circumstances. She hadn't seen a clear path until now—until Balladyn. He had shown her the way.

A Reaper. A *Fae*. She had hated anything to do with them for most of her life. And now, she wasn't just turning to him for security but for his wisdom, as well. His presence was comforting, his voice soothing. She trusted him as she did Sorcha—odd since she had only known Balladyn for a short time.

There were…feelings…developing that she was too afraid to look at too closely. They were probably due to him saving her. It was hard not to feel things for someone who acted so valiantly. He didn't see it in himself, but to her, it was a beacon that banished the darkness.

She swallowed, shaken to her core at the deep attraction she felt towards Balladyn. She had to be careful. He was there to help her, not start some sort of affair.

Then again, life was short. No one knew that better than she did. If she saw anything to make her think that Balladyn was interested, she wouldn't pass up the opportunity to know what it was like to be in his arms. The formidable Reaper was probably a masterful lover. Just thinking about it made her legs go weak, and her blood heat.

Rhona moved her cup to her other hand in an effort to get her desire under control. She cleared her throat. What had he said? She needed to stop thinking about sex and focus. Oh, yes. He'd asked if her ambiguity might be the cause of the current situation. "I might not like what you say, but I'm not too proud to admit that you're right. You did tell me to cut out fear before it spread. I'm sorry to say that it has spread throughout me. That doesn't mean I won't fight it until all of it is gone."

"Good," Balladyn said with a sexy grin that made her heart skip a beat. "Does that mean you've actually accepted your role as leader?"

"Don't look so smug," she retorted, but she couldn't stop the smile from tugging at her lips.

He chuckled. "I can't wait to see what you do next."

At that, her smile vanished. She knew exactly what she had to do next. "I need to find who ambushed me."

"I think they made an attempt on your life because of the power you hold, along with you being the head of the Skye Druids."

"As I told you, I can't do any special magic like others can."

"Could be someone wanted to make sure you didn't embrace the leadership role and discover your full potential," he said, his brows raising.

The more they talked, the colder she became. She kept warming her fingers on the mug, but it wasn't penetrating the rest of her. The knowledge that someone wanted her dead was chilling. "That circles back to the Druids."

"Not just any Druids," he said softly.

"Skye Druids." Her people. The ones she trusted. One or more could want her dead.

Balladyn lifted one shoulder. "Unless you have dealings with Druids outside of Skye."

"Some, of course. There are fewer and fewer of us every year, so we're trying to make sure no one gets left behind. But we're a tight-knit community here on Skye."

Balladyn's red eyes narrowed.

"What?" she asked hesitantly.

"Those without magic live among you."

She nodded. "They always have."

"Do they know about the Druids?"

Rhona thought about that for a moment. "Some, yes. Not all. Are you thinking it was them?"

"If one of them caught wind of the Others, they could fear for themselves if any Druids—but especially Skye Druids—had that kind of power."

She shifted to lean on one foot. "The only way that could happen is if they learned from a Druid what was going on."

"You said that people sometimes marry into the Druids. Could it be one of them?"

"It's a possibility. I can't rule that out."

He glanced outside. "The only thing I'm sure of is that there will be another attack."

She knew that, as well, but she didn't want to dwell on it right then. Her mind was too full of other things. "How would the Fae Others feel about Druids organizing groups?"

"Since the Fae intend to take over the realm and do with humans as they see fit, I can't imagine they'd be too happy."

Rhona grinned. "Precisely. That could mean it was the Fae Others."

"That faction is growing at an alarming rate. They're killing Fae and taking their powers, while the rest have no idea. If any of the Six discover the Druid Others, they could kill all of you with little preamble."

Well. That was terrifying. She had been so caught up with the Druids, she hadn't thought about what it meant if the Fae gained such power. Something else Corann would've been on top of. Damn. It was easy for the fear and doubt to stay rooted deep. She'd said she would eradicate it, but that was easier said than done.

"We're fighting the Fae Others," Balladyn said. "We'll keep fighting them until we've won or they kill us. They know of us, and they're coming, but we're ready for them. If we fail, the Dragon Kings will step in."

Relief shot through her. "You've spoken to the Kings? They know?"

"Erith will make that determination. Don't think for an instant the Kings aren't aware of what's happening, though. They'll take care of the Fae Others just as they did with the original group. They'll do the same to any Druid Others."

Rhona set her mug aside on the counter behind her. "I've been so blind to so many things. I've been so wrapped up in my issues that I failed to see the bigger picture. I'd like to be able to handle this on my own, but I don't mind asking for help. This is about more than just me."

"We're here because we want to make sure the Six aren't involved. Regardless, we'll be on Skye until we know who attacked you."

"I appreciate that, but I'm wondering if I should call in additional assistance."

"More? Than the Reapers?"

She fought to hide her smile at his offended tone as only someone with such magic and power would be. "The Druids from MacLeod Castle."

"Ah." His lips flattened for an instant. "They are formidable. Not to mention they'll come with the Warriors. That might not be a bad idea."

For the first time since Corann had told her she would be taking his place, Rhona felt as if she were a leader. Being on offense instead of defense would also be a nice change. Corann had often told her to trust her instincts. It was time she did just that.

A slow smile pulled at Balladyn's face.

She frowned. "What's that look for?"

"I just caught a glimpse of why Corann chose you."

CHAPTER NINE

Balladyn had only thought he knew torture until he was in Rhona's home, trying not to think about her in bed. The smart thing would probably be to leave her alone and go outside with the other Reapers. Instead, he welcomed the torment with open arms as he sat on the sofa, staring at the light from under her door.

She had grabbed her book and glasses after telling him goodnight. He hoped she was able to read. He had seen her eyes get a faraway look several times that evening. Balladyn didn't need to ask to know that she was thinking about her attack. That was one of the reasons he was still in the cottage. If she got to sleep, he wanted to be there in case she had a nightmare.

Night terrors had plagued him for months after Usaeil had killed him. Eoghan had confided in him that he'd also suffered from them for an extended period. And Eoghan wasn't the only Reaper who had. Aisling still fought with her nightmares. Balladyn's attention was focused on Rhona now. She had mental and emotional strength, but a person could only take so much.

Balladyn tried to make himself relax, bathed in the red-orange glow of the fire, but no matter what he did, he couldn't stop thinking about Rhona. It wasn't her blood-soaked body he had found in the rain. No, it was the shower fantasy from earlier that had him rock-hard. That, coupled with their trip to the Fairy Pools, had done something to him.

His every thought was of Rhona. Who might harm her, how Balladyn would protect her, and how he would tear apart the people who had tried to end her life.

Something touched his shoulder. He jerked his head to the side to find Rordan sitting beside him. "What the fek?" Balladyn bit out in a hushed tone so as not to alarm Rhona.

Rordan grinned knowingly. "You were deep in thought."

"There's a lot to think about."

"Hmm. Especially with a pretty redhead in the same house."

Balladyn glanced toward Rhona's door. The light was still on. "That isn't what I was thinking about."

"No need to get testy."

"I'm not *testy*," Balladyn snapped. Then he sighed when he heard his tone. Fek.

Rordan pushed to his feet and walked to the hearth where Balladyn had used magic to ensure the fire wouldn't go out. Rordan looked at one of the pictures on the mantel before turning to Balladyn. "Sorcha is worried about her cousin. Seems Rhona refused to keep answering the texts Sorcha sent every hour."

Which meant that Sorcha had reverted to using the Reapers to gain information. "She's doing as well as can be expected."

"Aye," Rordan said, his lips flattening. "We all understand what Rhona is dealing with. Cathal tried to explain it to Sorcha, but unless someone goes through it, they can't truly understand. It's good that you're here with Rhona. She doesn't need to be alone."

Balladyn looked at her door again. He got to his feet and walked to Rordan. "I've gone over and over in my head who might have betrayed and attacked her."

"Did you come up with anything?"

"I think things point to one of the Druids."

Rordan clasped his hands behind his back and nodded slowly. "We've been debating it, as well. Sorcha is sure it's a Druid, but

Dubhan and Eoghan think that's just a diversion and that it's really the Six. Specifically, Lena. Ruarc is also leaning that way."

"The Fae have more magic than Druids do. Even the Skye Druids. Why would the Six care about them?"

"That's what I asked. Torin's theory is that by creating this conflict, our attention will be focused on the Druids and not on the Six."

Balladyn ran a hand over his face. "I thought of that, too. We learned what happens when the Reapers get split up. I can't help but feel like the biggest battle with the Six is approaching quickly. Taking our attention from them is a strong move. It's one I would've made."

"There's a reason for the connection between you and Rhona. We're not leaving until that gets sorted."

"Aye. It's because she was meant to survive."

Rordan quirked a black brow, his silver eyes locked on Balladyn. "I think it's much more than that."

"The Ancients spoke to her after the attack. She didn't hear what they said, but they were there."

"Is that who reached across time and space to you?"

Balladyn frowned and hastily shook his head. "Since when have the Druid Ancients ever spoken to a Fae?"

"A lot of things are happening right now that are out of the ordinary. I'm in agreement, though, something wanted Rhona saved. It makes sense it was the Ancients."

Balladyn grew uncomfortable with the way Rordan was looking at him. He changed the subject. "Have any of you seen any Fae?"

"None. Some of the deputies have been driving past Rhona's. They're giving her time, but I'm not sure how much longer that'll last before they begin dropping in."

That was the one thing Balladyn wasn't looking forward to. "The answers we want are out there. Not in this cottage. Yet, at the same time, I'm not sure Rhona is ready to venture out."

"She seemed to do fine today at the pools."

"The pools calm her."

Rordan wrinkled his nose. "You know what needs to happen."

Regrettably, Balladyn did. If they were going to catch who had betrayed Rhona, she would have to put herself back into the spotlight to draw out the attackers. "I'll talk to her about it."

"Do you think she'll do it?"

"She doesn't strike me as the kind of person who backs away from a fight. She needs time to heal emotionally, but that won't happen now."

Rordan nodded slowly. "Anything else?"

"She mentioned calling on the Druids from MacLeod Castle. Rhona thinks the more allies, the better."

"What do you think?"

Balladyn lifted one shoulder in a shrug. "I think she has a good point. Besides, the MacLeod Druids might be the only ones we can trust right now."

"Aye. They've no interest in creating a group of Druid Others. If they come, they'll draw the attention of the Six. It's hard to ignore the power those Druids have, and they won't come without their Warrior mates." Rordan ran a hand through his short, black hair. "Ask Rhona to hold off on that for the moment. Let me share the news with Eoghan and the others."

Balladyn bowed his head in agreement.

"Oh, and one more thing," Rordan said. "A piece of advice. Don't fight it if something develops between you and Rhona. Something incredibly powerful connected the two of you. And before you try to argue that I don't know what I'm talking about, consider the fact that you won't leave her side. Or let any of us guard her. That should tell you something."

Rordan slapped him on the side of the arm before teleporting away. Balladyn turned to the fire and watched the flames dance. Rordan was right about one thing. He couldn't leave Rhona. Balladyn had thought it was only because she'd asked him to stay, but he now wondered if it was because he didn't want to be apart from her.

After so many years of being solitary and pining for Rhi, he had finally accepted that he was meant to spend his life alone. The time he got on his own allowed him to think about his poor choices so he could learn from them. Nothing had turned out as he had expected or hoped, but he felt as if he'd found his place among the Reapers.

Watching the couples sometimes made him lonely, but he was all right with that. He was better on his own. There would be more children on Death's realm. He didn't mind being the nanny while the couples spent time together. His time with Kyran and River's son, Breac, had shown him that he adored children. A surprise to be sure.

His head turned in the direction of Rhona's door. The memory of the urgent, pressing feeling that someone needed him would be forever stamped on his soul. Something had been shuttered within him that hadn't loosened until he found Rhona. Even after she was safe, the bond between them continued to grow and strengthen.

What did it mean? Who had called to him? Why had he been chosen to find Rhona? So many questions without answers.

Balladyn listened to the quiet of the house. The light beneath Rhona's door went out, blanketing the cottage in darkness except for the fire. His thoughts went to the Ancients. Everything he knew about Druids and Reapers told him that it couldn't have been the Ancients who'd reached across the realms to him. But it had been *something*.

He lowered himself to the floor and crossed his legs. After a moment, he closed his eyes. He didn't know what he expected to happen, but as the silence lengthened, he found himself sinking deeper into it. He needed to know who had called to him specifically. If there was any chance that it was something evil, he would get as far from Rhona as he could because he refused to bring that kind of darkness to her. He had lived with it. He knew how cunning and insidious it could be, how persuasive.

Rhona was all that was good. He wouldn't ruin her as he had everything else in his life—no matter how much he wanted to remain beside her. His chest tightened at the thought of leaving her. Of never seeing her lips curve into a smile or watching her soak up the magic at the Fairy Pools...of never looking into her green eyes again.

Never knowing her kiss.

"I know you can hear me," he said softly to the Ancients. "You see and hear everything. The future of the Druids is about to be tested, and I think you know that. Were you the ones who drew me to Rhona?"

Balladyn anxiously waited, hoping he might get an answer. Disappointment filled him when nothing happened. He had really thought it had been the Ancients who'd reached across time and space.

"When have they ever spoken to a Fae?" he reminded himself with a snort.

Balladyn started to get up when he heard something. He stilled, desperately straining to hear it again. Was it his imagination, or had that been the faint beat of a drum? Chills raced over his skin as his heart rate kicked up a notch.

He slowly resumed his seat. "Ancients?"

The minutes ticked by, but try as he might, Balladyn didn't hear anything else. He gave up after an hour. It must have been his imagination. The Ancients only spoke to Druids. When he regained his feet, something sharp and cold ran through him. His head whipped around to Rhona's door just as he heard a muffled scream.

He instantly teleported into her room and found her in the throes of a nightmare, her limbs tangled in the covers.

"Rhona," he said calmly as he tried to wake her. "I'm here. I'm here."

She shoved at him as she gasped for breath.

He gave her a shake, but she wouldn't open her eyes. "Rhona!"

CHAPTER TEN

They were there, surrounding her. She could feel their eyes, but she couldn't see their faces. Rhona wanted to scream, to run. She tried to prepare herself before the first dagger entered her body, but she couldn't. The pain of it took her breath.

She attempted to jerk away when the second blade struck. Then, there was a third. A fourth. The ache was excruciating. Agony wracked her body. Her limbs wouldn't work, and none of her muscles did as commanded. She knew she was going to die.

Rhona felt herself falling. She waited for her body to slam into the hard ground. Instead, she tumbled down an abyss with her attackers continually trying to stab her. Each time their blades found her, she tried to scream, only to have her voice muffled.

"Rhona!"

She fought against those holding her as she tried to call her magic. Nothing worked. She would die in darkness and pain. Alone. It was her greatest fear—and it was coming true.

"Rhona!"

She jerked open her eyes and stared into crimson orbs she knew well. Concern lined Balladyn's face as he sat beside her on the bed.

His fingers that clutched at her arms loosened as relief made his shoulders sag.

"I'm here," he whispered.

As much as she wanted to be strong and pretend that she hadn't clawed her way out of a nightmare, she couldn't. She pressed her lips together and threw herself at Balladyn. His strong arms wrapped around her, holding her tightly as she buried her face against his neck.

"You're safe. I've got you," he said, over and over.

Rhona didn't know if it was the sound of his voice or the fact that he held her, but she took in a shuddering breath and felt the knot in her stomach loosen as she cried. She had stayed awake for as long as she could, but her eyes grew too heavy. The dream had been worse than the attack because the ambush had lasted only seconds, while the nightmare had seemed to go on for eternity.

Finally, her tears halted, but she wasn't ready to release Balladyn. She knew the things she felt for him were partly because he had saved her. That didn't stop the need she had to be in his arms or to feel him near, though. She squeezed her eyes closed, fighting against the urge to hold onto him for the rest of her life.

How pathetic was she? Corann had believed she was strong enough to lead the Druids. Right now, she didn't care about them or anyone else. She just wanted to stop the emptiness and keep the cold taste of fear from her forever.

Rhona opened her eyes and looked across her darkened room. She realized that her fingers were still locked in Balladyn's long hair. If she were hurting him, he didn't say. Shame washed through her. She was stronger than this. She wasn't the type to cling to others.

"Don't," Balladyn whispered.

She stilled. Could he read her thoughts?

"There's nothing wrong with the fear you feel. There's no reason to be ashamed of it."

Rhona wondered what it would've been like to have Balladyn in her life years before. His calm presence was soothing. She didn't want to say it made her stronger or more in control, but that was exactly what it did. She had never known that she'd felt *out* of control until he was with her. Though, she should have. Corann used to tell her to control her emotions. And all this time, she'd thought she had.

Begrudgingly, she loosened her arms and sat back, meeting Balladyn's gaze. He smoothed the hair away from her face with gentle fingers and tucked it behind her ear. "I don't want to ever sleep again."

"It'll get better. I promise," he said.

Rhona didn't think she could handle it until the nightmares went away.

"I couldn't wake you," he admitted, a worried frown furrowing his brow.

She clasped her hands in her lap in an effort not to reach for him again.

"Do you want to talk about it?" he asked. When she hesitated, he said, "How about some tea?"

Rhona nodded, and in a blink, he held a mug with steam wafting from the liquid within. He smiled and handed it to her as he flipped on her light. She grasped the cup as if it were a lifeline. The heat of it stung her hands, but she didn't care. It was proof that she was alive.

"I've never been afraid of the dark," she said as she glanced at her light.

Balladyn hadn't moved from his spot beside her. "That's because you were attacked in the dark and left to die in it."

He was probably right. Rhona lowered her eyes to the mug and inhaled. Chamomile. It was what she would've made for herself. How had Balladyn known? The dream suddenly took over her thoughts. "The nightmare started just like the attack in Belfast. Then things…changed."

"How?" he asked softly.

"I started falling. There was no ground or anything beneath me, just deep, black space. My attackers fell with me, continuing to stab me."

Long, warm fingers covered her hand. Rhona lifted her gaze to look at Balladyn. Their eyes locked for several moments before he glanced away. But something had passed between them. His hand was warm and comforting. She missed the feel of his arms around her.

"It was just a nightmare. You survived the attack."

Barely. But she didn't say that. "What if the dream wasn't just a nightmare? What if it meant something?"

His brows snapped together in another frown. "Do you often dream of things?"

"No, but I'm trying to think of everything."

Balladyn nodded and dropped his hand away. She wanted to reach for him, to tell him that she needed his touch, but she gripped the mug harder instead.

"What do you think it means?" he asked.

She took a drink and felt the warmth of the tea slide down her throat. "In the literal interpretation, it suggests that the attackers didn't finish the job and will be coming back for me. But we already expected that."

"Our discussion could've triggered that part of your dream."

"That's true," she said. Still, she couldn't shake the feeling that she was supposed to know something more about the nightmare.

Balladyn pushed the tea at her to drink some more. "What else do you think the dream meant? Tell me the first thing that comes to mind."

"Darkness." A cold chill ran down her back.

"Easy," Balladyn said as he lightly gripped her wrists.

Rhona looked down to see that she was shaking. She handed the tea to him and tried to take in a calming breath but she couldn't.

"Talk to me," he urged. "Tell me what you're feeling. Tell me why that word made you react so."

She shook her head as she shrugged. "At the end of the nightmare, I knew I was going to die in the dark. Alone. It's my greatest fear."

"You said that you weren't afraid of the dark until now."

"That's just it. I'm not scared of anything but that darkness." That's when it hit her. She wrapped her arms around herself. "The darkness was alive. It wasn't like the night. It was something altogether different."

"Evil," he said.

She nodded, the coldness wrapping tighter around her. "Yes."

Balladyn rose and paced in front of her bed. He stopped and looked at her. "Did you see any faces, hear voices or names?"

"Nothing. I was trying to get away from the knives. The pain—"

"Aye," he said over her. "I understand."

The coldness had seeped deep into Rhona's bones, and she wondered if she'd ever be able to dislodge it. She reached for the tea, needing something to warm her. After a few sips while watching Balladyn, she said, "Maybe it's like you said. Just a nightmare."

His red eyes slid to her. "Maybe."

But they both knew that wasn't the case.

Rhona finished her tea and shoved her fingers into her hair to get the long length out of her face. "I have to go back to sleep, don't I?"

"No."

She wanted to hug him for lying. He was trying to protect her, but they both knew if she wanted the truth, then she had to go to the one place she didn't want to go—her nightmare.

"I can stay with you," he offered.

Rhona nodded as gratitude filled her. Somehow, he knew. Of course, he did. He'd told her that he'd suffered his own nightmares after his betrayal and death. He had intimate knowledge of what she was going through. No one had been there for him, though. Then again, maybe the other Reapers had.

She wanted to believe that, but she was sure that each Reaper had dealt with things in their own way. That made her heart hurt. If she had this much trauma, she couldn't imagine what Balladyn and the other Reapers had dealt with.

"I won't leave the room."

His husky voice startled her out of her thoughts. She watched as he walked to the chair in the corner that had clean clothes piled to be folded. *In the room* wouldn't be good enough. If she were going to do this, she needed him beside her.

Rhona patted the bed. "It's better than the chair."

He stilled in the process of moving the clothes to sit in the chair. The way he seemed to stop breathing as he turned and stared at the bed made her wonder if he felt the same attraction she did. He had touched her several times. She had been in distress, though. She didn't want to read into things that weren't there. But if they were…

Balladyn's gaze met hers. Slowly, he put the clothes back, straightened, and walked to the other side of the bed. He carefully sank down and stretched out on top of the covers. She started to turn off the light, then thought better of it. Rhona glanced at him to find his eyes locked on the ceiling. She slid back down and brought the covers up to her chin.

She had to force her eyes to close. Trepidation held her immobile, and that fear could get her killed if she didn't face it. There were a million other things she'd rather do, but Rhona forced herself to relax and close her eyes. Balladyn remained still beside her, but just knowing that she could reach out and touch him made it easy for her to face the next nightmare.

Her thoughts turned to the one subject she couldn't seem to get enough of—Balladyn. A Light Fae warrior who'd become the King of the Dark and who was now a Reaper. If she hadn't already known him, she would've wanted to. She didn't care what had sent him to her. All she knew was that his quiet strength, combined with his imposing power, made for a heady combination that she couldn't get enough of.

Rhona knew she was mixing her appreciation for his part in saving her with the dread of what she had to face. It was wrong to put him in a position where he'd have to turn her down.

But what if he didn't? What if there *was* something there? What if he was attracted to her, too?

She was so lost in her thoughts of Balladyn that she didn't realize she had fallen asleep.

CHAPTER ELEVEN

Wicklow, Ireland

Aisling stood on the docks and watched the anchored boats roll with the water, the moonlight reflecting off the surface. For weeks, she'd been unable to find Xaneth. She thought of her fellow Reapers. She had almost returned to Death's realm a few times, but then she thought about the certainty within her that she was meant to work with Xaneth.

If only she could convince him of that.

After he had fought Lena, the leader of the Six, he had disappeared. No matter where Aisling looked or how she tried to track him as she had done before, he was nowhere to be found. She thought he might be hiding from her. It was still a possibility. Then again, he couldn't seem to control when he went after the Fae Others. It was almost as if something inside him controlled him.

Her neck tingled slightly. This was the third time in as many weeks that she had felt it. The feeling never lasted long. The first time she had sensed someone watching her, she had whirled around immediately, searching for who it was. Unfortunately, she'd come up empty-handed. The second time, she had tried to be more discreet with little difference in the outcome. This time, she was going to do her best to ignore it. She had no proof, only the hope sprouting inside her, but she thought it could be Xaneth.

When she caught up with him the last time, he had made it clear that he didn't want her around. Something had flashed behind his silver eyes. She had thought it was fear at first, but surely that couldn't be. Xaneth faced off against the Others and their soldiers without hesitation. Why would anything cause him to be afraid of *her*?

The sensation on her neck intensified. Aisling forced herself to remain still. She recalled Xaneth asking if she had come to kill him. He had seemed genuinely surprised when she informed him that she had come to fight with him.

She thought about teleporting somewhere close in hopes of catching who watched her. Was it Xaneth? Just because she wanted it to be him didn't mean it was. He hadn't answered a single call from her. It was almost as if he were no longer on the realm. Yet she knew that wasn't the case. He was after the Six and anyone connected to the Fae Others. There was no way he would leave until that was done.

He had skills in battle, ones she hadn't expected of a royal Light Fae, no matter if he had been hiding for most of his life or not. When she first saw him, she had wondered why Erith had enlisted his help. Obviously, the goddess had known of his battle abilities. Something had changed inside him after his aunt, Usaeil, had tortured him. There was a ruthlessness in him now, a relentlessness that drove Xaneth. It was almost as if his very being hinged on wiping out the Fae Others.

Disappointment filled her when the tingling on her neck suddenly stopped. Whoever had been there was gone. If it weren't Xaneth, then she hoped she ran into whoever it was soon because she needed to burn off the growing frustration and anger inside her.

She had walked away from the Reapers. Aisling was still shocked that Erith had allowed her to go, especially after the vow Aisling had given to the goddess when she became a Reaper. Even when she had fought with the Reapers recently against Lena, Erith hadn't demanded that Aisling return to the fold. The goddess knew something. Otherwise, she wouldn't have given Aisling the opportunity to find Xaneth.

"Where are you?" Aisling whispered on the wind.

The knot in her stomach had been growing bigger with each week that passed and she went without locating the royal Light. She knew something big was coming. What she didn't know was whether it was for Xaneth or the Reapers. She was torn because she knew she was doing the right thing by tracking Xaneth, but she also knew her place was with her fellow Reapers. They were her family. She counted on them, and they counted on her.

And she had left them.

Aisling had been so sure of her path when she left to find Xaneth. Now, she was far less certain. Xaneth somehow determined where the Fae Others were because he was always there, fighting them. Maybe she had done the wrong thing in leaving the Reapers since they were continually in the midst of fighting the Others.

She fisted her hands, wanting to scream her irritation. Aisling turned her back to the water and looked over the city. The lights and cloud cover prevented her from seeing the stars. Her gaze moved slowly from one side of the metropolis to the other. The Fae Others were out there. She knew it, just as she knew Dark Fae were killing humans that very second. Some things would never stop.

No matter how much everyone wanted a utopia, it would never happen because there had to be balance. There was always dark with light, evil with the good. Neither could ever be completely wiped away. The scales could be tipped in one direction, and it sometimes took some time to correct the balance again, but it always happened. Always.

She should know.

"If you don't want me to find you, Xaneth, then I need to be with my family," she whispered into the night. "I came to help. I couldn't tell you for what, but I just knew that I was meant to aid you in some way. I still know that to be a fact, but perhaps I'm going about this wrong. The closer I get to you, the farther you run. But you can only run for so long. We're both seeking the same thing. Why then, do I get the feeling that you'll…?"

She let the words die. Aisling couldn't even say them. Thinking them was difficult enough.

Xaneth had thought Death had sent her to kill him. He had looked confused and mildly annoyed when she hadn't. These past weeks, she hadn't wanted to consider that Xaneth wished to die, but the truth had been staring her in the face the entire time. He didn't want anyone near him, he refused to talk, ran anytime she got near, and sought out the Fae Others, jumping into battle without thought or plan.

The truth of it all cascaded down on her like ice water. Anguish made her nearly double over. How could the thought of Xaneth dying make her feel like that? She didn't make connections with others. At least she hadn't until she became a Reaper. Those attachments with her brethren, her family, had been established one thread at a time until they formed without her even knowing. The Reapers gave her something she'd never thought she needed—family. None of them cared about her background, and she didn't care about theirs. They trusted her, just as she did them.

Unequivocally.

She could understand why she would be tracking one of her family. With Xaneth, what she felt was something altogether different and…special. Distinctive. She couldn't explain where it had come from or why it had developed—not to herself or anyone else. But there was a link between them. One that refused to be ignored.

"Xaneth," she called, knowing he could hear her and trace her voice if he wanted.

Aisling waited for several minutes, hoping he would show. When he didn't, she sighed and made her decision to return to the Reapers.

～

Xaneth rubbed his chest, confused by the ache that had begun when he heard Aisling's words. He had made sure to stay out of sight so she couldn't find him. However, he hadn't been able to stop checking on her wherever she went.

He'd started to follow her, which had hindered her search for him. He hadn't wanted to keep an eye on her, but he hadn't been able to stop himself. Between spotting her, he followed the scents of evil in whatever city she chose and ended any Fae Others or soldiers he stumbled across.

That was when he began to notice that there weren't as many sightings of Fae Others or the soldiers anymore. Something was going on, and he couldn't figure out what it was. He should be ecstatic since his sole duty was to eradicate evil. Why then did he have this gnawing, guttural sense of dread that this was the lull before the storm?

His gaze swept over Aisling from the lengthy braids of her black and silver hair, to her lithe body clad in all black, to her long nails colored blood red. The Reaper was beautiful and deadly, and he couldn't take his eyes off her. In another life, he wondered what might have occurred between them.

When she called his name, he had to fight not to go to her. He saw the resignation on her face. She was tired of not finding him. It was what he wanted. Why he had made sure she *couldn't* find him. The expression that passed over her countenance confirmed what he already suspected—she was returning to the Reapers.

Xaneth teleported behind her, half hoping that she would turn around and spot him, but he'd timed it so that he arrived a half-second before she jumped—just enough time for him to breathe in her jasmine scent and touch the end of one braid.

The instant she was gone, a great despondency overtook him. He tried to brush it off, but it clung to him like mist. With her near, all he could think about was Aisling, when he should be focused on finding evil. Xaneth pivoted, ready to get back to work, but he paused. He needed to know that she was gone from this realm first.

He closed his eyes and inhaled deeply, letting her scent fill him.

He followed it to a small island with a Fae doorway. He got there in time to see her disappearing through it. Xaneth hesitated. She was gone. Just as he wanted. Why then did it feel so…wrong? He stared at the doorway for a long time after she disappeared. He didn't know what he was hoping for. In the end, he returned to Wicklow to hunt the Fae Others. Aisling had gone back to the Reapers where she belonged. He should be pleased.

Except, he wasn't.

Would it really have hurt to speak to her? To let her tell him what she had been trying for weeks to say? He'd lost count of how close she had come to finding him, not to mention the times she actually had. That was before he'd made sure to keep hidden from her.

Xaneth shook his head in an effort to dislodge Aisling from his mind. He would see her again the next time there was a battle with the soldiers. The Reapers were always there. Except Xaneth would make sure he beat them to it. He knew his purpose.

He teleported from roof to roof as he waited for the stench of evil to reach him. Unfortunately, his mind kept drifting to thoughts of Aisling. She had only just left, and yet he already missed scanning the buildings to look for her. He would miss watching her from a distance, wondering what she was thinking while keeping out of sight.

Maybe he should've asked her what she was thinking those times she'd stared off into the distance, deep in thought. Or perhaps that time he'd happened to hear her cry out when she had been sleeping. After that, he rarely saw her rest.

Everyone had a story. His was one he never wanted repeated. He assumed Aisling felt the same about hers. Xaneth turned his head slightly, hoping he'd catch her call for him one last time. It was silly. She couldn't reach him across the realms. Even if she could, he wouldn't go to her.

Wouldn't you?

He ignored his inner voice and breathed. Xaneth choked on the reek of evil. He wanted to hold his breath and get the smell out of his head, but he had to locate it. Squatting, he put one hand on the roof and scanned the city as he breathed in. There. To the left. It wasn't just any evil, either. What he smelled was Fae Other.

A slow smile pulled at his lips as he jumped toward the scent.

CHAPTER TWELVE

Balladyn could feel Rhona's warmth beside him. He made himself lay perfectly still despite the urge to reach over and touch her or roll toward her. When she had patted the bed earlier, his heart had skipped a beat. Did she have any idea how alluring she was? Had she no concept of how desperately he wanted her?

He hadn't until the idea of being on the bed with her was presented to him. Now, all he could think about was what they could be doing. He squeezed his eyes closed, but he couldn't stop the images playing in his head of them together, tangled in the sheets, their bodies slick with sweat, and the room filled with moans of pleasure.

All the blood rushed to his cock. His body was aflame, and there was nothing he could do. Of all the places he'd thought he might find himself, in the bed of a flame-haired Druid with green eyes that made him feel as though he had found a safe harbor wasn't one of them. The ache inside him to taste Rhona's lips, to run his hands over her skin, and learn every nuance of her body engulfed him.

No, he thought, *it consumed him.*

He heard her breathing finally even out into sleep. Balladyn made himself relax, but the instant she rolled toward him, he

stiffened once more. This agony was worse than when he'd sat in
the living area, thinking of her in the shower.

Unable to help himself, he slowly turned his head to look at her.
The glow of the light behind her cast her face in shadow. His gaze
slowly moved from her flaming locks to her forehead, lower to her
long lashes, and then over her cheeks to her lips that were slightly
parted in sleep. Before he knew it, he was on his side, facing her.
Her courage inspired him. He wouldn't have gone back to sleep
after a nightmare, but she had lifted her chin and faced the situation
with determination.

In subtle ways, he caught indications of why Corann had chosen
her as his replacement. She was terrified and dealing with a
horrendous trauma, but she didn't hesitate to face the monsters of
her nightmare. He knew few who would attempt such a thing so
quickly. And Rhona didn't think she should lead the Druids. If only
she could see herself from his eyes. Maybe then she would
understand that she had more than what it took to hold the position.

Minutes stretched with nothing happening. Her exhaustion
might pull her under quickly so she could escape any nightmares.
However, that was usually when they struck the fastest. Yet, nothing
happened.

He glanced down to see that their hands were nearly touching.
She had asked him to join her on the bed to make her feel safe. The
last thing she needed was to be woken by his touch. Even as he told
himself that, he shifted his hand slightly so the back of his fingers
met hers. His gaze jerked to her face, but she didn't wake.

Balladyn breathed a sigh of relief. He couldn't believe that she
wanted him with her. At the pools, and now in her bed. No one had
ever wanted him to guard them before. He'd thought that after
telling her his story, she would find him abhorrent. That wasn't the
case at all. The compassion in her eyes had nearly been his undoing.

His thoughts drifted to the gift Erith had given him during the
holidays. One side of the globe had an image of him at the height
of his career as a Queen's Guard. The other when he had been
King of the Dark. When held just right, the two merged and
showed him as he was now. It had been Death's way of indicating

that he was both the Light warrior and the Dark King. Neither made him better or worse than the other.

It was such a special gift. Unlike anything he had ever received. He'd been so touched that it had brought tears to his eyes. He'd felt much the same way when Rhona had told him he had gone through everything because being a Reaper was his destiny. He'd never thought of it that way, but there might be a kernel of truth to her words.

Her fingers twitched, touching him. His eyes lowered to their hands. He waited for any indication that she was succumbing to a nightmare, but she remained blissfully still and calm.

Balladyn yawned. He'd had no rest since he'd first felt the need to get to her. He wouldn't sleep now, either. Anything could happen, and he didn't want to learn that he hadn't been there to protect her because he had drifted off.

He yawned again and decided the best thing would be for him to return to his back. He couldn't stare at Rhona all night. Besides, thoughts of *what-ifs* kept running through his head when he did. Like, what if he went to bed with her every night? Those kinds of thoughts were the last things he should be thinking. What he *should* be considering were ways to help Rhona if she got stuck in a nightmare. It was rare, but it did happen. Mostly to those with magic. And since she had more of it than she realized, it was a concern.

Or, he could make a list of ways that someone could reach another across realms. Even with all the books in his library, he had never read of it happening. It had been an impossibility. Until it hadn't been. He could only imagine it would be Rhona or the Ancients who had done such a thing. But did Rhona have that kind of magic? He wasn't sure. Nor did he believe the Ancients would speak to him, a Fae and a Reaper.

Still unable to work out that problem, he moved on to the next, which was who had tried to kill Rhona. It only made sense that it was the Druids, yet he couldn't cross out Lena and the Six. The only reason they had to do it was because it would draw the Reapers to Skye and away from Ireland.

Or get the Reapers in one place for an attack.

Balladyn couldn't believe he hadn't thought of that before. He started to rise from the bed to go to Eoghan but hesitated. Balladyn didn't want to leave Rhona, but it would only take a moment to teleport to Eoghan and tell him before Balladyn jumped back to the bed.

He turned his head to her for one last look before teleporting outside. That's when he saw the small frown between her brows. Her body stiffened, and her hand reached out to his, her nails digging into his skin and drawing blood. He didn't flinch as he was too engrossed in watching for what might happen next. Rhona needed to get answers, but he wouldn't let her get sucked into the nightmare.

She let out a sound that was a mix of a growl and a scream. Balladyn sat up and faced her. He reached for her shoulders to wake her when she flopped onto her back, an unholy sound coming from her throat. Then she was slowly rising from the bed. The covers fell from her as if an unseen hand yanked them away.

"Bloody hell," he murmured and jumped from the bed to his feet. Balladyn wasn't sure if he should touch her or not. She wasn't thrashing, but this was far from normal. "Fek!" he bellowed in frustration.

Suddenly, Rhona's back arched as she levitated several feet off the bed. Light began to pour from her fingers and toes, growing brighter and brighter until Balladyn had to raise his hand to shield his eyes from it.

Balladyn bellowed her name. Just as he took a step to wake her, drumming filled the silence. It was so loud he had to cover his ears. The beat was rhythmic, growing faster and faster in time with the brightening light. Balladyn squeezed his eyes closed, but it did no good. The luminescence was blinding, the drums deafening.

"Eoghan!" Balladyn shouted.

Surely, the other Reapers had seen the light and were in the cottage. One of his brethren would be able to get to Rhona. He hated that it wasn't him, but he couldn't get to his feet. It was as if the drums were pushing him down, and the light was purposefully keeping him blinded.

Just as suddenly as the drums had begun, they silenced. Only to be replaced by a multitude of voices that bellowed, "*They're coming!*"

A hand touched Balladyn. He jumped to his feet, a ball of magic in his hand ready to throw, when he found the other Reapers in Rhona's room, staring at him in confusion. He jerked his head to the side to find Rhona once more on the bed.

Balladyn's chest heaved. His ears rang from the drums and the voices. Every time he blinked, he saw black dots from the brightness of the light.

"It's just us," Eoghan said softly.

Balladyn frowned, hating that they were talking to him like he was on the threshold of madness. Then again, maybe he was. He made the orb of magic disappear and ran a hand through his hair.

"So," Ruarc said into the awkward silence, "anyone want to guess where that crazy white light came from?"

Balladyn took one more look at Rhona. She looked unharmed. There were no signs that she was caught in a nightmare. He should be pleased about that, but he felt anything but good at the moment.

Eoghan touched him lightly on the shoulder and jerked his chin toward the hall, silently urging Balladyn to follow them. Eoghan was the first out of the bedroom, with the others following. Balladyn swallowed and decided that a few minutes with them couldn't hurt. He slowly walked to the door and paused to look at Rhona. Then he went into the living area.

"What happened?" Rordan asked.

Balladyn shook his head, not sure he could put it into words yet. "You saw the light?"

"We all did," Bradach answered.

Ruarc snorted. "Bright as hell. I'm sure half of Skye saw it."

"And the drums?" Balladyn asked. "Did any of you hear them?"

The Reapers exchanged looks. It was Eoghan who said, "There were no drums."

"Druids hear drums when the Ancients are trying to speak to them," Dubhan stated.

Every eye was glued to him. Balladyn shifted his feet. Fek. Fek! Without a doubt, he'd heard drums. What did that mean? "If you saw the light, how could you not hear the drums? They were thunderous."

"No drums sounded," Torin replied.

Balladyn felt sick to his stomach. If they hadn't heard the drums, then they certainly hadn't heard the voices.

"What is it?" Eoghan urged.

Rordan's nose wrinkled as he looked at Balladyn. "You just went a shade paler than when we found you a few minutes ago."

"Fek," Balladyn said and briefly closed his eyes. "Earlier, I asked the Ancients if they were the ones who'd called to me across the realms. I heard nothing. Well, I thought I heard drums for an instant, but it must have been my imagination because nothing else happened. Rhona then had a nightmare. She said she felt something in the dream. It was different than the attack, and she suspected there were answers there."

Ruarc nodded. "She went back to sleep in hopes she'd find what she was searching for."

"Except what I thought was turning into a nightmare became something else. She floated off the bed and emitted a strange sound. Then there was the light. The drumming came after. I had to shut my eyes, and I covered my ears. It felt like I was being pressed into the ground. Then the drums halted and…" Balladyn paused. There was no getting away from sharing this next part—even though it would sound farfetched. "Hundreds of thousands of voices surrounded me. They yelled at me."

Eoghan's quicksilver eyes sharpened. "What did they say?"

"*They're coming.*"

There was a beat of silence as everyone took that in. Eoghan's lips tightened a fraction before he asked, "Were they speaking about the Fae Others?"

Balladyn shrugged.

"Fek that," Torin said. "I want to know if that was the Ancients speaking to you."

Balladyn swallowed, his throat dry. "I'm Fae. Why would they speak to me?"

"Someone did," Dubhan said.

Ruarc crossed his arms over his chest. "Regardless of who it was, we got a warning."

"It might be the only one we get," Bradach replied.

CHAPTER THIRTEEN

Rhona wasn't sure what'd woken her. Her eyes felt swollen and scratchy, as they always did when she hadn't gotten enough sleep. She knew better than to rub them, but she couldn't help it. She winced at the pain she caused herself and reached for Balladyn. When she met an empty, cool bed, she sat up.

That's when she sharpened her hearing. She caught the sound of Balladyn's deep timbre, but she couldn't make out what he said. Other voices joined in. She caught the word *Ancients*, and her stomach clenched. Rhona swung her legs over the side of the bed, then paused as she glanced back at the covers. It wasn't like her to kick them off, and she knew Balladyn wouldn't have done that. So, why was she outside the covers on a chilly winter night?

More confusion filled her. She shivered from the cold and the knowledge that something had happened she hadn't been aware of. After shoving her feet into her slippers, she reached for her cardigan. Once it was on, she felt marginally warmer, but she couldn't shake the fear that it would be a long time before she got rid of the cold that had seeped deep into her soul.

On silent feet, she walked toward her door that stood ajar. The low voices became clearer then.

Balladyn said, "I'm a Fae. Why would they speak to me?"

"Someone did," Dubhan replied.

Ruarc said, "Regardless of who it was, we got a warning."

"It might be the only one we get," Bradach countered.

That's all Rhona needed to hear. She had to know what was going on. She slipped through the opening of her door and walked to them. No one noticed her at first. They were all deep in thought. Then Balladyn's head swung to her.

He pushed away from the counter and faced her. "We didn't mean to wake you."

"What happened?" she asked, not taking her eyes off him. She knew he would tell her. She couldn't say how, only that she would stake her life on it.

Balladyn's red gaze lowered to the floor briefly as a frown marred his brow. "We're trying to figure that out."

"It sounded like you already had." Rhona couldn't explain why she was angry that the Ancients had spoken to someone else, but the emotion burned hotly inside her. She hated that she felt that way. She had begged the Ancients to speak to her all her life. The closest she had come was when she lay dying. Now, they were talking to Balladyn? A Fae?

"Did you have a nightmare before you woke this time?" Eoghan asked.

Rhona glanced at Eoghan before returning her gaze to Balladyn. He must have told them everything. All the Reapers were there to help. She should be grateful for their involvement, not jealous because the Ancients *might have* spoken to Balladyn.

She realized that everyone was waiting for her to answer Eoghan's question. "No."

"Did you feel anything?" Bradach asked.

That made Rhona frown. She crossed her arms over her chest and slid her gaze to Balladyn. "Again, I'm going to ask, what happened?"

"You floated off the bed," he answered.

She blinked, shocked. Had he just said…? As far as she knew, she had never done anything like that before.

"And light shot out of you," Balladyn continued.

Rhona reached for the nearest wall to keep herself on her feet. "Light?" she asked, her voice faint and wobbly, even to her ears.

Balladyn slowly nodded. "It seared my eyes."

"The entire house lit up," Ruarc said.

It was difficult to breathe. She wanted to sit down. Rhona didn't think she would make it to a chair, but neither did she want to collapse in front of the Reapers. So, she'd floated and had light shoot out of her? What in the bloody hell did that mean?

Balladyn cleared his throat. "That's when I heard the drums."

Drums? Rhona searched his eyes, looking for the lie, but there wasn't one. Something had happened. She had known it the instant she woke. She glanced at the Reapers. "Did any of you hear them?"

They all shook their heads.

Rhona's knees began to shake, but she kept herself upright. Barely. She took it all in, assimilating slowly. Just when she thought that was it, Balladyn continued.

"I felt like I was being pushed down from all sides. I was on my knees when the drums suddenly halted, and voices replaced them."

Her lips parted in shock. Though, she shouldn't have been surprised. She had heard the whispered end of their conversation before she left her room. But now she had pieced it all together. The Ancients had chosen Balladyn, a Dark Fae and Reaper. The betrayal cut so deeply she bent at the waist and sucked in great gulps of air.

Why? That one word kept ringing through her head like a tolling bell. Why had the Ancients chosen Balladyn instead of her? What did he have that she lacked? She was the head of the Skye Druids, but the Ancients wouldn't talk to her. Maybe them ignoring her was their way of telling her Corann had gotten it wrong.

Rhona closed her eyes. She didn't want to ask her next question, but the words tumbled from her lips anyway. "What did the Ancients say?"

"They're coming."

Her eyes snapped open as she straightened and looked at

Balladyn. There was something about those words. Her entire body felt as if it were vibrating.

As if her thoughts were written on her face, Balladyn took a step toward her, his gaze sharpening. "You've heard them before?"

"I-I don't think so. At least not their voices. The drums I heard as a child. And yet, it feels as though I have."

"Maybe when you were injured after the attack?"

She searched her mind. She *had* heard the Ancients, but she hadn't been able to make out what they said. "I can't be sure."

"If they did say that to Rhona, could they have been talking about us?" Torin asked.

Rhona felt everyone's gazes on her. "Maybe. I don't know."

"Then why say it to me?" Balladyn asked, his frown deepening. "It was a warning. I heard that in their tone, but that's all I can say for sure."

The more she learned, the more Rhona felt as if the rug had been yanked out from under her. She had barely been keeping it together since the attack, and now this? She pushed away from the wall and walked woodenly through the gathered Reapers to the sofa, ordering her legs to hold her. Somehow, she made it without falling on her face. When she lowered herself to the couch, she felt cold all the way to her bones.

"We'll be outside on guard," Eoghan said.

Out of the corner of her eye, Rhona saw each Reaper leave until it was only her and Balladyn. He didn't immediately walk to her. When he took the chair beside her, she couldn't quite meet his gaze. It was stupid, really. She had no reason to be angry at him. The Ancients had made their decision. She only wished she knew why they had spoken to him.

"I'm sorry," he said into the silence.

She looked down at her hands. "For what?"

"Because of the Ancients. The distress coming from you is palpable."

What could she say to that? It was the truth. So, she decided to remain quiet.

He sighed softly. "I tried to communicate with them earlier. I wanted to see if they were the ones who'd sent me to you in Belfast, but I didn't hear anything." He paused. "You think them speaking now means you aren't meant to be the leader."

Bloody hell. Was he a mind reader? She curled her fingers into fists.

"The words they gave me have meaning to you. Maybe they couldn't get them to you, so they used me. Focus on that, not that they spoke to me."

She snapped her head up, her gaze finally meeting his. "I'm not going to fall to pieces if that's what you're worried about."

"I'm not."

But she talked over him. "If someone else is meant to lead, then it'll happen. Until then, I'm going to perform the duty I was handed."

"Good," he said with a soft smile.

He was agreeing with her, but she wanted to scream. It wasn't his fault. She knew that, and yet she couldn't calm the raging storm of emotions within that threatened to consume her. Mostly because Balladyn had nailed each and every one as if he could see straight into her soul.

She looked at the fire, needing something other than his handsome face to stare at. She felt his gaze on her. It was on the tip of her tongue to ask him what he was thinking, but she couldn't manage the words. Her anger wasn't really directed at him. It was for the Ancients. But he was here. He had heard them.

Could he be right? Had they been unable to reach her, so had used him? It didn't seem plausible since the Ancients only spoke to Druids. Then again, how did they know that? It wasn't as if the Ancients had told them as much.

The more Rhona thought about all of it, the more confused she became. Everything she'd thought she knew had been wiped away. The world was in flux, and she seemed to be at the center of it. It was a position she didn't like or want. Yet she couldn't—*wouldn't*—walk away. She had promised Corann she would protect Skye and their people. And she would.

Even if it claimed her life.

"I think the Ancients shared that warning with you," Balladyn said into the silence. "I also think that, for some reason, it didn't get through to you."

"And so they used you?"

She saw him shrug out of the corner of her eye. "I know very little about the Ancients, but I sense they needed to get the warning to you, and they knew I would tell you. They wanted to make sure I heard, so they spoke loudly enough to burst my eardrums."

Rhona swung her head to him. "I only heard them as a whisper."

"You felt the importance of their warning, though, didn't you?"

She nodded, unable to deny it. "But who is coming? You said it sounded like an alarm. Could it have been a declaration?"

"They shouted the two words at me. I took that to mean a warning, but you're right. It could have been an announcement."

Rhona threw up her hands. "So, it could be a warning that we should prepare for, or it could be a declaration that help is on the way. Or, it could be something else entirely. That's how the Ancients usually communicate. They never spell things out just as they are. It's up to the one receiving the message to decipher it."

"Did Corann give you any details about how to interpret their words?"

"I wish I could say that Corann trained me to take any part of his position, but the truth is, I didn't learn anything different than any other Druid on Skye. I had no idea he had chosen me until it was done."

Balladyn sighed. "Is there anyone we can ask?"

"Yep," she said with a nod. "The ones the Ancients seem to talk to a lot. The MacLeod Druids."

CHAPTER FOURTEEN

Balladyn should've seen that coming. Then again, he hadn't paid too much attention to the Druids, no matter where they lived. All Fae knew about the Warriors and Druids of MacLeod Castle, but knowing *of them* and knowing them were two different things. Obviously, he needed to dig deeper into everyone at the castle.

"You don't seem thrilled with that news," Rhona said.

Balladyn looked into her green eyes and shrugged. In the past, he would've come up with a cool quip so no one would know what he was really thinking. It never crossed his mind not to be honest with her. "I know little about them."

"That surprises me."

"Does it?"

It was her turn to shrug. "You strike me as someone well informed of a lot."

"When it comes to the Fae, I am. I have an extensive collection of books and scrolls dating back to the original Fae families."

"That sounds like it took a long time to acquire."

He chuckled as he thought about the lengths he'd gone to in order to acquire some of the books. "Many didn't have a clue what they had in their possessions. If they had, they never would've let them go. And I stole a few."

"Somehow, that doesn't surprise me," she replied with a smile. "I have a feeling you make use of them."

"I've read every one at least once. Many dozens of times. It's how I knew the spell to slow your bleeding."

Her brows snapped together. "Can Fae not do healing magic?"

"On ourselves, yes. On a Druid who already has magic hindering her, no."

Rhona rubbed her hands together as if to warm them. "I don't understand."

"We don't need to use spells for our magic."

"But…you just said you used a spell."

He raised his brows briefly. "That is something we learned from Druids on Skye through our friendship at the Fairy Pools."

"Really?" she asked in surprise. "Tell me what you know about the Druids."

"As I said, very little. I know humans were brought to this realm by a Druid named Moreann. Her realm was losing magic, and she found this one. Unfortunately, it already had dragons on it. So, she came up with an idea for how to rid the realm of them. She dumped humans from her planet here, those born without magic, and wiped their memories. The Dragon Kings aided the mortals, helping them get settled. Through the years, some humans were born with magic."

"The first came to Skye," Rhona interjected.

Balladyn nodded. "While the Dragon Kings were fighting with the humans, Moreann formed the Others. Two Druids from Earth, two Fae—a Light and a Dark—and herself and one other Druid— a *drough*—from her realm. Together, they merged their magics, which was the only thing that could match a Dragon King's. And plans were laid far into the future to begin an attack on the Kings."

Rhona leaned her head to the side and popped her neck. "What was meant to be the downfall of the Dragon Kings was the ending of the Others. Corann was the one who killed Moreann, giving up his life in the process. So, you know some of our history, then. What about the Warriors and Druids?"

"I know even less. I know who they are. I also know that the Druids brought about the Warriors."

Rhona looked pained by that statement. "There's a debate in the Druid community about whether that was our finest hour or not."

"What do you mean?"

"When the Romans landed on the shores of England, they swept over the land like a scourge, working their way up to Scotland. There were many Celtic tribes at the time, each with Druids who were their trusted allies and advisors. The *mies*. Our magic comes in the purest form from this realm. However, there were those who wanted more power and control."

"*Droughs*," Balladyn said.

Rhona licked her lips. "The *droughs* had a solution for the invading armies of Rome. Each Celtic leader called their greatest warrior forward as *droughs* cast their spells and called up gods long-buried in Hell. The gods were happy to be free at last, even if by answering the *droughs'* call, they bound themselves into each tribe's fiercest warriors.

"Those men became Warriors, who then attacked Rome, winning battle after battle until the Romans finally relented. Just as the *mies* had suspected, the gods wouldn't relinquish their new freedom. They were still thirsty for blood. Still hungry for battle. With no Romans to fight, the Warriors turned on each other and anyone else. The Celts demanded that the *droughs* reverse their spell. While the *droughs* had enough magic to release the gods, they didn't have nearly enough to return them to their prison. With every kill, the gods took over the men.

"A gathering of Druids was called. It was the first—and last—time such an assembly ever occurred. The *mies* and *droughs* set aside their differences and tried everything they knew to release the men from the gods. But nothing freed the warriors. The Druids had one last option. If they couldn't send the gods back to Hell, then they could bind them. So, *mies* and *droughs* united their magic and created a spell that bound the gods inside their hosts. The Warriors returned to the men they had once been with no memory of what had occurred, while the gods were loose."

Balladyn quirked a brow. "The gods were still there, however."

"Oh, yes. With every generation, the gods moved from warrior to warrior, passed down and forever a part of the family's bloodline. The Druids hadn't solved a problem. They had merely created a new one that could be unleashed in the future. A decision was made that a Druid would always stay near the Warriors, forever keeping watch. They did it even when their faith, the very thing they were, caused them to hide in fear of being killed. They watched, keeping all of mankind safe."

Balladyn suspected that the Dragon Kings had known, but he didn't say that. "Is that the end of the story?"

"Far from it. Many, many years later, a power-hungry *drough* named Deirdre found a scroll written in secret by another *drough* with the spell to unbind the gods and control them. She used it, which gave her the army she wanted as she set her sights on ruling the world and becoming a goddess before which all men would tremble. Yet there was one drawback. The scroll didn't list all the families. It only had one name."

"MacLeod," Balladyn guessed.

Rhona nodded. "Deirdre turned her sights on them. There were three brothers, equal in strength, cunning, and intelligence. The god split himself between the siblings. When Deirdre used the spell, she awoke the god within the siblings. The three hid themselves away for three hundred years until a woman came to their ruin of a castle —one who had no idea that she was a Druid."

"And Deirdre?"

"The spell woke other gods inside men, and she rounded them up, one by one. But she couldn't get her hands on the MacLeod brothers. She decided to go after them, which was her mistake. It made the brothers realize what was going on, and they took a stand. Other Warriors who had been fighting Deirdre joined them. Druids were drawn to MacLeod Castle, to the Warriors. They eventually defeated Deirdre and those who tried to take up the gauntlet after her. The Warriors and Druids have since remained at the castle in peace. Though they did come to Skye when the final battle with the Others was taking place."

Now that interested Balladyn. "Why?"

"The Ancients told Isla to come."

"Which is why you think you should contact these Druids?"

Rhona shrugged. "One of them might have learned something from the Ancients that neither of us has."

"Trust your instincts."

"If I contact them, they'll come."

Balladyn tried not to smile. "That's what you want."

"What if I'm pulling them into something dangerous? They've suffered enough. They deserve their peace."

"Everyone can say that. Contact them. We'll fill them in on what's going on. Then let them make the choice of what to do."

She yawned, covering her mouth as she nodded. "Right. That's a good idea."

Balladyn spotted the dark circles under her eyes. "You need to sleep."

"I'm not sure I want to try again."

"You won't be good to anyone if you aren't rested."

She twisted her lips. "And if I levitate again?"

"Then maybe we'll get another message from the Ancients."

"Or everyone on the island will see the light from this house and start asking questions."

Balladyn leaned forward, resting his forearms on his knees. "Maybe they need to see that."

"So, if someone here betrayed me, they'll get scared?"

"Aye."

"It could galvanize them to try again sooner."

He dared them to try. "Let them. I'll be waiting."

Her expression softened at his words. "I can't hide in my cottage forever. I have to face this."

"We have no idea what's coming for you. You were singled out and betrayed. Not here on Skye, but in a place where no one was there to help you. Someone wanted you out of the way."

"They'll have to try harder."

Balladyn was impressed by her courage. "Why did you go to Belfast?"

"This wasn't the first time the Druid leaders were set to meet. Corann used to go once a year. This instance was about the Others. It was a special meeting, and I had no reason to think it was anything but that."

"And the location?"

She lifted one shoulder in a shrug. "It rotates."

"Have you thought about contacting the other Druid leaders to see if they received the same invitation?"

"It crossed my mind, but I quickly decided against it. If they set me up, they'll lie."

"We probably won't know who is after you until you're attacked again."

She rolled her eyes. "That makes me feel all warm and gooey inside."

It was a struggle for him not to smile. He had always appreciated sarcasm. Rolmir, Rhi's brother, had been one of the best at it. It was what had made them such fast friends.

"You should smile more."

Her remark drew him out of his thoughts. "What?"

She jerked her chin to him. "Whatever thoughts made you grin just now, think on them more. You look good with a smile."

Grinning was the last thing he was thinking about now. He didn't want to hear that she thought he looked good. He was already doing everything he could not to think about her sexually—and failing epically.

Her grin slipped as they stared at each other. He forced himself to remain still because he wasn't sure he wouldn't reach for her if he moved. Balladyn bit back a groan when he saw her pulse beating rapidly in her throat. Damn her. Was she trying to drive him mad with need? Because it was working.

Rhona cleared her throat. "You were right. I need to rest."

Balladyn leaned back in measured, stilted movements. The only way he could get himself under control was if they were in separate rooms. "Of course."

He watched as she awkwardly got to her feet, but instead of leaving, she grabbed the throw blanket, spread it over the sofa, then crawled beneath it. His body went rigid with shock. No. No, nononono. She needed to go. Or he did.

"I can't sleep in my bed tonight. I think the only way I'll get any rest is with you near. Thank you for staying," she said and glanced at him before laying her head on the pillow.

He stared at the top of her head, cursing himself. He wasn't about to leave her now.

CHAPTER FIFTEEN

Somewhere in Ireland

Lena couldn't stop thinking about how Chevonne had managed to cut off part of her ear. Lena hid the deformity with magic. If any of the other Six learned what she had done, they would attack her. Lena had enough power now after taking her family's magic as well as their lives that she would most likely win against the other members of the Six. She wasn't quite ready to take that chance, though.

Yet.

It was coming. Very, very soon. If only she had gotten Chevonne's magic. If she had, she would be able to kill the members of the Six and take command of the Others. It was such a simple and elegant plan she couldn't believe no one else had thought of it.

Like most times when her mind plotted and planned for takeover, her thoughts drifted to Moreann—the Druid from another realm who had dared to take on the Dragon Kings. Moreann had been intelligent and cunning, and from what Lena knew, she had been extremely powerful after taking magic from others on her realm. That was what had given Lena the idea. If Moreann had been as formidable as everyone said, she could've—and *should've*—been the only one in charge of the Others.

Lena wouldn't make that mistake. From the very first, the Dark Fae on the Six were at constant odds with the Light. Lena suddenly pressed her lips together in an effort not to laugh. The fools were so fixated on themselves and their role in the Six that they had no idea she was no longer Light.

It was as easy as Usaeil had made it seem to fool people into believing whatever she wanted. Lena hadn't trusted the rumors surrounding the former Light Queen, but she had tested things herself. Her glamour hadn't slipped once. None of the Six paid her any heed. Or noticed the magic had shifted.

And that would be their downfall.

"I'm tired of sitting here. We should be attacking," Nola stated from her position in the circle.

Lena looked at the Dark female who stroked one of the thick strands of silver on either side of her head. She detested Nola.

"She's not wrong," Enya replied.

The Dark were always ready for a fight. That came in handy at times. Lena slid her gaze to Barry. The only male of the Six, he was the strongest of the Dark, the one who challenged Lena any time he could. Barry. She almost snorted in derision every time she thought about him. For such a potent Fae, he had the worst name. It certainly didn't strike fear into anyone. Barry held her gaze as if daring her to say something. Lena never fell for that trick. She was too smart for that.

"We should remind the Reapers that they can't take one of us without retribution," Sheila added.

Ah. Finally, one of the Light spoke. Poor Sheila was finally showing signs of aging, and she wasn't taking it well. It did grate on Lena's nerves that, despite her age, Sheila was still immaculately elegant and breathtakingly beautiful.

Lena then turned to their newest addition, Oona. Lena quirked a brow at the Light female who spent most of her time in silence listening and watching. It was a wise move, and one Lena would've made herself. It was why she kept a close eye on Oona. If anyone was a threat, it could be this Light.

"We should have a plan first," Oona replied. "If the goal is to kill the Reapers, that is."

Barry chuckled. "The first wise words we've heard."

Lena immediately prickled. But that's what Barry wanted. She tamped down her anger and smiled. "You claim to be the battle expert, and yet we've heard nothing from you in the way of plans."

The grin on his face turned into a sneer. "Why don't you tell us where you were recently? You disappeared and refused to answer our calls."

"I'm the leader of the Six. I don't need to tell you every detail of my life."

Oona said, "We should answer to each other. Otherwise, one of us could try to take power."

"Aye. I wonder who that might be," Barry said as his red eyes narrowed on Lena.

Lena smiled at Oona. "You're absolutely right. We've been dealt a blow with the loss of your predecessor. We thought we had the Reapers and Death, but things didn't quite go our way. None of us wants a repeat of that. The sooner they're out of the way, the quicker we can take command of things."

"Speaking of that," Enya said with a satisfied smile and a flip of her long, black-and-silver ponytail. "The formation of the Fae council isn't making any progress. The Others we've sent to spread the rumors have done a great job."

Nola's red eyes crinkled. "Not to mention the members of our organization trying to get on the Council to make sure it doesn't work."

"I say that's progress," Barry stated.

Oh, yes. Lena could hardly wait until she sucked all the power out of each and every one of the five around her. It would almost be as good a feeling as it had been taking her family's. "Progress, yes. But not enough. The Reapers will continue causing problems for us until we make sure they're out of the way."

"Which led us to our current plan," Oona said.

Lena met the Light's silver eyes. She wouldn't underestimate any of them, but especially not Oona. "Exactly."

"A Druid," Barry replied with a loud snort. "Once we're in command, we'll wipe them out with a snap of our fingers. Who cares if one is connected to the Druids?"

Sheila lifted a brow as she glared at Barry. "Because we're striking at them in a way they won't expect."

"They're smart. They're going to consider we started this," Nola said.

Lena smiled then. "They certainly will. I'm counting on that."

Barry's eyes narrowed on her. "You changed the plan?"

"It wasn't as if I had a choice. The Reapers saved Rhona," she replied.

His nostrils flared as his anger simmered just beneath the surface. "Without running it past us? I thought we all answered to each other."

Lena really loved riling him up. It was almost too easy, and he fell for it every time. She smiled softly. "I had to think quickly."

"What's this new plan?" Oona asked.

Lena's smile grew. "One that won't fail."

~

Death's Realm

Cael stretched out his legs in the chair and watched Erith rearrange the flowers in the vase for the fifth time. She was anxious about what was happening with the Skye Druids. All of them were.

"We can go," he said.

She glanced at him and shook her head of blue-black hair. "No."

"It would make you feel better."

Erith sighed and lowered her hands to the table. "I want to go because I think they're going to need all of us."

"But?" he urged when she paused.

"I can't shake the feeling that if we do, something terrible is going to happen."

Cael rose and walked to her. He set his hands on her shoulders and turned her to face him. He might have some of her powers now. She called him a god. All he knew was that he was no longer a Fae. Sorting out what he was had proven more difficult. He was still learning so much about his abilities. But he had trusted Erith from the day she'd come to him and offered him a position as a Reaper. "Your intuition has never led us wrong. Trust it."

"I would. Except I also sense that if we don't go, something terrible will happen."

The confusion and doubt in her lavender eyes broke his heart. He kissed the top of her head as he brought her close and held her tightly. "It's the Fae Others, then?"

"I can't tell."

The last time she had been this conflicted had been when Bran was siphoning her powers and slowly killing her. Cael had nearly lost her then. He, himself, had almost been killed. He'd held on because of his love for Erith and, somehow, had remained alive. They'd fought Bran together with the other Reapers and ultimately won. Since then, he and Erith had been together.

"I have to do something," she said.

He nodded and loosened his hold so she could lean back. "You're a goddess, my love. You command a group of men and women unmatched by any other Fae. We've fought many foes and won. We'll triumph against the Six."

"I wish I had your confidence."

"You have it from me and everyone on this realm. Every Reaper, every mate. You've given all of us a second chance as well as a safe place to live. Trust your instincts."

Erith drew in a shuddering breath and squeezed her eyes closed for a long moment. Then she said, "I can't tell one way or another."

"Then we wait. We can get to Eoghan and the others quickly if need be. Until then, we wait to make sure it isn't a trap set by the Six."

Her eyes grew troubled. "And if something happens to the Reapers on Skye?"

Cael chuckled. "I told you to trust yourself. You should also trust your Reapers. You chose each of us. You know what we're capable of."

"What they're capable of." Erith winked, showing a hint of a smile. "Darling, you aren't a Reaper anymore."

"Aye, but I was for a very long time. In many ways, I always will be. Eoghan and his team are on alert."

She drew in a breath and slowly released it. "You're right. About all of it. I want someone on Earth the Reapers can call to in order to bring everyone else. Despite what happened with Balladyn, the Fae have never been able to communicate across realms before."

"Fair enough. Who do you want to send?"

"Us."

Cael grinned. "I was going to suggest just that."

CHAPTER SIXTEEN

The sky was clear and the sun bright as Davie played a raucous song on his fiddle while Fraser, Drew, and Jamie beat on their drums. Laughter filled the air. Rhona tried not to spill her ale when Sorcha attempted to pull her out to dance a jig. Rhona managed to free her arm from her cousin's firm grip, preferring instead to enjoy the drink and watch this go-round since she was out of breath from the last three.

Rhona lifted her face to the sun, basking in its warmth. It had been a long time since they'd had cause for celebration. They should do this more often. Everyone needed a reason to lift their spirits, and there was nothing more uplifting than free-flowing alcohol and loud, Scottish music.

She finished her ale but opted for some water next. The wind blowing over the land cooled her heated flesh, but she didn't want to wake with a headache the next morning. If she did, though, it would be worth it. Already, her cheeks hurt from laughing so hard, and no doubt her body would be sore from all the dancing.

"A good memory," she murmured to herself.

Her parents used to host such parties all the time, and Rhona and Sorcha used to get into all sorts of trouble as children. The thought made Rhona smile. Her gaze landed on her cousin to see Sorcha's curls stuck to the side of her face from sweat. Sorcha threw back her head and laughed loudly at something her dance partner said. Something seemed slightly wrong, but Rhona couldn't pinpoint it. She was having too much fun to want to ruin it, so she quickly forgot the thought.

Rhona downed her water and turned to grab another bottle. The sight of a woman in a white cloak with her back to Rhona caught her attention. She was inexplicably drawn to the figure.

The music around her became muffled as she heard the beat of drums. She knew that sound. It heralded the Ancients. Her heart rate accelerated. The woman looked out of place, almost as if she were from another time.

"Rhona."

Rhona jerked and looked around. Who had said her name? She hadn't heard it with her ears. It had been in her mind.

The lady turned her head to the side. She had the hood of her mantle pulled up, hiding her face, but a strand of long black hair fell against the white material of the cloak. Rhona glanced back at her friends, all dancing and laughing. None of them had seen the woman in white.

"Rhona."

That voice again. Rhona knew it. She had heard it before. Not as clearly, but she recognized it from after the attack in Ireland. A memory tried to surface as fear rushed through her like a warning. Almost as soon as it came, it faded away. The memory that had begun to form also vanished.

The drums of the Ancients grew louder, drowning out everything else. Rhona couldn't stop her feet as they started walking to the woman. The visitor's cloak billowed with a gust of wind, giving Rhona a glimpse of a dark green gown beneath. As she drew near, a sense of calm overtook her.

The woman suddenly turned and faced her with a welcoming smile. *"I've been waiting a long time for you,"* she said in Rhona's mind.

~

Balladyn paced the kitchen, glancing at Rhona every few minutes to make sure she was slumbering soundly. She had fallen asleep quickly and had barely moved since. He was glad she hadn't suffered from another nightmare. Why then was he so edgy?

He had gone over everything in the cottage. There was no hidden magic from the Six or Druids anywhere. Everything seemed as it had been before. And yet he couldn't sit still or shake the thought that something was about to happen.

"Eoghan," he whispered.

In a blink, the Reaper stood before Balladyn. "What is it?"

Balladyn put a finger over his lips and pointed to Rhona on the sofa. When Eoghan nodded in understanding, Balladyn asked in a soft voice, "Do you sense anything?"

"Nothing. Do you?"

Balladyn shrugged. "Not exactly."

"What does that mean?"

"I'm not sure." Balladyn looked at Rhona.

Eoghan caught his attention. "Do we need to get her out of here?"

"Maybe." He wasn't sure.

"You aren't making sense."

Balladyn heard the frustration in Eoghan's voice. He sighed and looked at the Reaper. "She's sleeping, without any hint of nightmare, levitation, or glowing. Everything seems normal. I might be looking for something that isn't there."

"Or you could sense something the rest of us don't. You did hear her across the realms." Eoghan looked at Rhona and pressed his lips together. He turned back to Balladyn. "The cottage is surrounded by Reapers. No one is getting to Rhona from the outside. You're guarding her inside, which means nothing is getting to her without you alerting us. A lot has happened in the last twenty-four hours, especially to her and you."

Balladyn nodded, wishing he could accept Eoghan's words as truth. "How long did it take before you could sleep an entire night without the nightmares after you became a Reaper?"

"Well over a year."

"Exactly. She shouldn't be."

A frown marred Eoghan's forehead. "Druid magic healed her. Perhaps that altered her trauma."

Balladyn swung his head to Rhona. That was a possibility. Since he knew little about Druids or humans, Eoghan could be right. It was plausible enough, but it didn't loosen the knot in his gut.

"I'm going to talk to Sorcha. She would know," Eoghan said before teleporting out.

~

"Me?" Rhona asked in surprise.

The woman's smile grew. *"Why does that shock you? Corann chose you because of me."*

"What do you mean?"

"There is much you don't know yet, but it will all become clear soon."

Rhona tilted her head as she thought she caught a hint of an Irish accent. Maybe she was just thinking about… The thought vanished, seemingly unimportant. She had no idea who she knew that was Irish, but for just a heartbeat, she had been about to say a name.

"You don't believe me."

"Who are you?"

The woman clasped her hands together before herself as her beautiful face fell into a serene expression. *"Names mean nothing where I am."*

Did that mean she was an Ancient?

The woman chuckled softly. *"You are from magic. None of this should surprise you."*

"Who are you?" Rhona took a step back, suddenly cautious.

"A friend," she said.

Instantly, Rhona was calm. She tried to recall what she had been upset about, but she couldn't. "Are you an Ancient?"

"You have no idea how important you are to the future of the Druids, Rhona."

"Why are you talking to me now? Why didn't you come to me all those times I needed you?"

"I come when it's time, and not a moment before. Are you ready for the next step?"

Rhona looked behind her at her friends. They hadn't noticed that she was gone. Sorcha was still dancing. Rhona then faced the woman. "What next step?"

"A lot is coming to rest atop your very capable shoulders. The way of the Druids should be remembered above all else."

"It has always been thus on Skye."

"Has it?"

"Of course."

"But you don't know if it will stay that way."

~

"Rhona, wake up," Balladyn said as he gently shook her.

Sorcha, Cathal, and Eoghan arrived in the next instant. Balladyn moved away from the sofa and faced them.

"I filled them in," Eoghan said.

Sorcha's green eyes looked troubled as she gazed down at her cousin. "I don't have an answer. I don't know anyone who has been brought back from the brink of death with our magic."

"Fek." Suddenly, Balladyn had a thought. "What about the Druids at MacLeod Castle?"

Sorcha's head swung to him. "If anyone knows, it would be them."

"Then I need to talk to them."

Eoghan grabbed his arm. "We go together."

Balladyn nodded as he looked at Cathal.

"Don't worry," Cathal said. "We won't leave Rhona."

Balladyn and Eoghan teleported to the east coast of Scotland and MacLeod Castle. An invisible shield surrounded the castle, similar to what the Fae used at the Light Castle and the Dragon Kings used around Dreagan.

"I'm sure they already know we're here," Eoghan said.

Balladyn shrugged and stepped through the shield. "Guess we'll find out."

The instant they were through, six Warriors met them, each with a different skin color. The entirety of their eyes was the same color as their skin, giving them an otherworldly look. Balladyn noted the long claws, and the fangs protruding from their lips. Three of the Warriors had black skin. One had indigo skin and huge, leathery wings. Another had silver skin, and the last had gold.

"Fae aren't welcome here," said one of the black-skinned Warriors.

Balladyn had expected this. Still, it didn't make things easy. "We didn't come to fight. We're here for information from the Druids."

"You expect us to believe a Dark Fae?" This from the Warrior with the gold skin.

It was Eoghan who answered. "We're Reapers."

"It's about Rhona," Balladyn said, not wanting to wait for the Warriors to respond.

The Warrior who had spoken first stepped forward. As he did, his black skin, eyes, and claws melted away to reveal short, dark hair and deep green eyes. "I'm Fallon MacLeod."

"I'm Eoghan, and this is Balladyn."

"As in the previous King of the Dark?" the gold-skinned Warrior demanded with narrowed eyes.

Balladyn bit his tongue to keep the retort from spilling from his lips. It seemed his reputation had reached MacLeod Castle. He had to get help for Rhona, and if that meant he left so Eoghan could do it, then Balladyn would. "Aye. And you are?"

"Phelan."

"Like I said, we're Reapers," Eoghan replied, his voice hardening only slightly.

Another of the MacLeod brothers shifted back to his human self. He held Balladyn's gaze with his sea green eyes. "What happened to Rhona?"

Balladyn swallowed, grasping at the small hope the Warriors had given him. "She was betrayed and attacked in Belfast. We found her and returned her to Skye to be healed." There was so much more to the story, but that could come later. That same urgency that had driven him when he went looking for Rhona returned.

Balladyn heard something behind him and turned around to see a Warrior with dark green skin walking through the barrier.

"They're telling the truth," the Warrior said and joined the others.

Fallon nodded. "That was Galen. His ability is to read minds."

There was a shimmer as a form took shape with iridescent skin. To Balladyn's shock, it was a female Warrior. She shifted and came to stand beside Fallon, her eyes locked on Balladyn. He wondered what other powers the Warriors had. If there was time, he would get to know all of them, but he had to get back to Rhona first.

"Welcome. I'm Larena. The Druids are waiting for you at the castle."

Fallon turned around and said, "Come with us."

One hurdle passed. Balladyn exchanged a look with Eoghan as they followed the Warriors across the land to the imposing castle perched on the side of a cliff.

CHAPTER SEVENTEEN

Something passed through Rhona like a hand from somewhere beyond. And there was no doubt it was a warning of some kind. She glanced around. Everything *seemed* right. Why then did she *know* it was wrong?

She wanted to believe the woman because her words made sense. Rhona had been grasping for anything to confirm that what she had been doing was right. She didn't care if someone told her it was wrong. All she wanted was confirmation either way.

From the moment she'd understood that she was a Druid, she had known her place on Skye. She had never doubted it, never wondered. Then Corann died and told her she was in charge. Deep down in her soul, she knew he had chosen wrong. But she'd wanted the position. Mostly because it gave her relevance—when she really didn't have any.

Rhona clung to the wrongness, searching for anything to help sanction its validity. Instead, she found her gaze drawn to the woman once more. Her silver eyes were locked on Rhona, her gaze searching. Silver?

"Something is wrong."

"I'm just thinking," Rhona answered. It wasn't really a lie. She had merely omitted *why* she was thinking, and that bothered her. If this woman was an Ancient, then Rhona should feel a connection.

And she didn't.

"Why are you here?" Rhona asked.

The woman smiled. *"I already told you."*

"Actually, you haven't." The smile on the woman's face tightened a fraction. Rhona might have missed it if she hadn't been looking for it. Her words had angered the Ancient.

The woman's shoulders expanded as she took a deep breath. Possibly to calm herself.

"I've never heard of one of you visiting us." Rhona intentionally left off *Ancient* and *Druid* to see how the woman reacted.

"You doubt who I am."

"I do."

"That's a pity."

The same warning as before rushed through Rhona, this time stronger. Thicker. She took a step back with the force of it. Her head turned to the side to watch Sorcha and the others still drinking and dancing, unaware of what was happening. Were they farther away? She couldn't tell. Rhona's gaze slid back to the woman. She had an ethereal look about her, but did that make her an Ancient? Since Rhona had never heard of any Druid seeing one, she had no idea.

"You can see me because you're special."

Rhona froze. Had the woman just read her mind? She really didn't like that. She gathered her magic and surrounded herself with it to use as a block. It didn't matter if the woman was an Ancient or not, Rhona wanted this to stop.

"Why have you gathered your magic?"

Was that a hint of anger in her tone? Rhona began to worry that she was overreacting. "I don't like anyone in my head."

"Is that what you think I'm doing?"

Rhona knew she was doing it. Instead of saying that, though, she simply stared.

The woman grasped her hands before her. *"I've watched you for a long time, Rhona. I know you better than you know yourself. You're going to take the Druids in a direction no one will see coming. You, alone, will be the reason for what is to come. Not even someone as powerful as Corann could do that. That should tell you why I'm here, why I'm speaking to you. And why I think you're so important."*

~

Balladyn walked up the castle steps and trailed the MacLeod brothers through the large double doors and inside. Eoghan was behind him, followed by more Warriors. Balladyn's gaze swept the grand hall. He could practically feel the history of the place. He would've asked to explore it thoroughly if he had come for any other reason.

Long tables had been set up in the shape of a U. Tapestries older than the MacLeod brothers hung on the walls, displaying bright colors to liven up the castle. Ancient swords, maces, axes, spears, and shields were artfully displayed. Colorful rugs of various sizes were everywhere, along with potted plants. An enormous chandelier hung from high above, casting the area in warm light reminiscent of the sun—no doubt Druid magic.

Balladyn's head swung to the side and the staircase as a woman descended it. She wore jeans and a dusky pink sweater. Her long, black hair was pulled away from her face to hang midway down her back, and her violet eyes watched him.

The Druid walked through the gathered Warriors, pausing beside the silver one to touch hands. She glanced at him before turning her attention back to Balladyn. "The wind has been very vocal the last few hours," she said in an American accent.

So many questions filled his mind, but Balladyn remained silent.

"It warned me you were coming," the Druid continued as she walked to stand before him.

"The wind spoke to Gwynn as the trees spoke to me," a soft voice from above said.

Balladyn lifted his gaze to see another Druid at the top of the stairs. She had curly red hair. "They warned you we were coming?"

The Druid didn't answer until she was in the great hall. The indigo Warrior with the bat-like wings walked to her, shifting to his human appearance as he did. The Druid took his hand and smiled at the Warrior for a moment. Then she went to stand beside Gwynn.

"I'm Sonya. And to answer your question, yes," she replied.

Balladyn glanced away from her amber eyes to Eoghan, who stood beside him. Eoghan met his gaze but didn't offer anything. Balladyn had commanded armies and had ruled Fae. But he had never felt so out of his depth as he did at that moment.

"I—we," he corrected, "need help. Something is wrong with Rhona."

Gwynn's head tilted to the side as she studied him. "Explain."

"Shouldn't the other Druids be here?" Eoghan asked the Warriors.

Fallon simply said, "They are. They're listening."

They obviously weren't going to show themselves. Balladyn couldn't blame them. He regretted coming. If Eoghan or another Light Reaper had arrived instead, the Warriors and Druids might be more welcoming. But all they saw were his red eyes and the silver in his hair, proclaiming the Dark Fae he had once been.

The need to protect Rhona was so thick it choked Balladyn. He wanted to be there, to hear what the Druids had to say. But what he wanted didn't matter in the grand scheme. This was about Rhona.

He turned to Eoghan. "I'll wait outside the perimeter."

"Why would you do that?" Sonya asked.

Balladyn glanced at the floor before he looked at her. "None of you know us. You may not understand what Reapers are. You see a Light and a Dark who have invaded your home. You're being cautious, as I would be. Discovering what happened to Rhona and how to help her is more important than me being here."

"Because you were King of the Dark," Gwynn stated.

Eoghan blew out a breath. "If it would make things easier, I can call Death. She can speak on our behalf."

"There's no need," Fallon said. "It's true we are no' used to having verra many Fae visitors—other than Rhi—but that's no' why we're acting this way."

At the mention of Rhi, Balladyn frowned. Somehow, he shouldn't have been surprised that she knew those at MacLeod Castle. Then the rest of Fallon's words registered. "What do you mean?"

"There's a dark force out there," one of the Warriors answered.

Sonya nodded her head. "It's growing larger."

Balladyn felt his stomach clench in dread.

"And directed at Skye."

He hadn't been prepared for the rest of Sonya's statement. Balladyn felt all the air leave his lungs because he *knew*—the kind of comprehension he felt all the way to his soul—that whatever this force was, it was aimed at Rhona.

"You have a connection to Rhona," Gwynn said.

Balladyn nodded, unable to find words.

"Can you help us?" Eoghan asked. "We might be Reapers, but we're out of our depth when it comes to Druid magic."

It took two tries before Balladyn found his voice. "Rhona doesn't trust anyone on Skye."

The Druids turned to the Warriors and simply nodded.

"Right, then," one of the MacLeod brothers said as he stepped forward. "It's time for introductions. I'm Lucan. The ugly one beside me is my younger brother, Quinn. There's Ian, Ramsey, Hayden, Logan, Arran, Galen, Charon, Camdyn, Broc, Malcolm, and you already met Phelan as well as Larena and my elder brother, Fallon."

Balladyn filed all the names away, trying to match the Warrior to each name, but his attention was riveted on Sonya and Gwynn, who faced him once more. "Can you help Rhona?"

"Maybe," Sonya answered.

Gwynn's lips softened into a smile. "We won't make any promises, but we're going to try."

"We need to know every detail," Sonya said.

Eoghan began to speak, but he paused when women began walking into the hall from doorways off each side. He and Eoghan had been surrounded the entire time, and Balladyn hadn't even realized it. He'd been too focused on the Warriors and the two

Druids before him. He didn't need to feel the magic of those surrounding him to know that it was potent and powerful.

And he felt sorry for anyone foolish enough to try and attack.

The Druids lined up next to Gwynn and Sonya so there were fourteen in all. Balladyn ran his gaze over their faces. Ice blue eyes snagged his. The Druid was petite with long, straight, black hair. There was a power about her that belied her size.

"You know Rhona," Balladyn stated.

Surprise flickered in the Druid's eyes. "I do."

"The Ancients chose Isla to speak through when the Others were attacking the Dragon Kings and Corann on Skye," Hayden said.

A small frown creased Isla's face. "The Ancients were shouting to all of us the other day. Then, they suddenly cut off."

Balladyn glanced around the room. "Is that normal?"

"No," Sonya said.

Eoghan blew out a breath. "When, exactly?"

"Two nights ago," Gwynn replied.

Balladyn could barely breathe. His chest felt as if it were being crushed. "That's when they tried to kill Rhona."

CHAPTER EIGHTEEN

"Why won't you tell me your name?" Rhona didn't know why that was important, but it was.

And she wasn't going to let up.

"I'm beyond names."

"What do I call you if I need to speak to you?"

The woman's serene mask didn't slip. *"I'm always here. There's no need to call to me."*

Drums sounded faintly behind Rhona. The erratic and rapid beats sounded like a warning. She saw alerts everywhere she looked, but maybe she spotted them because she was looking. This woman had sought her out. There was no reason for anyone to do that other than an Ancient.

"Your destiny is approaching rapidly, Rhona. You must be ready."

Rhona took offense to those words. She was always ready to defend Skye, the Druids, and indeed, the entire world if need be. "I am."

"You're too wrapped up in other things."

"Other things? Stop talking inside my head. Talk to me like normal."

"This is normal."

Rhona rolled her eyes.

"Patience has never been your strong suit, but you must adhere to it now."

"For what? When? How can I do anything when I know nothing?" Rhona was frustrated, and agitation expanded inside her. She couldn't shake the feeling that something was very, very wrong.

Which was why she kept up her magic.

"I'm here to teach you."

Balladyn had to get back to Rhona. Immediately. His chest tightened with the pressing urgency. "I have to go," he said through clenched teeth.

"What is it?" Eoghan asked.

Balladyn felt a bellow rising in him.

"Easy," Eoghan said. "Get a hold of yourself."

Balladyn wanted to ask how Eoghan knew he was about to lose it, but his thoughts swiftly returned to Rhona. She was in danger. "Rhona," he ground out.

"We need to go to Skye," a Druid said.

Balladyn's attention shifted to the woman, taking in her straight, wheat-colored hair and hazel eyes. She sat beside Arran, the white-skinned Warrior. What was her name? He forced himself to focus and remember. Ronnie, short for Veronica.

"We have no idea what's there." Malcolm, whose god favored the color maroon, had a scarred face and astute azure eyes. That gaze was focused on his mate, Evie.

Evie had her curly brown hair pulled into a low ponytail, and determination lit her blue eyes from the inside as she looked at Malcolm. "We were always going to Rhona."

"Why no' bring her here?" Fallon asked.

Balladyn's response was past his lips before he even thought about it. "Nay!"

Every gaze in the hall turned to him. Eoghan grabbed him. "Easy," he whispered again. Then, to everyone else, Eoghan said, "We need to return to Skye now."

"What's happening?" someone asked.

"Now isn't the time," Eoghan hurried to say.

Balladyn squeezed his eyes closed. He couldn't breathe. Rhona. He had to get to Rhona.

"I agree with Balladyn," Isla said into the silence. "Rhona is Skye. Skye is Rhona. We take her away from the island only when we have no other option."

Balladyn drew in a deep breath and concentrated on his breathing to center himself and get his emotions under control. The bellow was there, waiting to be released. The Druids and Warriors talked amongst themselves. No matter how many breathing techniques Balladyn did, nothing was working. Something inside his head screamed. It wasn't a voice, exactly, more like a feeling. He jerked away from Eoghan.

"Balladyn?"

He forced his eyes open and looked at Eoghan. "I…have to go to her."

"Go," Eoghan said.

Balladyn didn't wait for the others to make a decision. He teleported back to Rhona's cottage to find her in the same position he'd left her. The tightness released, but only barely. The bellow loosened its hold, and he felt more like himself again.

"About bloody time," Sorcha snapped from behind him.

Balladyn looked over his shoulder to find her pacing before the hearth. He then swung his head back around, searching for Cathal. He found the Reaper in the kitchen with his arms crossed over his chest, and his face lined with concern. "What happened?"

"Not a damn thing," Cathal said in a soft voice.

Sorcha threw her arms out in frustration before letting them fall to her sides. "That's right. Not a goddamn thing happened." Sorcha's face crumpled as she looked at Rhona. "Something is wrong. I can feel it."

So could Balladyn. He knelt beside the sofa and started to reach for Rhona. He hesitated, wondering if he should try to wake her once more. Then he touched her, giving her a soft shake. "Rhona?

You need to wake up now. Open your eyes. Can you hear me? I need you to look at me."

~

Rhona felt herself being pulled. It was a nice feeling. A comfortable one as if she knew that where she was going was safe. She didn't fight it. In fact, she was turning toward it when the Ancient was suddenly right in front of her.

"I thought you would do anything for your people."

Rhona hated how the Ancient kept offending her. "I am, and I will."

"Prove it."

"What else do you want from me?"

"There are things you need to learn. Only I can teach you."

"Then teach me."

"This isn't a simple spell I can tell you and send you out to do."

Something disturbing and worrying crawled down Rhona's spine like bony fingers from some creepy horror flick. Was it another warning? Or was it just her imagination?

As Druid leader, she put the fate of Skye above herself. The island, the people, their very way of life were more important than anything else. An Ancient stood before her. Why wasn't she eager to learn what the Ancient had to say?

Rhona strained to hear the drums, but they were gone. It was only then that she realized she couldn't hear the music and laughter from her friends either. She looked over her shoulder, but they were so far away, they were barely a speck in the distance. When had she and the Ancient moved?

"It's normal to fear that you'll fail them."

Rhona faced the Ancient. "Everyone is counting on me."

"The enemy will come soon. I'll make sure you're prepared."

A loud drum banged as if it were right by her ear. Rhona winced and jerked away. A millisecond after, a memory of her being stabbed filled her head. Just as quickly as the drum had come, it was gone. Snuffed out.

But the memory remained.

Rhona's blood ran cold. How could she have forgotten that? Or…she struggled to remember who had helped her. It was someone she trusted deeply, someone she felt safe with, but she couldn't remember their name or recall their face.

Her eyes locked on the Ancient. "What is happening to me while I'm here with you?"

"Nothing."

"You aren't taking memories from me?"

The Ancient laughed softly, her eyes reproachful. *"Why would I do such a thing?"*

Rhona noticed that the Ancient didn't answer the question. That feeling of being pulled happened again, this time more insistent. And just for a heartbeat, Rhona thought she heard a voice. A male voice with an Irish accent.

"Time isn't on our side. You must focus, Rhona."

"Who betrayed me? Who sent me to Belfast to be killed?"

"That isn't why you're here."

"I'm asking, though."

"Since when does an Ancient give such knowledge?"

"You brought me here. You keep telling me I'm important, that enemies are approaching. Those enemies are the ones who tried to kill me. Tell me who they are so I can fight them," Rhona demanded.

"You must put aside your wants and desires. You're leader of the Skye Druids. It's time you act like it."

~

She wouldn't wake. Balladyn had given Rhona a hard shake. He'd screamed her name. And still, nothing. That bellow rose within him again.

A soft hand touched his shoulder. He looked up into Cara's eyes.

Lucan's wife gave him a soft smile. "We need to be somewhere powerful on the island. Standing stones, if you have them."

"Loch Eyre," Sorcha hurriedly answered. "It's on the northwest coast."

Cara looked to her right where Eoghan was and nodded. Eoghan vanished in the next instant. Cara then turned to Balladyn. "Gather Rhona. Sorcha, come with us."

Balladyn carefully lifted Rhona into his arms, keeping her wrapped in the blanket. He stared down at her face, silently begging her to open her eyes. Balladyn looked at Cathal when Rhona didn't respond.

"Ready?" the Reaper asked.

"What of the others?" Balladyn looked out the window to the rest of the Reapers.

Cathal nodded. "They're coming."

That's all Balladyn needed to hear. He teleported to Loch Eyre. There, he found the two ancient stones that stood ten feet from the edge that dropped down twenty feet to the loch's shore. The stones themselves stood thirteen feet apart. Both stones are just over five feet. The tallest was the south stone. It was irregularly shaped and tapered toward the top. The north stone was four-sided.

The Druids stood in a large circle around the stones, the Warriors surrounding them. Around *them*, the Reapers. Balladyn walked through the Reapers, Warriors, and Druids until he stood between the two stones. He glanced at Rhona. Her hair blew in the wind, tickling his face. He didn't want to release her, but he made himself lower to his knees and gently place her on the cold ground.

He stood and found his place among the Reapers. That's when everything began.

One of the Druids started chanting. Balladyn didn't know which Druid, but soon, all of them were chanting. The words were foreign but also almost recognizable.

The incantation was rhythmic, the cadence nearly palliative. Until the Druids clasped hands. It was as if something electric passed through them and then moved outward to anyone near. And though Balladyn couldn't see anything, he could've sworn the magic bounced between the two stones.

The Warriors had all released their gods, their colored skin on display for anyone to see. While the Warriors kept an eye on the Druids, the Reapers scanned the area, watching and waiting for someone to appear.

Balladyn's heart leapt when he saw Rhona move, but it soon dropped to his feet when he heard her cry out.

"It isna working," one of the Warriors said.

Without thinking, Balladyn rushed to Rhona.

Something was happening. Rhona gasped when she felt as if some invisible hand had grasped her arms and was trying to pull her back. She looked at her friends, but she couldn't see them anymore.

"You made a commitment, Rhona. I thought you wanted your people to survive."

"You know I do," she yelled above the wind that had suddenly sprung up to whip around her.

"Then you must prove it. Fight to stay with me so I can teach you what you need."

"I'm trying!"

But was she? Even now, she was torn. She wanted to know how to save her people—and possibly herself—from the enemy, but at the same time, she couldn't shake the feeling that not all was as it seemed.

"If you leave now, I can't bring you back. This is your test to prove yourself to me, to everyone."

Rhona would have to make a decision. Corann had once told her that being the leader of the Skye Druids meant he had to put aside the things he wanted to ensure their people endured and their magic continued. How did she think she could stand in his shoes and not do the same?

Her decision made, Rhona concentrated on fighting whatever pulled at her.

Balladyn pushed against the forces swirling around Rhona. All he'd heard were the Druids' words, but between the stones, wind whirled and whipped. He gave up fighting it and teleported to Rhona, only to be struck again and again by magic. The pain was excruciating, agonizing.

But he bore it all.

"Rhona!" he bellowed over the wind. "I know you can hear me."

Her hair slapped at his face along with his long strands. Balladyn leaned over her so their faces were only inches apart. He closed his eyes and thought of the link that had called to him between the realms, the connection that had brought him to her as she lay bleeding. He let it envelop him and expand outward until it covered her.

"Rhona. Come back to me," he whispered.

The deep voice was like a bucket of ice water. She knew that Irish accent.

Balladyn.

Then Rhona felt him. *All* of him. She didn't know how or why. It was like a cord bound them to each other, and he was pouring all of himself into it. The uncertainties that had plagued her with the Ancient were gone. She knew she had to return to Balladyn, to whatever awaited her there.

"Don't do this," the Ancient warned.

Rhona grew dizzy when she felt a different kind of magic mix with hers. It was Balladyn's magic. Fae magic. All she wanted was to return to him. She smiled as excitement ran through her at seeing his crimson eyes once more.

Suddenly, a hand roughly gripped her arm. Rhona found herself staring into the Ancient's eyes.

"You aren't going anywhere."

CHAPTER NINETEEN

Balladyn gritted his teeth and pushed back against the fierce wind that endeavored to move him away from Rhona. He shifted until his knees were on either side of her hips, his hands braced near her head. That's when he felt it—magic.

But not just any kind. Dark magic.

Fury coiled within him at the thought of it touching Rhona. He shoved against it, fighting to keep it from Rhona. To his shock, he felt *his* magic mingle with Rhona's. It was the barest of touches, but it was the most amazing thing he had ever experienced. Rich. Vibrant.

Pure.

He sought out more of her magic, but it retreated. Balladyn knew he was losing her. He didn't know yet if this was the Six or someone else, but *someone* was attempting to take Rhona. There was no time to tell the Druids, Warriors, or his fellow Reapers. He wasn't even sure if he could've gotten the words out.

He dug his fingers into the soil. His magic rushed through him. He felt the power of it, the potent force of it—and he feared it still wouldn't be enough.

Please, he silently prayed to whoever might be listening. *If I can do one thing right in my life, let me do this.*

Balladyn didn't hold back as his magic answered his call, coursing through him in a rush and shoving back against whatever held Rhona.

~

"Get your fucking hands off me," Rhona demanded as she glared at the Ancient.

The woman smiled. Gone was the ethereal being who had been so careful with her words. Rhona's stomach dropped to her feet as she realized she wasn't talking to an Ancient. Once more she had been betrayed.

"You can try to leave, Rhona, but now that I have you, you aren't going anywhere."

Rhona shoved away from her, adding her magic as she did. The woman didn't budge. The smile that widened on her face enraged Rhona. How could she have been duped again? How could she have missed the clues?

"You should be better at hiding your emotions. They're like a billboard over your face. You're wondering how you were deceived. It was easy, really. You fear you aren't the right person to lead the Druids. You gave me the in I needed."

"Who are you?"

"The one who is going to make sure you never return to the Druids."

Rhona lifted her chin and called to her magic. "We'll see about that."

"Your magic can't come close to competing with mine. Give in to your fate."

Once more, the other magic brushed over Rhona. It felt like Balladyn. Fierce and brilliant. She didn't know how it was happening, but she grabbed hold of what was offered. She opened herself and let the magic meld with hers. The rush that swept through her was like a warm glow infusing her from the inside out. She felt the strength of it, the sheer might it held.

And she let it fill every inch of her.

The woman must have sensed the new magic, too, because the

smile vanished, and her brows drew together worriedly. Rhona spread her fingers as she called to her magic. The force in which it came to her nearly knocked her on her face. She controlled it, but just. There was no time to think about the intoxicating experience of Reaper magic mixing with hers. She had one thought—get back to the Druids.

And Balladyn.

Rhona locked her eyes on the woman then released her magic.

The wind howled violently, deafening Balladyn. He squeezed his eyes closed and dug his fingers deeper into the soil in an attempt to remain with Rhona. Magic from the stones pummeled him while the Dark magic tried to dislodge him, but he fought them both because he knew he had to be there. He had to help Rhona. If he didn't, then she would be lost to him forever.

Balladyn no longer knew if they were in Scotland. His body rebelled against what he was attempting, but still, he remained. He had made so many bad choices in his life. Saving Rhona wouldn't erase everything, but it was a start.

Rhona's first shot of magic dislodged the woman's hand from her arm, but it didn't do the damage Rhona had wanted. Balladyn's magic was so strong that she didn't know how to wield it properly. If she were going to get back to her people, back to Balladyn, then she had to learn quickly.

"What did you just do?" the woman demanded.

Rhona widened her stance. She didn't smile at the fact that the woman no longer spoke inside her mind, nor did she answer. Instead, Rhona ground her teeth as the magic swelled inside her again. She knew she had maybe two more chances before the woman figured out what was going on. Rhona let the magic gather within until she felt as if she were bursting with it.

Then she unleashed it.

The woman shrieked in fury as she was thrown backwards. Rhona barely had time to rejoice gaining some semblance of control over Balladyn's magic before she was struck. Rhona gasped for breath as she reeled with the impact of the woman's magic. She could feel herself fading, falling. The black hole she had dreamed about awaited her.

Rhona steeled herself. "One more time," she whispered.

Balladyn's lungs couldn't expand to take a breath. He felt as if he were being torn into a million different pieces at the same time he thought his body might implode. Everything urged him to let go, to stop fighting, but it only made him hold firmer.

He thought of Rhona, of her smiling green eyes and how her red hair looked against the angry Scottish sky. He remembered her soft voice and the way she had clung to him, how she'd told him that she felt safe with him.

He would not fail her. He had found himself with her, rediscovered who he was without the weight of his past restraining him. All he had to do was stay with her. If he could protect her one more time, that would be enough.

With that thought, a bellow threatened to break free of him. Balladyn was so intent on remaining with Rhona that he couldn't control it. He threw back his head and let it loose as he gave her all his magic. He saw lightning flash in an awesome display above him. The release of the shout made him feel better, but he already felt another forming.

His attention returned to Rhona when a bright light chased away the night. Balladyn watched as the same light from earlier emanated from Rhona again. He barely grasped what was happening when something dark and malignant struck him square in the chest. He had experienced enough Dark magic to know what it was.

He fought to keep his eyes open even as the magic sank through muscle and into bone and then into his organs. Balladyn clenched his teeth as he fought against the agony sizzling through his body. He willed Rhona's eyes to open so he could see her one more time, but she lay unmoving.

His heart valiantly tried to keep pumping. It became impossible for his arms to hold him up. Dimly, Balladyn was aware of the wind dying. Was it over? Why wouldn't Rhona open her eyes?

"Rhona," he whispered before his arms gave out.

Rhona's eyes flew open. She found herself staring up at the sky. As she listened, she heard her own breathing and the lapping of nearby water. Then she felt the weight of something atop her. She lifted her head and saw Balladyn collapsed over her.

"No," she whispered as she took hold of his face. "Balladyn?"

But he didn't respond.

She lightly tapped his face, trying to get him to wake. His magic still swirled within her, and though she was loath to relinquish it, it didn't belong to her. She wasn't sure how to give it back, though. The only thing she could do was try. So, she thought of the magic moving from her back to Balladyn.

Rhona anxiously waited. Tears burned her eyes as tense minutes passed without him moving. She'd never considered that he might die. He was a Reaper. That meant he was invincible. He had to be. He couldn't be gone. He just couldn't. She wouldn't accept it.

"Please," she said.

His lids slowly lifted, and deep crimson eyes gazed back at her.

She released a wobbly breath as a tear leaked from the corner of her eye. "Hi," she said, not able to think of anything else to say.

One side of his lips lifted in a grin. "I knew you'd make it."

There was so much she wanted to say. She parted her lips when the sounds of others reached her. They both glanced to the side to see Druids, Warriors, and Reapers racing toward them.

Rhona jerked her gaze back to Balladyn. "Thank you. I know what you did."

"I might have helped, but you did the hard part."

She saw his face squinch as if in pain as he sat up. Before she could say anything, he gently wiped the tear from her face and moved off her. Rhona lost sight of him as Druids surrounded her and all spoke at once.

Someone helped her to her feet. Without Balladyn's heat, she shivered against the cold. Sorcha noticed and called to Cathal. Rhona searched the group for another sign of Balladyn. She needed to know that he was all right. Cathal touched her, and when she blinked next, she was back in her cottage.

With the fourteen Druid and Warrior couples from MacLeod Castle, who all looked at her expectantly.

"What happened?" Sorcha asked.

Rhona held up a finger to tell them to wait before hurrying to her bedroom. She turned in a slow circle, waiting for Balladyn. Everyone wanted answers, and she wasn't sure she could give them. She only knew what had happened with her. She didn't know what Balladyn had done, but she knew it had been something incredible. Without him, she wouldn't have gotten free.

A knock sounded on her door. Rhona sank onto her bed when she realized that Balladyn wasn't there. It felt like a band tightening around her chest when she thought she might never see him again.

"Rhona?"

She turned to the door to see Sorcha leaning her head around it, her expression worried. Sorcha slipped into the room and closed the door behind her before walking to the bed and sitting beside Rhona. Then she took Rhona's hand in both of hers, and they simply sat.

"Where is he?" Rhona finally asked.

Sorcha shrugged and shook her head, not having to ask who *he* was. "I don't know."

"Is he coming back?"

"Maybe. I'm not sure. We're still reeling over him going into the stones."

So was Rhona.

Sorcha shifted to face her. "What did he do?"

"He saved me."

"From whom? And how?"

It was Rhona's turn to shrug. "I don't know who it was, but she was powerful. As for the how?" She paused as she turned her head to her cousin. "I felt his magic with mine."

"What?" Sorcha asked in disbelief, her eyes wide. "How is that even possible?"

Rhona lifted one shoulder as she fought a sudden onslaught of tears. "How did he find me when I was dying? I don't have an answer for that either."

"Something is developing between the two of you."

Rhona swallowed and glanced at their joined hands. "This is going to sound silly, but I've carried a heavy burden since stepping into Corann's position. It doesn't feel quite as heavy when Balladyn is with me."

"He's a Reaper," Sorcha said cautiously.

The tears finally fell as Rhona forced a smile. "And I'm the leader of the Skye Druids. My place is here. His is with the Reapers. I know."

And yet, Rhona knew what she wanted. Surely, it meant something that Balladyn had been there for her twice. Fate had intervened in their lives for a reason. It couldn't be merely to break her heart.

CHAPTER TWENTY

Lena opened her eyes and smiled.

"Don't ever do that again," Barry ordered angrily.

She looked in his direction and shrugged. "We're in this together. We share our magic. Or have you forgotten?"

"There's a difference between sharing and taking," Sheila snapped.

Enya nodded, her nostrils flaring in fury. "And that was taking."

"I had a plan," Lena replied coolly.

Oona turned her silver gaze on Lena. "One you did not share."

"Being leader doesn't give you the right to make those kinds of decisions yourself," Nola said.

Lena rolled her eyes. "What's our goal?" When no one answered, she looked pointedly at Barry.

He glared back but answered, "To rule the Fae and this planet."

"What is the first step in doing that?" she pushed.

Barry's eyes narrowed. "We take out the Reapers and Death."

Lena smiled as she looked at each of the Six. "I found our way in."

"Explain," Nola demanded.

Lena couldn't wait until she could put Nola and the rest of the Six in their places. Until then, however, she had to play by the rules. Ones she was beginning to detest. "We've tried to ambush the Reapers, which didn't work. They've tried to do the same to us, and we lost one of our own. I don't want to spend years playing this cat and mouse game. I knew we had to get to the Reapers in a way no one would think of."

"What did you do?" Sheila asked warily.

Lena glanced down at her arm, thinking of the magic she had blocked from Rhona. It had felt much different than what she'd thought Druid magic would feel like. "I told you the Reapers have a connection to the Skye Druids. It's why we targeted them."

"And I thought you said you wanted them taken care of so they didn't threaten us," Enya replied.

With a shrug of her shoulders, Lena smiled. "I was counting on the Reapers going to help the Skye Druids, and they did."

"Lena, I'm getting tired of your cryptic answers. You aren't above us," Barry threatened. "We can remove you anytime."

They couldn't, but she didn't tell them that. Yet. She was waiting for when they actually tried it. By then, she would have enough power to kill them simultaneously. So, she forced her face to relax and shoved aside her irritation. "When the Reapers managed to save Rhona, I suspected they would stick around to help. I counted on that, and it paid off. I used our magic to bring Rhona to a place none of the Druids could reach."

"With our magic," Oona said.

"As I just said," Lena snapped. Then she took a breath and calmed her voice. "I waited until a Reaper attempted to help her, and then sent a little surprise. He'll be ours when we need it. We can also now track the Reapers."

Barry slowly clapped, but anger still burned in his red eyes. "Your plan worked, but in the future, we discuss things. You won't be taking my magic again without my consent. Remember, we can all do that to each other. But we don't as a rule."

Lena smiled coldly. Yes, her plan had worked. Sort of. None of them needed to know that she had designed it to keep Rhona with her indefinitely. She'd underestimated the Druid, and she had lost her.

In the end, however, Lena had gotten what she wanted—a Reaper.

CHAPTER TWENTY-ONE

"Fekking hell."

"What the bloody hell were you thinking?"

"Do you have any idea what could've happened?"

"Fekking insane. Or heroic. Not sure which."

"Erith is going to have your arse."

"Fek me."

"Are you all right?"

The last question was from Eoghan. Balladyn forced himself to look away from the Druids surrounding Rhona. He glanced down at his chest where he had felt the Dark magic. "I don't know."

"I'm taking Sorcha and Rhona to the cottage," Cathal said. Before he left, he pinned Balladyn with a hard look. "I'm not sure whether to hug you or hit you. Fekking insane."

Balladyn swallowed past the pain coursing through his body. It took everything he had to stay on his feet. There was no wound, but he knew he had been hit. The instant Rhona was gone, Balladyn leaned over and braced his hands on his knees. If he sat down, he wasn't sure he'd ever get back up.

"Talk to me," Eoghan urged as he leaned down next to him.

Balladyn swung his head to look at the Reaper. "I was hit with Dark magic."

"I fekking knew it," Bradach grumbled.

Eoghan lifted his head and snapped, "Enough. We're all on edge right now, but until we know something, there isn't a damn thing to do."

Despite Balladyn's efforts, his knees gave out. He fell on his ass and leaned his head back to look at the sky, breathing in deep lungsful of cold air. Fek, he hurt.

"What did you see?" Eoghan asked.

Balladyn just wanted to be left alone, to let his body heal and try to determine what had happened for himself. But that wasn't to be. He licked his lips and lowered his face to find the Reapers, including Cathal, sitting or squatting in a semicircle in front of him. They weren't alone, though. Several Warriors were with them.

He rubbed his chest over the spot where the magic had hit him. "I didn't see anything. It's more what I felt."

"No one has ever dared to go into the standing stones while Druids were using their magic on someone," Charon said.

Balladyn swiveled his head to look at Charon. The Warrior's brown gaze met his. Balladyn sighed before he returned his attention to Eoghan. "I can't explain it. I just knew what I had to do."

"Like you knew you had to get to Rhona when she was dying?" Ruarc asked.

Balladyn shoved his hair away from his face. "Just like that."

"Why?" Quinn MacLeod asked.

Balladyn shook his head. "I wish to hell I knew. It wasn't as if I had a choice. I knew if I didn't go to Rhona, she wouldn't wake."

"Fek me," Dubhan murmured.

Eoghan ran a hand over his jaw. "Maybe you should start at the beginning."

Balladyn took a deep breath and told them all of it. When he finished, he looked around to find a mixture of incredulity and bewilderment on the faces staring back at him.

Eoghan looked at Quinn. "What do you think this means?"

"That is a question posed to our wives, no' us," the Warrior answered.

Balladyn rubbed his chest again. "Something powerful had Rhona, and they weren't going to let go. Combine that with the Dark magic that struck me, and I think it's the Six."

"But why?" Rordan asked.

Ruarc snorted. "It could be any number of reasons or nothing at all. They want power. This we know."

"I need to know Rhona is okay," Balladyn said.

Torin made a sound in the back of his throat. "You gave your magic to Rhona, which, as far as I know, has never been done before. Something reached between the realms to you and brought you to Rhona. And you were struck with Dark magic, but you don't have a wound. I don't know about anyone else, but I'm having a hard time with all of this."

"You aren't the one going through it," Eoghan said before looking at Balladyn. "How do you know Rhona got away from whatever had her?"

Balladyn glanced at the Warriors. "I felt it. When she lit up like she did in her bedroom."

"Lit up?" one of the Warriors asked.

Dubhan's brows knitted together. "That didn't happen."

"We didn't see or hear the wind, either," Bradach pointed out. "We did see your lightning display again when you bellowed."

Balladyn frowned as he shook his head. "What are you talking about?"

Eoghan sighed and ran a hand down his face. "When you first felt the pull to Rhona. You gave a shout on Death's realm."

"Aye," Balladyn said. "What of it?"

Cathal grunted. "You lit up the sky. Lightning, wind. It was quite a display."

"And you saw lightning when I yelled again?" Balladyn asked.

Everyone around him nodded.

Charon asked, "Why did you bellow?"

"It's just something I felt I had to do." Balladyn rubbed his chest as the ache intensified.

"Let's get back to why we didna see Rhona light up," Quinn said.

Ruarc shrugged. "I think it's because we weren't between the stones like Balladyn was."

"We saw it at her cottage," Dubhan added.

"I don't care about the why," Balladyn said as he climbed to his feet. "I need to make sure Rhona is fine."

The others stood with him. It was Cathal who said, "She's fine and surrounded by Druids."

"You should go talk to Erith," Eoghan told Balladyn.

Charon asked, "Is that wise? He's saved Rhona twice now. It's likely that whatever is coming for her will strike again. I'd say there's a reason for Balladyn to remain."

"He makes a valid point," Torin agreed.

Eoghan blew out a breath. "None of it makes sense. I don't like being on the defensive."

"No one does." Dubhan slapped Eoghan on the back. "We'll get the Warriors to Rhona's cottage."

Balladyn was about to go with the others when Eoghan caught his attention. They remained behind until it was just the two of them.

"I need to know if I should be worried," Eoghan said.

Balladyn swallowed and looked at the loch. "I wish I could say you had nothing to be concerned about."

"Bloody hell." Eoghan turned away, then swung back around to him. "You didn't see any of the Six? Soldiers? Anyone from the Fae Others?"

Balladyn shook his head. "It was pure instinct that made me go to Rhona in the stones. It was also instinct that told me to share my magic."

"Did Rhona use it?"

Balladyn glanced between the two standing stones. "I know she accepted it, and I sensed it mingle with hers. I felt her use it. Like it was an extension of me."

"Did you have any of *her* magic?"

"I don't think so. But..." He paused. "She returned mine."

Eoghan's face was lined with shock. "How is any of this possible?"

Balladyn didn't have a different answer than he'd had before. "I have no proof, but I think whoever attacked Rhona this time was of the Six."

"Was the hit you experienced meant for Rhona?"

"I can't say either way for certain. What I *can* tell you is that it packed a punch. Like one of the soldiers but stronger."

Eoghan's liquid-silver eyes narrowed. "Was it Lena?"

"I think we should assume that it was. Whether it was her or all of the Six, I think they've found a way to strike at us."

"Fek!" Eoghan shouted with his hands on his hips. He released a long breath and looked at Balladyn. "You and Rhona have both been through a lot in a short period. What do you need?"

Balladyn answered immediately. "Some time to think. I need to sort things out without answering questions in between."

"And I suppose you want to do that with Rhona?"

"I need to talk to her about what she experienced and match that up with my memories."

Eoghan nodded and dropped his arms to his sides. "If you're right, then the Six need to be dealt with straightaway."

"Aye. Whoever this is got to Rhona as she slept. That takes powerful magic. They were Fae, though. There's no getting around that."

"Do you think it was this same entity who set Rhona up in Belfast?"

Balladyn licked his dry lips. "I think it's all connected."

"Even calling to you across realms?"

"There's a good possibility."

Eoghan's lips twisted. "I'm not as sure as you. A lot doesn't make sense."

"Only Rhona has been attacked. No other Druid."

"Aye. There is that." Eoghan paused and stared into the distance for a moment. Then he looked at Balladyn. "I'm going to fill Erith and Cael in."

Balladyn waited until Eoghan teleported away before turning to look at the stones. Rhona had been the focus of the attacks, but now he wasn't sure if she had been the intended target all along or if it had been the Reapers.

He rubbed his chest again. He didn't know if it was being in the midst of a Druid enchantment, sharing his power with Rhona, or being struck with Dark magic, but he didn't feel like himself. His hand moved to his cheek where Rhona had touched him.

Staring into her eyes had made him want to shout with joy. She had woken. His plea to the universe had been answered. He thought about the tear that he had caught with his thumb. If he'd thought something had bound the two of them before, there was no denying it now. It was as if someone had tied their destinies together.

His head turned in the direction of her cottage. Of all the people, why him? After all the things he had done, he didn't deserve to be in this role. It should go to someone who warranted it. Everyone knew that wasn't him.

But he wanted to be with Rhona. To hear her voice, watch the way she moved with such grace, and to see her smile.

No, he didn't merit his current situation, but he was in it, and he would do everything to keep Rhona out of the hands of the Six.

CHAPTER TWENTY-TWO

She was spinning out of control. That was the only way Rhona could describe her current state. Her small cottage was bursting at the seams with Druids and Warriors, and they all wanted answers.

They hounded her with questions. While she understood their concerns, she wanted to scream in frustration. Everything was happening to *her*. She was the one enduring each attack, and she hadn't had any time to digest the latest.

"Go over it again."

Rhona didn't know which Druid had asked that, and she didn't care. She squeezed her hands together and bit her tongue to keep from unleashing her irritation, anger, and bone-deep fear. She couldn't stop thinking about Balladyn and the pain she had seen in his eyes before he carefully hid the emotion behind the walls he'd erected around himself.

Not that she could blame him. She wanted walls of her own—anything to have some time to soak everything in.

"Give her a second," Sorcha stated. "All of you have been pestering her since we arrived. Look at her! She's barely had time to take in any of it herself."

Rhona glanced at her cousin with a silent *thank you* in her eyes.

She'd thought Sorcha's words would put an end to the endless questions for a short while.

She was wrong.

"We have to know what happened."

Rhona squeezed her eyes closed. She didn't care who was talking now. She was done. Finished. She needed to get her own spinning emotions in some semblance of order before she proceeded.

When she opened her eyes, she spotted Eoghan next to Cathal. They shared a look, but no words passed between them. That's when Rhona felt it. Balladyn. He was there. She didn't need to look for him. She felt him in her bedroom.

Without a word, Rhona got to her feet and pushed through everyone to dash into her room. She shut the door softly and then turned to the far wall where she felt him. Two heartbeats later, Balladyn dropped his veil. They stared at each other across the room. Her gaze raked over him, but she didn't see any wounds.

She flattened her hands on the door behind her lest she rush to him and throw her arms around him. The need to have him enfold her in his embrace was strong. She wasn't sure how she managed to remain on her side of the space, especially after she had felt him on top of her and had held his face in her hands.

Gazed into his expressive eyes.

"Are you hurt?"

The sound of his deep, smooth voice made her shiver. She shook her head. "I don't think so. You?"

"I'm uncertain."

She frowned. "What?"

"I was struck by Dark Fae magic."

"Where?" Rhona ran her eyes over him, searching for a wound.

Balladyn swallowed. "There is no wound."

Her eyes snapped to his. "That we can see."

"Aye."

They were back to gazing at each other. Words burned on Rhona's tongue. None came out because she didn't want to bombard him as she had been earlier and because she wasn't entirely sure she was ready for answers.

In the end, she blurted, "I felt your magic."

He blinked in response.

"How?" she asked softly.

Balladyn's shoulders sagged as he sighed. He ran a hand through his long hair, shoving it out of his face. "I knew you needed it. As to the how? I have no idea."

"Have you done that before?"

"As far as I know, no Fae has ever shared magic like that before. We know the Others and Fae Others combine their magic, which means they pool it together to be used jointly. Usaeil killed Druids to consume their power just as Lena consumed her family's. But to have my magic flow into you as if it we were one body, and I feel yours? Nay. Never."

Rhona's mouth was suddenly dry. She tried to swallow but couldn't. "My life has been in jeopardy twice now. And twice you've saved me. How can I ever repay you?"

"Live," he said. "Don't succumb to whatever is after you."

Something in his words drew her up short. "You know who it is."

"I've a hunch."

And then she knew. "The Fae Others."

Balladyn's gaze briefly lowered to the floor. "It makes sense."

Rhona tucked her windblown hair behind her ears. She glanced down at her socks. "Why me?"

"Because you are the leader of the Skye Druids. Because Corann chose you. Because you have a connection to us. We may never know."

Her eyes returned to him. "She was strong. Very strong."

Balladyn was across her room and before her in a blink. He was so close she could touch him. It was too great a temptation to resist. Rhona placed her palm on his chest. He covered her hand with his. Whatever kept drawing them together wouldn't be denied.

And neither would she.

The one thing Rhona was sure of was Balladyn. Saving her life

—twice—had bound them, but there was something else there. Something that was as sure and strong as the magic of Skye.

"I'm not the man you think I am."

She blinked up at him. "I know exactly who you are." She smiled. "A hero."

"I'm nothing of the sort."

"Funny since you keep acting like one."

Her other hand rose to his chest. A tremor ran through him. Knowing she affected him as much as he did her gave her the courage to proceed. She smoothed her flattened hands over his expansive chest to his muscular arms. As she gazed into his crimson eyes, she saw desire war with hesitation.

She slid her fingers over his shoulder, around his neck, and into his thick, black and silver hair. Rhona inwardly smiled when his hands came to rest on her hips.

Then a knock broke the spell holding them.

Balladyn hurriedly stepped away. Rhona wanted to scream.

"Rhona?" Sorcha called through the door. "We're all going to leave to give you some time. It's been decided to let you rest. We'll be back tomorrow."

"Thank you," Rhona said.

No one had to tell her that the Reapers would be watching her house, or that Balladyn would be inside with her. Bright sunlight filtered through the blinds, announcing the dawn. Rhona hadn't taken her eyes from Balladyn. He could've left. But he hadn't.

They stood in silence for several moments until the cottage grew quiet, neither of them looking away from the other.

"Are they gone?" she asked.

Balladyn nodded. "You should rest."

"What are you afraid of?"

His brows snapped together. "What do you mean?"

"You feel what's between us. I know you do. It's impossible for either of us not to. Why are you fighting it?" she beseeched as she took a step toward him.

His eyes closed for a heartbeat. "I told you. I'm not the man you think I am."

"And I told you that I know who you are."

"You're vulnerable right now. You've been attacked and came close to losing your life two nights in a row."

Anger shot through her. "So help me if you say I feel beholden to you because you saved me. If you do, I'm going to scream."

"It's true."

"Do you feel indebted to *me*?"

His brow creased once more. "No. Why would I?"

"You came to my rescue twice."

"It's not the same."

"Isn't it?" she pushed. Rhona glanced away and sighed. "I knew the instant you arrived tonight. No one had to tell me. I even knew where you were while veiled. I felt your magic earlier. It was inside me, mixing with mine."

"And you gave it back to me."

She nodded slowly. "You knew I was hurt across realms. You found me in that alley. I don't know why any of this is happening. What I *do* understand is that I have to know the taste of your lips."

In the next instant, he had her against the door. His body pressed against hers as his red eyes burned with longing. Her heart thudded with excitement. He put a hand on her hip and slowly slid it around her as his mouth descended upon hers. The ache inside Rhona to know his touch, to feel his kiss, finally loosened when his lips met hers. The kiss was heat and passion.

And *need*.

Her arms wound around his neck, clasping him tightly in case he tried to pull away again. His tongue slid between her lips and dueled with hers. His hard body pressed hers against the door as he deepened the kiss. Her nipples hardened; her sex clenched. *Yes*. This was what she wanted, what she craved above all else.

Balladyn suddenly ended the kiss and leaned his head back. He was breathing rapidly. She licked her swollen lips, and his eyes followed her tongue as he panted. His red eyes lifted to hers. The hunger she saw made her knees go weak.

His arm tightened around her as he lowered his head once more and brushed his lips against hers. He bent and grasped behind her knee with his free hand, lifting her leg as he rocked against her. Rhona gasped when she felt the long, hard length of his arousal.

"In case you had any doubts," he murmured.

She cupped his face with both her hands as he lifted her and spun. Rhona wrapped her free leg around his waist and leaned in for another kiss.

CHAPTER TWENTY-THREE

Balladyn knew he shouldn't give in to the yearning for Rhona.

He knew it, and yet he ignored it.

Her taste was everything he had fantasized it would be. Sublime. Exotic. Irresistible.

Utterly Rhona.

Her sighs inflamed his already heated body. The way her hands moved over his shoulders and back caused heat to race across his skin. He wanted all of her. He craved to sink deep inside her, to claim her body as his. In all his long years, he'd never felt anything so primal, so savage. But once the thought was there, he couldn't dislodge it.

Balladyn walked to the bed and put a knee on the mattress before slowly lowering Rhona. The feeling of him sinking against her softness made his cock twitch. He rolled to his side and splayed his hand on her lower back before moving it up her back.

It wasn't enough. He wanted—no, he *needed*—her naked. To feel her. All of her. Every beautiful inch. He almost used his magic to remove her clothes, but since he had imagined peeling each layer from her, he wasn't going to miss the chance.

He broke the kiss and looked down at her. The sight of her kiss-swollen lips made him moan. Her eyes were heavy-lidded, her desire palpable.

She was so beautiful. He wanted to remember this exact moment. To have it burned in his memory. He knew he was crossing a line, but he couldn't keep away from her. She was…everything he wanted.

Balladyn saw the question in her eyes. He answered by kissing her forehead. Then he leaned to the side and kissed behind one ear, lingering to softly run his tongue along her skin. Her soft sigh and the way she moved her head to the side made him smile. He shifted to the other side and repeated the kisses.

Then he moved down her body and took one foot in his hand. He tenderly removed the sock before grasping the other. His hands shook when he reached for the waist of her pants. Balladyn moved her shirt up just enough to see her stomach. He placed a soft kiss on her belly as his fingers hooked in the waistband of her joggers.

Before he pulled them down, he ran his lips along her midriff where her skin met her pants. Her stomach clenched, and her nails dug into his shoulders. He took his time lowering the lounge pants, pausing to kiss the exposed skin of her thighs, knees, and shins before tossing the clothing aside.

When he looked up, he saw her eyes locked on him as her chest rose rapidly. Desire blazed in the green depths. He'd only meant to give her a quick peck before removing her cardigan and shirt, but the instant he kissed her, he had to have more.

From the first kiss, he was instantly and irrevocably addicted. There was no turning back for him.

A groan tore from him when she wound a leg around him and ground herself against his cock. He was holding on by a very thin thread that was unraveling even then. He tore his mouth from hers and slipped his hand under her shirt.

Her breath hitched. Balladyn found his gaze locked with Rhona's as he slowly pushed up her shirt. He lost patience and removed the shirt and cardigan with a thought, leaving her in only her nude bra and white cotton panties with tiny rainbows.

All thought left him as he gazed at the beautiful Druid. Pale skin dotted with freckles made him want to count each one—and he would. One day soon. He moved to his knees as he swept his gaze from her flaming hair spread haphazardly on the bed, her face filled with unadulterated need, then down her neck and over the swells of her breasts to the indent of her waist and the flare of her hips. He paused, licking his lips when he came to her panties that hid her most delicate parts.

Balladyn rested a hand on her leg and skimmed down the limb, his eyes following the movement. "I could look at you forever."

"I like the sound of that," she said huskily. "Only if you keep touching me."

His attention snapped to her face. "I couldn't stop if I tried."

She rose to her knees before him and reached around to unclasp her bra. The straps loosened on her shoulders before she tossed the garment aside.

His breath left him in one fell swoop. It had been so long since he had felt anything this profound, this…true. He had wondered if he would ever feel passion again. It seemed that he had only needed to find Rhona to discover it had simply been waiting.

Balladyn wound a hand around her waist and pulled her to him. The sight of her pink nipples, hard and waiting, had him fighting to stop from taking her right then. He cupped one of her breasts, testing the weight as he learned that it fit perfectly in his hand. He ran his thumb over the taut nipple.

Rhona gasped and covered his hand with hers. "Not yet," she said breathlessly. "If you keep doing that, I won't get to look at you. And I really want to see you."

How could he refuse such a request? He had the solution. Just like with her clothes, he would remove his with magic.

"Don't," Rhona hurriedly said.

He frowned at her. "Don't, what?"

"Don't use magic." Her gaze had lowered to where her hands rested on his chest. "I want to do this."

The instant her hands moved beneath his shirt, Balladyn knew he would go up in flames.

Oh, yes, Rhona thought as she felt the ridges and valleys of Balladyn's washboard stomach. She flattened her palms against his skin and heard his sharp intake of breath. A glance at him showed his struggle to remain still. She knew exactly how he felt since she had been in his shoes just moments earlier. It had been the purest form of torture, the most exquisite torment for him to remove her clothing item by item.

And she was going to repay it in kind.

The way he took such care in touching her, learning her, made her hunger for him grow with each second. If this was his foreplay, she couldn't wait for what came next. Her attention returned to his stomach and the shirt that hid it.

Rhona slid her hands up, taking the tee with her as she did. With every inch of exposed skin, heat moved to the center of her body. In her haste to get the shirt off, Rhona ripped it. Then she was taking in his broad shoulders that tapered to trim hips. Every muscle was finely molded as if it had been individually worked to its optimum strength.

"Oh," she whispered.

She tore her eyes from his chest to see the thick sinew of his shoulders and arms—arms that she had dreamed of holding her. Now that she could see him, she took advantage of being able to run her hands over him. She heard his shallow breathing and soft groans, but she couldn't get enough of him.

Her hands hit the waistband of his jeans. She unbuttoned them before looking at Balladyn's face. His eyes blazed with such fierce desire that her heart missed a beat as it answered the sight before her.

He moved off the bed, waiting for her to finish undressing him. Rhona scooted to the edge of the mattress and noticed that his boots were gone. She was thankful because she didn't think she could have waited the time it would have taken to remove them. She eagerly returned to Balladyn's jeans. After grasping the edge of the pull, she began to unzip his pants, exposing more skin beneath.

"Rhona," he said tightly.

Did she torture them by continuing?

Or did she give in so they could both experience the pleasure that awaited?

With a growl, Balladyn used his magic to remove the last of his clothes as well as her panties. She took in his arousal that jutted upward. Rhona reached out to touch it when he grasped her hands and pulled them over her head as he pressed her onto her back. Her legs parted, waiting. Eager.

Hungry.

"Woman," he ground out in a rough tone that made her sex clench in need.

Rhona gazed into his crimson eyes. "Don't make us wait any longer."

Fek. He was in way over his head, but Balladyn didn't care.

His fingers tightened around Rhona's small wrists as he held himself over her. She lifted her hips and rocked against him. He squeezed his eyes closed at the contact. Without a doubt, he was going up in flames.

But what a pleasurable death it would be.

He opened his eyes and looked down at her willing body. All Balladyn had to do was shift his hips and he could enter her in one thrust. And he would. Just not quite yet.

Rhona bit her bottom lip as he slowly lowered his body to hers. Then he shifted and licked a nipple. Her back arched as she moaned. Balladyn then wrapped his lips around the peak and gently suckled. Only when she was breathless did he move to the other nipple and begin teasing it.

She ground against him, seeking release. Each time, his cock jumped. Needy and impatient. It was becoming harder and harder to rein in his desires, but Balladyn wasn't giving in quite yet. His lips wanted to taste another place on her body. He thumbed her nipples as he kissed down her belly.

The instant he released her wrists, Rhona clutched the covers. She stilled the closer he came to her center. He hovered over her as their breathing filled the room. Then he leaned down and gently ran his tongue along her sex.

A low moan fell from her lips as her back arched. He grasped her hips to keep her still as he found her clit and began moving his tongue over the swollen nub. He didn't relent until her body stiffened, and the first orgasm rushed through her.

With the taste of her pleasure on his tongue, Balladyn rose over Rhona. Her body still convulsed with the climax in a stunning, erotic sight.

Then he pushed inside her.

～

She was dying the most beautiful, satisfying death. Rhona was still experiencing her first earth-shattering orgasm when she felt the blunt head of Balladyn's cock against her. He slid inside her with one thrust. She sucked in a breath at the exquisite feel of him stretching and filling her.

The weight of him settled over her. She tried to open her eyes, but she was too lost in sensations. Every nerve ending sizzled, anxious for more.

Because she knew there would be more.

"Hold on, *mo stór*," he whispered.

She found him and wrapped her arms around him as he began rocking against her. Rhona found herself drifting as he gradually increased his rhythm. He didn't change positions, didn't alter his thrusts as he pushed her closer and closer to her second climax.

The feel of his lips on her neck forced her eyes open. Their gazes locked. His crimson orbs reflected the depths of his longing. The walls he so carefully erected around himself were gone. She saw him. *All of him.*

And she never wanted to look away. In that instant, that very second, he captured the last of her heart.

The orgasm took her by surprise, wrapping her in its embrace and once more taking her to a place of ecstasy and delight. Waves of decadent pleasure infused her. It stole her breath and robbed her of thought.

She came back to herself to discover Balladyn still moving inside her. His breathing was ragged, his thrusts hard, fast, and oh, so deep. His body rubbed against her clit, causing tendrils of bliss to zing through her, prolonging her orgasm.

Rhona looked down at where their bodies joined, slick with sweat, and groaned at the sight. Balladyn made a sound that brought her attention back to him. When their gazes met, he drove deep inside her and stilled, his face contorting as he climaxed.

She wrapped him in her arms when he lowered himself atop her. Rhona grinned when he kissed the side of her neck and rose on his elbows to look at her. They shared a smile. She tugged at his long hair, loving having it around her.

He moved off her and held out his hand. A towel appeared. She laughed and took it to clean herself. Only then did he move them so their heads were on the pillows. He lay on his back, but Rhona faced him.

He turned his head to her. "You should sleep. There is much more I want to do to your body."

A thrill went through her at his words, but the thought of sleep made her uneasy. "Be prepared, because there's a lot I'm going to do to you, as well."

"Tease," Balladyn said, his eyes crinkling.

"Oh! It's okay for you, but not me?" she asked with a laugh.

He nodded once and put a hand under his head as he looked at the ceiling. "Exactly."

She sobered as she looked over his unbelievably handsome face. As if sensing the change in her mood, he looked at her and then shifted to face her. With tender fingers, he tucked her hair behind her ear. Rhona alternated between wanting to cry and climb atop his body.

"Twice, they came for you. Twice, you beat them," he said.

She moved closer to his warmth and strength. "With your help."

"I'll be here if they try again." He pulled her against him. She rested her head on his chest as his arms held her tightly against his side. "You will win if they come again. I know it because I felt your power."

Rhona closed her eyes, wondering if those words were platitudes or the truth. Then she realized that Balladyn would never give false words.

"Use your magic," he said. "There has to be something in your arsenal that will prevent someone from getting to you in sleep again."

Why hadn't she thought of that? Rhona kissed his chest in thanks. She called up her magic. The feel of it rushing through her was reassuring and relaxing. She began to whisper a protection spell but altered it to strengthen as she slept.

Balladyn's arms tightened around her when she finished. "I've added my magic as another barrier to protect you. Sleep. I have you," he promised.

She took a deep breath and settled into his warmth as exhaustion weighed heavily.

CHAPTER TWENTY-FOUR

Balladyn released a breath as his gaze lingered on the ceiling, where it had been for hours while Rhona slept beside him. The sun moved across the sky and descended again. She slept soundly, her breathing even and deep. He glanced at her, wanting to pleasure her again but loath to wake her after all she had endured.

A soft knock at the door alerted him that someone had grown tired of waiting for her. He didn't dare move because he had promised he would remain with her. Nothing would make him break that promise. Not even Erith.

"Enter," he whispered after using his magic to cover them with a blanket.

The knob turned, and the door opened quietly. Eoghan poked his head around the edge. His gaze landed on the bed and Rhona's sleeping form. Eoghan raised a brow in question. Balladyn motioned for him to enter, but also put a finger to his lips, urging the Reaper to remain quiet.

Eoghan walked to Balladyn's side of the bed and squatted down beside it before whispering, "The MacLeod Druids are getting antsy."

"They can fekking wait."

"We asked them here."

Balladyn shot Eoghan a dark look. "I don't care. Not after what Rhona has been through two nights in a row. This is the first time she's truly rested, and she needs it."

"I'm not arguing the point. I'm merely stating facts."

"We know where to find them. Let them return to the castle. When Rhona wakes, we'll let them know."

Eoghan's lips flattened. "I've already told them that. The Druids are insisting they remain."

"Then they're going to have to wait. Look at her," Balladyn said as he jerked his chin to Rhona. "She's not moved in hours."

"How do you know she wasn't taken again?"

Balladyn grinned. "She used her magic, and I added mine."

Eoghan glanced away with a small sigh. "I spoke with Erith."

"And?"

"She's concerned about you."

"She need not be."

Eoghan gave him a baleful look. "Don't forget who you are now, what you're a part of."

"I haven't."

"You don't have to do anything alone."

Balladyn thought about Rhona's naked body pressed against his under the covers. "It feels like I've been alone for an eternity."

"Whatever happens here, whatever happens with her, and between the two of you," Eoghan said as he glanced at Rhona, "we're with you. Always. We're a family."

It had been so long since Balladyn had anyone he could trust to have his back. Now, he had an entire family. It was an odd sensation. One he could get used to. "And I am with all of you."

"We know," Eoghan said with a grin. It vanished, his face lined with concern. "Something is happening here at Skye. I'm not sure what it is, and the Druids won't say anything until they've spoken with Rhona."

Balladyn debated waking her. In the end, he knew she needed the rest because there might not be time in the future for it. "Let her sleep some more."

"It's already been over twenty-four hours."

"She was attacked physically and mentally. Both took a toll on her emotionally. If there's a chance of her standing against her opponent, she has to be restored and revitalized."

Eoghan nodded slowly. "I agree. It's why I came to talk to you."

"Thank you."

Eoghan grinned. "Cathal is occupying Sorcha for the moment, but that won't last. She's worried about her cousin."

"Remind everyone who Rhona is and what she's sustained. That should hold them back for a little longer."

"Let's hope." Eoghan paused. "By the way, I'm glad."

"Glad for what?" Balladyn asked with a frown.

Eoghan's gaze jerked to Rhona before returning to Balladyn. "The two of you. It was impossible to miss the looks that passed between you. Whatever is going through your head now, stop it. Everyone deserves some happiness. Most especially you."

Balladyn wanted to believe Eoghan, but he couldn't.

"It took a long time before I was able to believe that about myself. Finding Thea was part of it. I didn't speak for thousands of years after I lost my family. In our battle against Bran, I took a hit that was meant for Cael. It sent me to another realm, one filled with darkness and death. I expected to die there. A part of me wanted to put an end to the grief I'd carried. Then, I heard music. A violin. It was Thea. Her playing transcended dimensions and entered the realm I was in, allowing me to find my way back to this planet. That's when Erith showed me the second group of Reapers she had and told me I was to be in charge of them."

"Bloody hell," Balladyn murmured in surprise.

Eoghan's lips twisted ruefully. "Aye. In the end, I set aside my anguish, took the role Erith demanded of me, and found myself falling hopelessly in love with Thea—who happens to be Usaeil's daughter."

Balladyn blanched. "What?"

"Usaeil killed all her offspring, but something stayed her hand with Thea. It came back to haunt her later when Usaeil attempted to use Thea, and Thea didn't want any part of it. Usaeil tried to kill her. With Thea's Fae blood, she survived."

"I knew Thea was a Halfling like most of the Reaper mates, but I didn't know she was Usaeil's daughter."

"It's not something we discuss, as I'm sure you can understand. My point in telling you all of that is to let you know that you can be happy. If you want to be."

Balladyn swallowed. He hadn't given much thought to his happiness. He'd been too absorbed in finding his way with the Reapers. "I appreciate it."

"I'll hold the Druids and Sorcha off until you call for me." And with that, Eoghan teleported out of the room.

Balladyn considered what Eoghan had told him. While Rhona slept, he had gone over what had happened to him at the standing stones. He had begun to plot out several actions to take moving forward, but, oddly, he didn't feel as antsy as he had in the past. Was it because he had yet to hear Rhona's side of things? Was it because of the Warriors and Druids? Or could it be because he had no firm proof that the Six had attacked Rhona?

His gaze lowered to look at the top of Rhona's head that rested on his chest. There was a very real possibility that it was because he was simply content to lay in bed with her.

Balladyn hastily looked away. He had given in to his desires, and his wanton need to know Rhona's body. But that was all it could be. He accepted that. But while he could, he would bask in the simple indulgence of holding her as she slept. Knowing she trusted him made it all the sweeter.

His thoughts returned to the troubles at hand. The Reapers were actively searching for—and fighting—the Six. The Six also hunted them by sending soldiers to attack. So far, the Reapers had come out ahead, but after the last encounter with Lena, things had been taken up a level.

Balladyn thought about how Lena had been able to take her family's magic with minimal effort. And if she could do that to a Fae, what could she do with the Druids? The thought left him sick to his stomach. The Reapers knew the Fae Others' end goal of ruling the Fae and ultimately believing they could destroy the Dragon Kings. But none of them had stopped to think about the consequences to humans during all of that.

If it hadn't been for Rhona, Balladyn never would've given mortals a second thought. Could they have missed an important detail? Could the humans, specifically the Druids, be the key?

His mind spun with possibilities. Yet he kept coming back to the attacks on Rhona. Why her specifically? He might be certain that the Six were responsible for the latest violence, but nothing pointed to them for the first. He and Rhona both believed Druids had instigated the attack in Belfast.

What if it had been? What if the Six had coerced Druids to go against Rhona?

Sweat broke out across Balladyn's body. If he were right, then some Druids wrongly believed they could take out those like Rhona and place themselves in positions of power. All they were doing was removing the most powerful from the board and giving the Fae Others a chance to step in.

The Fae, as a rule, believed that mortals were beneath them. For the Dark Fae, humans were merely there to have their souls consumed. To the Light, they were toys, playthings to pass the time. Though a few Druids did have immense power, the Fae generally disregarded them.

Balladyn ran his free hand down his face. He went through every angle to see if he was reading too much into things because of his connection to Rhona, but each time he did, he became more certain of his findings.

CHAPTER TWENTY-FIVE

Rhona blinked open her eyes and found herself staring at her bedroom wall. She yawned and stretched. Her lamp on the bedside table was aglow. She blinked, wondering why she had left it on. Then she remembered everything. The attacks, Balladyn saving her again, and the amazing, toe-curling sex with the handsome Reaper.

Her euphoria waned when she recalled how he had promised to remain with her. She rolled onto her back and looked to the side to find him lying there. He raised his brows as his red eyes met hers.

"You stayed."

Balladyn's lips curved into a sexy grin. "I gave my word."

Rhona glanced to the window to find the curtains drawn. No sunlight peaked in from the sides, which meant it was night. "I hope I didn't sleep too long and keep everyone waiting."

"Don't worry about them. You needed the rest."

She frowned at how he'd said those words. "How long have I been asleep?"

"Almost twenty-eight hours."

Her lips parted in shock as she blinked up at the ceiling. Then she took stock of her body. She felt rested. Both mentally and physically. Rhona inhaled deeply and slowly released the breath. Maybe Balladyn was right. She had needed the rest.

Rhona rolled to face him and propped her head against her hand. She studied Balladyn's face, her eyes caressing the contours and strong jaw, and she knew he had kept the others from waking her. "I can't hide in here any longer."

"You weren't hiding," he corrected her. "You were taking care of yourself. When the next attack comes, you need to be ready. You couldn't do that as taxed as you were."

Neither mentioned the trauma of her near death in Belfast. She set that aside and closed the door on it until she could give everything she had to sorting through the ordeal. Rhona sat up and sniffed. She needed a shower, food, a gallon of water and another of tea, and then she had to tell Balladyn about the woman.

He rested a hand on her back. "What is it?"

"I'm thinking of everything I need to do."

"Like what?"

She glanced at him with a grin. "Shower."

"Is that all?"

Rhona rolled her eyes and slipped from the bed, stretching muscles that hadn't moved in over a day. "You'll thank me later."

"Use magic."

She shook her head as she opened her closet and pulled out a pair of black jeans and a chunky gray sweater. "We don't use magic like that."

"You sound like the Dragon Kings."

Rhona chuckled and glanced at him as she went to her bureau and opened a drawer for a pair of panties and a bra. "It's not a bad thing."

"Maybe. Maybe not. If you won't, I can."

That stopped her. She wanted to stand underneath the spray of hot water, but washing her hair was an event. It was thick and now tangled from sex and sleep, so it would take forever. Never mind drying it. Her gaze slid to Balladyn.

He smiled as he sat up and swung his legs over the side of the bed to stand. "Is that an aye?"

"It is."

In the next blink, she was dressed in the clothes she had laid out. She sniffed, happy that she smelled nice. Then she looked in the mirror. Her hair looked immaculate. Better than when she went to the salon.

"Well?" Balladyn asked as he came up behind her.

She caught his reflection in the mirror and noted that he wore a new olive-green pullover and dark denim. His boots were on, and when she looked down, she saw she also had her boots on. "I'm going to be hard-pressed not ask you to do this again."

"I'd be willing to do it anytime," he said in a soft voice as he moved aside her hair and placed a kiss on her neck.

Rhona turned in his arms, her hands on his chest. "I'd like us to talk before I face anyone else."

"Eoghan is keeping everyone out of the house until I say otherwise."

"I need food, but I can talk while I eat."

They walked out of her room to the kitchen. Rhona set about heating water for tea as she downed several glasses of water.

"What would you like to eat?" Balladyn asked as he poured the hot water over tea bags.

Rhona almost balked, but then decided to just go with things. "Sushi."

There was a smile on Balladyn's face when he glanced at her. He nodded toward her small table. "Help yourself."

She looked to find various plates on the table, her stomach growling. Rhona hurried to the chair and grabbed some chopsticks as she chose her first bite. Her eyes closed as her mouth exploded with flavor.

"I take that face to mean you like it?"

Rhona opened her eyes to find Balladyn sitting in the chair opposite her. She nodded and took another mouthful.

"You eat. Let me tell you my side of things," he told her.

She was too hungry to argue. Rhona listened raptly to his tale. When her stomach was full, she set aside the chopsticks and leaned back.

"It's a lot to take in." Balladyn watched her carefully.

Rhona shrugged one shoulder and took a sip of tea. "It is, but I'm thinking how it meshes with what happened to me." She paused and set her cup on the table. "I don't remember falling asleep. Suddenly, I was with Sorcha and some other friends. There was music and drinking. We were outside. The day was beautiful, the weather fair. We were laughing."

"A memory?"

"No," she said softly. "It didn't feel like a dream, either. It felt real. Like sitting here with you now. Yet something didn't feel right. Nothing specific, just a feeling inside me. That's when I saw her."

Balladyn held her gaze. "Who?"

"I don't know. She was just standing in the distance. A woman in a white cloak. I heard the drums of the Ancients. I was drawn to her. She said my name, but it was in my head. The voice was familiar but I couldn't place it. It was like I'd heard it before. I thought she was an Ancient." Rhona paused and drank some tea. "Her head turned to the side, and I saw long, black hair. Then she faced me. Every time she spoke, it was in my head."

"What did she say?"

"That she had been waiting for me for a long time. That Corann had chosen me because of her. She said everything, *did* everything to make me believe she was an Ancient. She told me the continuation of the Druids rested with me, and that she would show me how. But I had to stay with her."

Balladyn didn't move, but Rhona sensed the tension in him. "Did she give you her name?"

"I asked," Rhona said. "She told me she was beyond names."

Balladyn snorted.

"She kept telling me I was special. That I would take the Druids in a new direction."

"Did she say what direction?"

Rhona shook her head. "Then I felt something, as if it were pulling me away from her."

"That was the Druids."

"I felt them, but it didn't make me want to leave. It wasn't until you were there. I recognized you, somehow. Even though I couldn't see you, I knew it was you. I knew that if I went to you, I'd be safe."

Something dark and primal flashed in his eyes. Rhona's body heated instantly.

Balladyn's voice was thick with emotion when he asked, "What happened next?"

"She grabbed my arm. Threatened me. But that's when I felt your magic. I took it and let it combine with mine."

"I was hoping that's what you'd do," he murmured.

Rhona swallowed, the sound loud to her ears. "She wasn't prepared for that. She was shocked when my battle magic sent her flying backwards. I thought that was the end of it, but then she struck me. I could feel myself fading, and I knew I only had one more chance to sever whatever hold she had on me."

"You did just that."

"Not without your help."

Balladyn looked down at the table for a moment.

Rhona asked, "Do you know who she was?"

He didn't answer right away as he tapped his finger on the table. Then he looked at her. "Would you remember her face if you saw it again?"

"Without a doubt."

Balladyn then produced a 3D image of a woman's face about six inches tall in the palm of his hand.

Rhona's stomach clenched in dread. "That's the woman I thought was an Ancient. Who is she?"

"Her name is Lena," he murmured and lowered his hand, the image vanishing.

At least Rhona had a name to go with the face now. "Is she Light or Dark Fae?"

"She was Light, but we recently battled her and watched as she took the magic of her husband, son, brother, and nieces. She's Dark now."

Rhona's hand went to her stomach as she fought to keep her food down. "Lena said my magic couldn't compete with hers. It wouldn't have, either, but then I had yours."

"Mine isn't just any Fae magic. It's Reaper magic."

She wrapped her arms around her middle as she considered everything she had learned. "What now?"

"Now we call everyone here. The MacLeod Druids are eager to speak with you."

"They told me you went to them."

Balladyn shrugged as if it were nothing. "It seemed the logical thing to do."

"Whatever you and Eoghan said convinced them to come."

"I'm not sure it was us. They said something about the wind and trees telling the Druids we were coming."

Rhona drew in a deep breath and released it. "Call everyone. We need to make plans for what's going to happen next."

Balladyn got to his feet and held out his hand. When she took it, he pulled her against him and held her tightly. "You aren't in this alone. No matter what, don't forget that."

"I won't." She leaned back to look at him, remembering how it'd felt to have him inside her, sliding in and out of her body.

He pressed his mouth to hers, moving his lips softly. She opened for him, and his tongue swept in. He kissed her as if there were no tomorrow, as if it were the last time he would see her. And she answered in kind.

Balladyn was the one who ended the kiss. They were both breathing hard as she rested her forehead against his chest. They stood in silence for several moments before Rhona released him and stepped back.

She caught his eye and said, "One night with you isn't enough. There will be more."

"Is that a promise?" he asked with a crooked smile.

"Definitely."

He winked at her before saying, "Eoghan."

Seconds later, her home was cramped with Warriors, Druids, and Reapers, along with Sorcha. Rhona had to grab hold of a wall to keep upright when Sorcha rushed to her and enveloped her in a hug.

"I'm okay," Rhona whispered to her cousin.

Sorcha pulled away and stated, "Of course, you are."

Then Rhona found everyone staring at her. She forced her hands to her sides in a bid to look relaxed. "By now, all of you know what transpired with me and Balladyn during this second attack. Thank you for allowing me to rest, but now it's time to figure out who is doing this and why. It's the Fae Others."

"We've thought of that," Eoghan said. "The Six know about Sorcha and Cathal, which means they know we had a reason to be protective of you. Harming you was a way to get to us."

"Then why didn't they? Why didn't they attack in Belfast?" Sorcha asked.

Cathal's lips twisted. "It's something I've been thinking about since it happened. It was the perfect time. We were concentrated on Rhona."

"We were also on the lookout," Torin added.

Balladyn then spoke. "There's something no one has thought of."

"What's that?" Lucan asked.

Balladyn met Rhona's gaze for a heartbeat. "The Fae are self-absorbed. They don't care about any other being unless they directly impact a Fae's life. The Fae came to this realm because of the humans. The Light use mortals as entertainment, as a distraction from everyday life. But the Dark..." He trailed off.

"To a Dark, humans are a meal," Cathal replied.

Fallon's brows drew together. "We know this."

"What are you getting at?" Rordan asked.

Balladyn swallowed. "Mortals mean nothing to the Fae. They consider humans beneath them. Even powerful Druids don't give Fae much pause."

"And especially not Fae like the Six," Bradach said as his face tightened.

Eoghan's face paled. "Bloody hell."

"Someone tell me what's going on," Rhona demanded.

Balladyn turned to her. "I think the Six targeted you to have the Druids kill you. The Fae Others could be influencing certain Druids with the promise of them being able to take your place if you're removed."

"It'll never happen," Ruarc continued. "All it will do is make sure no Druids can stand against the Fae Others."

Rhona's head was spinning with this latest news. "That doesn't make sense. You said yourself that few Druids have enough power to give the Fae pause."

Before anyone could reply, a knock sounded on the door. Rhona looked through the crowd of people as Bradach opened it to reveal a beautiful Dark Fae with long, black and silver braids.

"It's about damn time, Aisling," Bradach said as he pulled the Dark against him for a hug.

CHAPTER TWENTY-SIX

Aisling blinked back the sudden tears that sprang forth when the Reapers each embraced her. Balladyn was the last. They shared a look before he walked to her and gave her a hug.

"Thank you," she whispered.

He grinned as he stepped back. "I didn't do anything."

"We both know that's a lie."

Aisling then looked around at the Warriors and Druids. She had gotten a glimpse of one of the Druids—Isla—many, many years ago. The fact that they were all on Skye didn't bode well. Aisling's gaze moved to Rhona. The Druid leader bowed her head in greeting. Aisling returned it.

"We have a lot to catch you up on," Sorcha said.

Eoghan caught her attention. "Did you succeed? Is Xaneth with you?"

She hadn't wanted to get into this, but there was no help for it. Xaneth was the reason her family knew she had abandoned them. They deserved a straight answer. She just didn't want to do it in front of the Warriors and Druids. "No."

Thankfully, no one asked her to elaborate.

Yet.

They would. She wasn't ready to talk about it any more than she had been with Erith and Cael, but there was no getting around it. Every Reaper deserved a proper response.

"So," Aisling said to take the attention off her, "I hear we have a Fae Other problem."

Lena paced her lavish bedroom in the house the Six had commandeered as theirs. Fury consumed her. She had planned everything perfectly, but her niece, Chevonne, had somehow escaped. Lena touched the missing part of her ear. When she got a hold of Chevonne, she would make her suffer terribly before taking her magic.

The only thing that calmed Lena was remembering the horror on her niece's face when she'd watched her father, mother, sisters, uncle, and cousin die in an instant. Now, all their magic coursed through Lena. She had thought the ancient magic she'd found would work, but once she knew it did, she hadn't hesitated to use it on those she knew could help her get where she needed—the top.

Lena would miss her husband and even her son, who had been a disappointment. But she wouldn't miss her brother and his side of the family. She remembered her roots and what the Muldowney family was truly about. Hugo had forgotten that. Everyone in their family had. They wanted to forget the greatness of who they had been, and they believed that changing their name would give them that.

But she had learned the truth. She was the one loyal to their ancestors. She was the one who would bring the Muldowneys back to the glory they had once had.

Lena stopped pacing and stared out the window to the night beyond. She'd contemplated telling the rest of the Six who she really was. Barry and the other Dark wouldn't care. They would likely rejoice in her admission. Then again, if everything she'd read about how her family had once been hated by the Dark and Light alike was true, maybe not. It was why she hadn't said anything yet.

It said something about her power that, even now, none of them guessed she was Dark. The dynamic of the Six should've shifted. *She* would've noticed because she would've been looking for anyone trying to succeed their place. It showed how oblivious her partners in the Six really were. If they were that ignorant, then they deserved to die. The time was drawing close for that. She could hardly wait until the magic of each of them was coursing through her body.

The smile on her face slipped when she thought of Rhona. The Druid was another thorn in her side. Everything with the Druids should've been simple and easy. Lena had known that bringing the Reapers into the mix would cause a few hiccups but not the kind she'd faced. Still, knowing where the Reapers were was an advantage that was too good to pass up.

Lena turned at the sound of a knock. She put her hands behind her back and formed orbs of magic in each. Just in case.

"Enter," she called.

The door opened to reveal Oona. The newest of the Six smiled in greeting. "May I have a word?"

"Of course," Lena said and softened her features. It was imperative that the Light believe she was still one of them.

Oona stepped into the room and closed the door behind her. She remained by it as she clasped her hands in front of her. Oona had an ethereal look about her. It wasn't just the soft clothes she wore or her manner. It was in her very bearing—the way she walked and even how she spoke.

"What's on your mind?" Lena asked when Oona didn't speak.

Oona glanced at the floor. "I've been thinking about your plan with the Reapers."

"I suppose you're angry that I didn't share it."

Oona lifted one shoulder in an elegant shrug. "We've already discussed that. What we know is that the Reapers are clever."

"We're shrewder," Lena snapped.

Oona paused as she stared. Then, she continued. "You knew the Reapers would go straight to Skye to help the Druids, and they have."

"We have them right where we want them."

"Do we?"

Lena held back her temper. With control, she said, "Yes."

"I'm not so sure. You nearly captured the Druid and permanently locked her in her mind."

Something Lena had gotten from studying Usaeil. The former Light Queen might have been a royal bitch, but she had been gutsy.

"But you didn't."

The anger within Lena snapped. It took great effort to rein it back in and not eradicate the Light in an instant. "No. I didn't."

Oona tilted her head to the side. "I've made you angry by stating a fact."

The Fae was toeing the line. Lena didn't know how much more she could take. "I don't need it thrown in my face."

"That isn't what I'm doing. I'm pointing out a fact to tell you that there's a chance the Reapers know it was you because your plan failed."

At least Oona realized who the real Fae in control was. Lena shrugged. "Your point?"

"They'll be expecting the soldiers."

Damn, if she wasn't right. Lena hated when others saw something that should've been right in front of her face. She had been too caught up in the feeling of the magic Rhona had used. It'd felt distinctly like Fae magic.

Which was impossible. Rhona would've had to be awake and with a Fae to mix their magic. But what Lena had felt wasn't what she and the other Six used to twine their powers. It had felt like Druid and Fae magic, fused together and not merely combined, bound on a cellular level that didn't seem feasible.

If a Reaper had managed to meld their magic with Rhona's while Lena had control of the Druid, then that changed everything. It meant there was something special about Rhona, something Lena hadn't realized before.

"So, they will," Lena said with a smile. "Perhaps it's time we joined the soldiers in their attack. The Reapers won't be expecting that."

Again and again, Xaneth found himself facing east. Something drew him toward Scotland. He straightened from killing another Fae Other, ridding the world of one more evil person. Xaneth looked toward the east. Why did he feel as if he needed to get there immediately? Was it the Six? Lena?

He hated that he hadn't taken Lena out when he'd had the chance. The leader of the Six had used magic that'd knocked him out. It was the last time that would happen. Xaneth had to take out the Six, had to remove every Fae Other. It wasn't an option. Something drove him, a force he didn't know how to control.

Xaneth hoped that when he killed the Fae Others he would find the peace he longed for. The kind of serenity that only happened in death.

His mind drifted to Aisling. In another life, they might have been happy together. What he had to do would take him to places that would shred him. And her, too. Being a Reaper wouldn't save her.

Xaneth was eager for what was to come. Not only would he fulfill the emptiness within, but he would also end the monster he was becoming. Aisling looked at him as if he were normal, but he knew differently. Xaneth felt the changes within himself. There was no going back, no escaping from what Usaeil had done to him. She had wanted his death.

Instead, Xaneth had become something every being on the realm should fear—especially the Fae Others.

Lena's added power had taken him by surprise. It shouldn't have. He had seen her consume her family, their magic entering her. It was a mistake Xaneth wouldn't make again. He couldn't. The Reapers were fighting the Fae Others, but they didn't fully realize the consequences of what would happen if Lena and her group gained control.

The Six thought that with the Reapers gone, nothing would stand in their way of complete domination. They hadn't counted on him. Unfortunately, he had used up the element of surprise with Lena. She would be waiting for him the next time.

Once more, his thoughts skated to Aisling. Maybe he should team up with the Reapers. It had nearly worked in their battle with Lena.

Xaneth frowned as he teleported to a rooftop and looked out over the sea toward Scotland. If he went to the Reapers now, they would see exactly who he had become. They would accept his offer to help, but the minute they realized the monster he was, they would kill him.

And they might do it before he could end the Fae Others.

It was a chance Xaneth couldn't take.

He turned his back to the sea and whatever Scotland might hold.

CHAPTER TWENTY-SEVEN

Balladyn was glad that Aisling had rejoined them, but given the way she refused to meet anyone's gaze, things hadn't gone well. Now wasn't the time to discuss it, however. That would come later. They took the time to fill her in on their latest discussion.

"How did you push your magic into Rhona?" Aisling asked him.

Balladyn shrugged. "I don't know."

"Nor do you know how you knew she was injured in Belfast," Sonya said.

Balladyn turned to the red-haired Druid and shook his head. He had been over this dozens of times. "I don't."

"Let's not forget that he knew something was wrong while Rhona slept," Cathal added.

Rordan's lips twisted. "There has to be something we're missing."

"I've never known a Fae, much less a Reaper, to have that strong of a connection with a Druid," Fallon said.

Dubhan snorted. "Us, either."

"It happened. We need to get past that part and look at *why*," Ruarc said.

Quinn MacLeod's brows drew together. "I think the *how* is as important."

Balladyn watched Rhona closely as the debate continued. Her expression remained impassive except for the slight puckering of her brow. Her green eyes suddenly clashed with his. Her lips softened as her forehead smoothed.

"There can only be one explanation," Rhona said over everyone.

The room grew quiet. Finally, Balladyn asked, "What is it?"

"The Ancients."

The Druids exchanged looks. It was Isla who said, "That's possible. The Ancients speak to whoever they want, but we've not heard them since the night you were attacked in Belfast."

"Could the attempt on her life have caused them to go quiet?" Eoghan asked.

It was Gwynn who shook her head. "We can't know for sure. The Ancients aren't exactly forthcoming with clear, concise answers. Most of the time, if they speak to one of us at all, we have to sort out their meaning."

"I heard the drums as I lay dying in Belfast," Rhona said. Her gaze returned to Balladyn. "I heard them when I was with the woman. They were faint, but they were there."

"Could this woman have sounded them to make you think they were real?" Balladyn pressed.

Rhona shrugged. "It's possible."

"Are the drums always part of the Ancients' visits?" Dubhan asked.

Sorcha nodded. "Always. Sometimes a Druid will only hear the drums."

"That doesn't make any sense. Why just the drums?" Torin asked.

Isla blew out a long breath. "Some Druids go their entire lives without hearing the Ancients or the drums. As I said, the Ancients decide who they speak to."

"They chose Balladyn," Rhona stated. "And nearly burst his eardrums in the process."

Eoghan nodded. "With a warning of: *they're coming.*"

"Who's coming?" Aisling asked.

Rhona threw up her hands. "It's anyone's guess."

"Could Lena have blocked the Ancients from getting through to the Druids?" Balladyn suddenly asked.

The Druids frowned collectively as if no one had thought of that.

"None of you realize how powerful Lena is," he continued. "The Six are killing hundreds of Fae at a time and consuming their magic. Lena took it a step further and slaughtered her family to take their power."

Lucan jerked his chin to Balladyn. "What's so important about her family?"

"She's descended from a powerful Fae family who committed heinous acts. Eons ago, the family changed their surname and tried to move on. Lena discovered the truth and has been walking the same path as her ancestors," Ruarc said. "Also, the Muldowney family had incredible power."

Fallon ran a hand down his face. "Bloody hell. So, what you're saying is that she might have the power to block the Ancients?"

"We should assume so," Eoghan said. "Whether she did it on purpose or not, I can't say."

Balladyn saw Rhona approach out of the corner of his eye. He turned to her as the rest of the room continued deliberations. "What is it?"

"I want to know how we seem to be connected, but I agree with Ruarc. Right now, the *why* is more important. I can't imagine something like this being done without a reason."

"I agree," he said as he glanced at the Druids who were still debating whether Lena could've hindered the Ancients. "What do you want to do?"

Rhona licked her lips and moved closer, lowering her voice even more. "I think we can all agree that Lena used me to get the Reapers in a place of her choosing."

"As an ambush. She'll have guessed that we deduced that by now."

Rhona smiled. "That's right. She'll have guessed that you Reapers will be waiting for her. She won't be expecting Skye Druids, as well."

"No."

Rhona quirked a brow, her anger sizzling beneath the surface. "Excuse me?"

"Battling her won't be like Moreann or the other Druids you've faced. Lena is powerful in her own right, but then she became one of the Six, and her magic grew with every Fae they killed. That isn't even counting what she took from her family. No Druid stands a chance."

When he finished, Balladyn realized that the entire room watched him and Rhona.

She lifted her chin. "Need I remind you that I was used?"

"And nearly died. Twice. The Skye Druids need you."

"They survived after Corann died, and they'll continue after my death."

Balladyn jerked back. "Are you so casual about your mortality that you freely offer yourself up to die?"

"I'm doing what any good leader would do," she retorted angrily. "I'm taking a bloody stand. I don't need your permission."

Balladyn stared at her, trying to find words that would make her understand that this fight wasn't one that she—or any Druid—could win. How could he begin to explain what the thought of her death did to him?

Quinn cleared his throat and said, "I'm going to step on some toes here, but I have to say that both of you have a point. Each of us Warriors was used by Deirdre. We got our revenge in the end, so we understand where you're coming from, Rhona. If the Six are targeting you, perhaps it's best no' to be there."

"But," Lucan added, "Lena and her group will think they're only facing Reapers. They'll never expect us. I like those odds."

Eoghan nodded once. "I like them, too."

"It's been a while since we've been in battle, but it isna something you forget," Fallon said.

Rhona threw up her hands. "And the Druids are supposed to do what? Sit back and watch?"

"As if," Gwynn replied.

"We still don't know if it was someone on Skye who set you up," Sorcha told Rhona. "Do you really want to invite them to a battle so they can warn the Fae Others?"

Rhona's lips pursed, her face tightening in anger because she had forgotten about that. Balladyn parted his lips to speak, but Rhona brushed past him and out of the house. He met Eoghan's gaze before following her. Balladyn found her down the hill from her cottage. The glen had a small stream running through it with a handful of sheep dotting the hillsides. He was surprised when she hiked up the next incline and simply stood there, staring. He approached, making sure she heard him coming so he didn't startle her.

"I left because I didn't want to talk to anyone," she snapped. "Especially you."

Balladyn halted behind her. "I understand your anger, but you've not fought the Fae Others."

"I fought Lena in my head. Things were done to me, Balladyn. This is my fight. You won't keep me out of it."

"I know."

She sighed loudly.

"I've watched a lot of friends and enemies die during my lifetime. For whatever reason, I've been allowed to help you stay alive. I think it's because you're important to your people."

She turned to face him. "Did you ever think it might have been so we could fight together?"

He hadn't. Why would he? She was a Druid, a human with magic but still mortal.

"I saw her face," Rhona continued. "When I let your magic mix with mine and fought Lena. She was scared. It was our combined magic that broke me loose. Not me. Not you. *Us.*"

Balladyn closed the distance between them and took her hands in his. "I don't know how I pushed my magic into you. I'm not sure I could do it again. I certainly don't want to bet your life on it."

"What propelled you to do it? What did you feel?"

"That you were dying. That I…I would lose you," he admitted.

"I was able to break free when I felt your magic. You gave me that. Your presence. It won't matter if I'm on the battlefield or not. They'll use me again."

Balladyn briefly closed his eyes and sighed. Fek. She was right. If Lena did that, it would split his attention and weaken the Reapers.

"I will be at the battle," she stated.

He brought her closer, giving her his warmth. When he still felt her shiver, he called her coat to her. "We need to find out who set you up in Belfast. This is a good plan we're putting together, and I won't have it ruined."

"Agreed. That was one of the reasons I came out here. I'm trying to figure out who it could've been. How long do we have before the battle?"

Balladyn shrugged. "It'd be now if I had my way."

"We need the power of the Druids. Can you imagine what we could do if we combined the Skye Druids with those of MacLeod Castle?"

"An impressive show to be sure."

She smiled up at him. "Yes, it will be."

He held her when she tried to move away. "I need you to understand that I can't help myself when it comes to you. If you're harmed, I must get to you. Even if it means putting my team in danger."

"Something brought us together. For all I know, it was the Fae Others. Whoever did it, though, I'm thankful for it. What we've shared is extraordinary and rare."

"It is."

"Trust me," she implored.

He nodded once. "I do."

Balladyn didn't hold Rhona back when she pulled away a second time. He watched as she hurried back to the cottage. Once she was inside, he turned to look out over the land. The wind had died, and with the clear sky, the temperatures would plummet.

"I leave for a short while, and you manage to get yourself mixed up in some crazy shite."

He grinned as he looked over his shoulder at Aisling. "It's all your fault."

"I should've stayed," she said as she came to stand beside him.

"You did what you had to do. That's what I did when I went to Belfast."

Aisling grunted. "That is some insane shite. Erith and Cael are stumped. They have Fintan and the others going through Death's library, looking for anything similar in history."

"I don't think there is anything."

"There's something deeper than just the need to save her, isn't there?" Aisling asked after a brief pause.

Balladyn sighed, letting the truth settle around him. "I couldn't stay away from her if I tried."

"I know the feeling."

He turned his head to study her profile. Finally, he asked, "Did you find him again?"

"Xaneth made sure I didn't. Arsehole. If he would just listen to what I have to say…"

"What would you tell him?"

She snorted and met his gaze. "I don't know. I've already tried to tell him once, but he thought I came to kill him. He was… disappointed that wasn't my intention."

"He's hurting—soul deep. Usaeil broke more than just his mind. He may never be the Fae he once was."

"Then why do I have this need to find him? Why do I keep trailing him and trying to get him to talk to me?"

Balladyn shrugged. "Something bigger is driving you."

"Apparently, both of us."

They shared a smile.

After a few moments, Aisling said, "I gave up. I'm here with all of you, and at a good time, I see. Would any of you have called me for the battle?"

"Wasn't my decision."

"Xaneth is a lost cause. I gave a vow to Erith, and I let all of you down while on my quest to help a Fae who wants nothing to do with me or anyone else."

Balladyn wrinkled his nose. "To be fair, Xaneth seems pretty damned capable of handling himself with the soldiers."

"That's what scares me," Aisling whispered.

Balladyn might not have been a Reaper for long, but the one thing he'd learned quickly was that nothing frightened Aisling. Until this. "We have your back. When this is done, we'll all go with you to find Xaneth. We'll corner him if that's what it takes."

"Thanks." Aisling glanced at him, her eyes shining with what looked like tears, but surely it was a trick of the moon. Because the Fae warrior never cried. She jerked her head to the cottage. "Come on. It looks like we have Druids to investigate."

CHAPTER TWENTY-EIGHT

Nothing would be easy. Rhona knew it, but that didn't make what she had to do any simpler. Every Druid on Skye was a suspect until she decided otherwise.

Her talk with Balladyn had helped her form a plan, and she laid it out for everyone. The Reapers were less than pleased with it, especially Balladyn, but the Warriors and Druids seemed to be on board. So was Sorcha.

Yet, now, as Rhona stood outside Lyra's home in the early light of morning, Rhona wasn't sure she wanted to know the outcome of her investigation. She considered every Druid on Skye part of her family. But one or more of them had turned against her. Rhona couldn't help but wonder what she had done to deserve such a betrayal.

Was it Lena who'd turned the Druids' heads?

Or did someone hate Rhona that much?

Neither option was good, but she hoped it was the former. She could understand that. Having stood against Lena, she knew how manipulative and devious the Fae could be.

But…if one or more Druids had tried to kill her simply because they despised her, Rhona wasn't sure she would ever come to terms with that. Was she perfect? Absolutely, not. Far from it, actually. Yet every action she took, every decision she made, was for the Druids on Skye.

Her thoughts wandered to Corann. As far as she knew, everyone had loved and respected the former leader of the Skye Druids. No one would've dared to stand against him as they were doing to her. Not for the first time, Rhona wished that Corann were still alive to fight these battles. She was petrified that she would fail and be the Druids' downfall. No one had prepared her for anything like this. How did she know she was doing the right thing? Corann wasn't there to guide her. No one was.

"Rhona?"

Balladyn's voice, a mere whisper behind her, jerked her from her spiraling thoughts. He was veiled, as were the other Reapers, but only Balladyn would enter the homes with her. It calmed her a little knowing that she wouldn't be alone, but she also hated that she was deceiving her fellow Druids in such a way. But what choice did she have? Someone had tried to kill her.

"I'm all right," she replied in a low voice.

"You don't have to do this."

She closed her eyes for a moment and took a breath. "We both know I do."

"I'll be with you every step of the way."

Tears suddenly burned her eyes. She wished his whispered vow meant that he would be with her always. Sorcha and Cathal made it work, why couldn't she and Balladyn? The answer was simple. She wouldn't leave Skye.

And he couldn't leave the Reapers.

Rhona blinked away her sadness and quickly rapped on the door. She heard Lyra's steps as she approached. A moment later, the entry opened, and Lyra's face appeared.

"Rhona," the young Druid said in her sweet voice, a smile tugging at her lips. "How are you? I've been worried."

"I'm getting through each day. Do you have a minute? I'd like to talk."

Lyra moved aside. "Of course. Please, come in."

As Rhona walked over the threshold, she saw the symbols carved into the wood that kept the Fae out. She knew from experience that they did nothing to stop the Reapers. Rhona felt a brush of air as Balladyn moved around her and into the home.

"Tea?" Lyra asked.

Rhona nodded and walked farther into the cottage. She remained standing as Lyra moved about the kitchen. Lyra's mother had died when she was only three. Her father had passed just over two years ago, and his death had hit Lyra hard. It had just been the two of them, and they had been extremely close.

Rhona found her gaze roaming about the room, pausing at the sketches that hung on the wall. Lyra's father had been gifted with such a talent, and he had used it to support them. The Druid community was close, and anytime anyone was in need, the others quickly stepped in. They had done it when Lyra's mother died, which was why Lyra and her father had usually been the first to help others.

Of anyone, Rhona didn't think Lyra could be behind the betrayal or attack. That didn't mean she hadn't done it, though. When Rhona slid her gaze to Lyra, she found the Druid watching her.

"You're troubled," Lyra stated. "You have reason to be. I gather that's why you're here?"

Rhona nodded. No beating around the bush with Lyra. It was one of the reasons Rhona liked the young Druid so much.

The kettle beeped when the water reached the right temperature. Lyra poured the water into mugs. She carried the cups into the living area and handed one to Rhona.

Lyra's dark eyes met hers. "Please, ask your questions. I want you to be able to take me off your list."

"I don't want to do this."

"Want has nothing to do with it. You must. I understand. Once I have assured you that I had no part in it, I hope you'll let me help you find who did."

Rhona wrapped her hands around the mug, letting the heat infuse her cold fingers. She then sat when Lyra motioned to a chair.

Once both had gotten comfortable, Rhona said, "Thank you for healing me."

"It's what we do for one of our own."

"Someone on Skye wants me dead."

"You think it's a Druid?"

This was much harder than Rhona had thought it would be. "Yes."

"I can't even fathom someone turning against us like that. Especially another Skye Druid."

Rhona glanced away and took a long drink of the delicious tea. "You know what I need to do now."

"I do, and I willingly submit."

After setting aside the mug, Rhona drew in a long breath and then slowly released it. She had hoped to never use this magic on anyone, but especially a Druid from Skye. Yet here she was.

"It's okay," Lyra said with a smile as she scooted to the edge of her seat and held out her hands.

Rhona grasped them in hers. She hoped that Lyra's eagerness meant she hadn't been a part of the ambush. Though, Rhona had learned her lesson. She had already decided what her actions would be when she encountered those responsible.

"I'm sorry," she said.

Lyra shook her head. "Don't be. If Corann were here, he would be doing exactly what you are. I've been expecting this. The other deputies should be, as well."

That didn't make Rhona feel any better. Well, that wasn't true. It made her feel slightly less nauseated at the thought of what she was about to do. She swallowed and wrapped her fingers around Lyra's hands. Rhona closed her eyes and whispered the lie spell. Magic surged through Rhona and enveloped Lyra. The young Druid didn't fight it. She sat easily and calmly as Rhona's magic swirled around both of them.

When she'd finished the incantation, Rhona opened her eyes. She looked deep into Lyra's dark brown ones and asked, "Did you conspire with others against me?"

"No."

Rhona waited to feel the sting of a lie, but nothing happened. "Did you know that someone set a trap for me in Belfast?"

"No."

Again, no irritation. "Do you know who wants me dead?"

"No."

Relief surged through Rhona when no pain greeted her. "Have you spoken to any Fae Others?"

There was a brief pause before Lyra replied, "Yes."

Rhona felt as if she had been kicked in the stomach. She didn't let that show, however. She held Lyra's gaze. "When? What was it about?"

"A few months ago. I received a strange email talking about forming a group of Druid Others. I was curious, so I answered."

"And?" Rhona pressed.

"I can't say for certain it was a Fae, but the way they pushed seemed odd. I suppose it could've been a Druid. They wanted me to meet them. They promised to give me what I needed to convince those in power to form a group."

Rhona swallowed. Why hadn't Lyra come to her with this? More troubling was the question of how many other Skye Druids had received the email. "Did you go to the meeting?"

"No. I never wanted any part of a Druid Others group. I answered that email to get information for you."

"Yet you brought me nothing."

"There was nothing to bring."

"Someone contacted you, Lyra. That's something. If you got the message, others might have, as well."

Lyra's shoulders slumped. "I didn't think about that. I'm sorry. When I let them know I wasn't interested, the emails stopped."

Through it all, there had been no pain of lies from her deputy. Rhona released her grip on Lyra's hands, the spell ending when she did. "In the future, please come to me."

"I will. I told you I didn't have anything to do with your attack."

Rhona returned the Druid's smile. There were times that she forgot just how young Lyra was.

It was the malcontent who looked for something to latch their anger to. If a Druid on Skye had received the same email as Lyra had, then they could've set Rhona up.

"Can I help now?" Lyra asked.

Rhona got to her feet. "Let me speak to the rest of the deputies. Once I've done that, I'll contact you, and we can go from there."

"I'll be waiting."

Rhona showed herself out. As she made her way to her car, the conversation replayed in her head. Once inside her vehicle, she glanced at the passenger seat where she knew Balladyn sat veiled.

"Well?" he asked.

"There were no lies in her answers."

"Could she have used a spell before yours to prevent you from sensing them?"

She started the car and backed out of the spot to get on the road. "The lie spell is complicated. It took me years to perfect it because it's so powerful. Corann crafted it himself. For the longest time, he was the only one on Skye who could wield it."

"And, yet again, I'm hearing why he chose you."

Rhona glanced in Balladyn's direction as she grinned. "There are three of us now who can use the spell. Me, Evan, and Violet. Evan is the most recent one to be able to use it properly."

"Are you sure there isn't a spell that can block it?"

"Not one that I know of. We don't teach the spell to outside Druids."

"At least, none of you is supposed to."

She twisted her lips. "You have to reach a certain level to even know it exists."

"From my experience, when there's a spell such as your truth one, someone has developed another to block it."

"I really hope you're wrong," Rhona said. "Everything is riding on this spell."

CHAPTER TWENTY-NINE

It was a long, grueling day. Balladyn remained by Rhona's side. After each discussion and then the spell on all five deputies, he and Rhona would chat in the car ride to the next home.

"That's all five," she said as she sat in the vehicle.

Balladyn had bet money that Evan had been the one to betray Rhona, but there had been no indication that he'd lied while under the spell.

"You don't like Evan."

Balladyn snorted. He couldn't lower his veil with the cars passing. "He wants a group of Others for the Druids."

"Half the Druids on Skye want that."

"That doesn't make me like him more."

She chuckled and started the car. "Well, my next option is to head to Lyra's, where we'll gather the Druids in her area, and I can go to them one on one."

"That's going to take days. We don't have that kind of time."

"I don't know what to tell you. That's how it has to work."

He watched as she pulled onto the road and started back toward Lyra's. "You could ask Violet and Evan to help."

"You really don't like him," Rhona said with a smile. "You nearly choke on his name."

"There's something about him."

"He's very vocal in his dislikes and disapprovals."

Balladyn glared out his window. "Exactly."

"It doesn't make him the culprit. He sailed through the spell. All five of them did."

He swung his head back to her. "You were hoping it was one of them."

"Yeah," she said with a small shrug. "It would have been easier if it were one or more of them. Now, I have to sort through the rest of the Druids on Skye. And, no, I'm not going to ask Violet or Evan to help. I have to know myself."

"Even with the spell, you still doubt."

She paused before she said, "I do. And I hate that."

"You manage the spell, but I can see it taking its toll on you. And that's just doing it five times. How many Druids are in Lyra's area?"

"A little over eight hundred."

"For fek's sake," Balladyn stated. "It won't take days. It'll take weeks to get through everyone on Skye. And that's if you have help."

"What do you want me to do?" Rhona snapped. "I don't know any other option. Do you? Because, if you do, now is the time to spit it out."

He stared at her. Though he had watched her all day, his attention had been more on those she'd questioned. Because of that, he hadn't realized how she had carefully kept her apprehension and frustration tightly under wraps. She was fast losing control, though.

"I'm sorry," he said.

She shook her head as she turned. "No, I apologize. You're trying to help. I shouldn't have bitten your head off for stating the obvious."

"Return to your cottage. Let's discuss with everyone else."

"By *everyone*, you mean the MacLeod Druids."

"I mean everyone," he replied.

Rhona sighed. "Okay."

It didn't take them long to reach her home. Balladyn was glad to be back inside her cottage so he could lower his veil and have her look him directly in the eye. He liked that she knew his location, but it meant more when they could look at each other.

Rhona filled the others in on what she had discovered. Her small cottage was bursting at the seams with all the bodies inside. Eoghan sent half the Reapers to stand guard outside. Fallon did the same with the Warriors. It allowed for a little breathing room, but Balladyn wished they were in a larger space to accommodate everyone.

"The Fairy Pools," he said.

Rhona looked at him, a silent question on her face.

"We need a bigger space. One we can all move freely in."

"The caves," she said as it dawned on her. "That's a good idea."

It wasn't long after that everyone had been teleported to the caves at the pools. Reapers used magic to call furniture to the space so everyone could get comfortable. Hayden, the red Warrior, used his power over fire to create a large blaze that both warmed the area and gave it light.

"Now all of you know the issue and the next steps," Rhona said.

Ruarc shook his head. "I agree with Balladyn. We don't have the time."

"Yet can Rhona trust anyone else to get the truth?" Quinn asked.

Galen's mate, Reaghan, lifted her hand. The Druid stood calmly as she said, "In case anyone has forgotten, my magic is being able to tell if anyone is lying. Galen can read minds. We won't need to get anyone alone. If we're near, we can help determine if anyone in a group is someone we should look closer at. Rhona, then you can take them aside and use your spell."

"You would do that? Both of you?" Rhona asked, looking between the Druid and Warrior.

Galen bowed his head of dark blond hair. "It's why we're here. Let us help."

To Balladyn's surprise, Rhona looked at him. He nodded, letting her know that he liked what Galen and Reaghan had proposed.

Rhona licked her lips and said, "Then let's do this."

"Wait," Lucan said. "What about the rest of us? We can be of use."

Larena grinned. "The Reapers aren't the only ones who can be invisible. Put me where you need me."

"Gladly," Eoghan said.

Isla glanced at the other Druids. "Is anyone else worried about what the Druids will think when they see two newcomers?"

"As long as a Reaper is touching someone, they're shielded," Rordan said. "One of us will be with Reaghan, and the other Galen. We'll keep them hidden from the crowd."

Balladyn was pleased with how everything had come together. By the smile on Rhona's face, she was, as well.

"Let's get moving. I want this over with," Rhona said as she got to her feet.

The rest of the Warriors and Druids remained behind while everyone else teleported to Rhona's cottage. Balladyn veiled himself once more and followed her to her vehicle. On the way to Lyra's, Rhona called and had her gather the Druids in her area at the local school. It was the only place indoors that could hold everyone.

"This is a good plan," she said.

Balladyn watched as sleet began pinging against the windshield. "It is."

"We're going to find those responsible tonight. I know it."

He didn't have time to answer as she pulled into the school parking lot and shut off the vehicle.

Rhona paused with her hand on the door handle. Her head turned to him. "I'm glad you're here."

"Me, too."

"I'm going to be sad when you leave."

He really didn't want to have this conversation while he was veiled. Then again, maybe it was better this way. He didn't have to worry about hiding his emotions. "I don't want to think about that."

"I know, but I needed to say the words. I need you to know that…that…"

He wanted to touch her. "I know," he murmured.

She blinked hastily and looked away. "Do you?"

"Aye." More than she knew.

Rhona cleared her throat and kept her head averted. "None of this would be possible without you."

"You don't give yourself enough credit." He saw her smile in the reflection of the window as a single tear rolled down her face.

She flipped back her hair and sniffed. "Our community has been a strong one. Whoever is stirring shite needs to leave. Tonight."

"We've got four other groups to interrogate. Pace yourself."

"There isn't time for that."

"I didn't save your pretty arse twice to see you die because you were stubborn."

Her head turned to him, and she grinned. "You should know stubborn is part of a redhead's DNA."

Then she winked and got out of the car.

Balladyn teleported beside her. "Minx."

"Oh, I'm just getting started," she mumbled under her breath.

He found himself smiling. He didn't think too long on that, or on the fact that his time with Rhona was coming to an end. Whether they defeated the Six or he failed in protecting Rhona, he wouldn't be staying on Skye.

A pain in his chest had him rubbing it. It had been bothering him off and on since he had been sure that Dark magic had struck him at the standing stones. Hours would pass without anything, and then a deep, ache would stab through him. Then it would vanish again as if it had never been.

Balladyn hadn't heard of a ghost wound. Whatever it was didn't cause him to become weak or affect him in any way other than the twinge. He didn't want to worry anyone, so he kept it to himself. Eoghan had examined him after the standing stones, and there hadn't been a wound. Maybe it was all in Balladyn's mind.

To his surprise, Druids filed into the school. He leaned close to

Rhona and whispered, "How do you know that someone isn't refusing to come?"

"Lyra has been counting them as they come in," she answered with a nod in the Druid's direction.

Balladyn settled behind Rhona. Eoghan was with Galen, while Torin stood with Reaghan. Rordan, Ruarc, Dubhan, Aisling, and Bradach waited out of the way for everyone to take their seats. Balladyn had no idea where Larena was, but he knew the Warrior was in the room with them.

"Thank you all for coming," Lyra said as she walked to stand next to Rhona. "We don't call these types of meetings unless it's for something important. With that, I'll turn the floor over to Rhona."

Rhona stepped forward and looked from one side of the room to the other. She took a breath and began. Balladyn watched the crowd as he listened to Rhona begin asking her questions. Galen and Eoghan and Torin and Reaghan walked down the rows of chairs, searching for lies.

Rhona asked each question four different ways, giving Galen and Reaghan time to circle the room and determine that no one appeared guilty.

After thanking everyone, Rhona let them leave. Lyra remained behind as Evan arrived, and soon after, his group. They repeated the process with his and three other groups. Each time, no one came up as guilty.

"Did everyone come?" Rhona asked the five deputies.

Lyra nodded. "All of mine."

"Two of mine didn't," Roy said.

Violet looked at her file. "I have a family that didn't, but they've been on holiday for the past week."

"One from mine was absent," Evan answered.

Kerry shook her head. "All of mine were present."

"I need the names of the individuals who weren't here," Rhona said.

Violet frowned. "You think it could be one of them?"

"I don't see how asking a room full of people those questions gave you the answers you needed," Evan said.

Lyra shot him a hard look. "I doubt Rhona shares all her magic with us. I know Corann didn't. Why should Rhona be any different."

Rhona waved her hand to get everyone's attention. "The names, please."

CHAPTER THIRTY

Unease rippled through Balladyn. He rubbed his chest as he watched the concern wash over Rhona's features. Everyone had believed they would find the culprits in one of the Druid groups.

Balladyn suddenly got dizzy. He tried to focus on Rhona, to keep his attention on her, but the edges of his vision began to blur. Balladyn shook his head to clear it. It was the wrong thing to do as he stumbled backward. Someone grabbed him, steadying him.

"What's wrong?" Aisling whispered.

He shook his head as the pain in his chest intensified. He heard Rhona speaking, but he couldn't make out her words. Balladyn blinked several times, willing his eyesight to clear so he could at least see her. But not even that worked.

His ears started to ring loudly. Aisling's fingers gripped him tighter. Was she talking? He couldn't be sure. What he did know was that something was wrong.

Really wrong.

Balladyn swung out his arms, fearing an enemy was approaching. He had to get to Rhona. Orbs of magic formed in his hands. He would be prepared if anyone tried to attack him. It didn't matter that he couldn't see or talk. In a last-ditch effort, he opened his mouth to shout Rhona's name.

Suddenly, multiple hands held him.

Balladyn thrashed and fought like a wild man. Were the soldiers attacking? Had they come? Where was Rhona? Was one of the Reapers watching her? Were they being attacked, too?

Why couldn't he see?

Why couldn't he hear?

He managed to get one arm free and formed another ball of magic. Before he could throw it, the pain in his chest intensified. It took his breath, locking his muscles in agony.

"What the fek?" Dubhan demanded as he looked down at Balladyn.

Eoghan stopped holding Balladyn and began shaking him. "Balladyn! Come on. Talk to me."

"What just happened?" Aisling asked, her eyes wide with fear and worry.

Bradach got to his feet and shook his head. "He's not fighting us anymore, but I'm not sure that's a good sign. He looks to be in pain."

"We can't just stand around and look at him," Dubhan stated.

The Druids watched from the sidelines.

Malcolm, one of the Warriors, stepped forward. "Can we help?"

"We don't know what happened," Dubhan replied.

Eoghan was used to the Reapers being invincible, nearly indestructible. Watching something overtake Balladyn at the school had left him cold to his bones. The way Balladyn had fought them, Eoghan knew that something had a hold of him. This was far beyond his capabilities. "Erith," he called.

In the next instant, the goddess and Cael were in the caves at the Fairy Pools with them. Erith's gaze moved from Eoghan, who still knelt beside Balladyn's prone form. "What happened?"

"He went crazy," Aisling said.

Eoghan noted her pale face. "You got to Balladyn first. Did he speak?"

Aisling swallowed and tore her gaze from Balladyn to look at Eoghan and then Erith. "I saw him rubbing his chest. Then he stumbled backwards. I steadied him and asked what was wrong."

"Did he reply?" Cael asked.

Aisling glanced around the caves, seeming only just then to realize the Warriors and Druids were there. "He shook his head. I thought he was trying to tell me something. He started blinking, squinting his eyes. Then he jerked. Next thing I knew, he had knocked me back."

"That's when I saw him take a battle stance with the orbs," Dubhan added.

Eoghan looked down at Balladyn, who appeared frozen in pain. "We immediately brought him here."

"He fought us," Bradach said. "Like we were the enemy."

Erith knelt beside Balladyn and touched him. "His entire body is tense. Where were you?"

"At the school, helping Rhona find which of the Skye Druids had betrayed her," Eoghan answered.

"Was it a Druid spell?" Cael asked.

Isla spoke up then. "Targeting only Balladyn? How would any of them have known that he or any of the Reapers were there? They were veiled."

"She's not wrong." Aisling shook her head. "I don't think it was the Druids."

Eoghan caught Erith's gaze. "I don't either. This might have something to do with Balladyn entering the stones the other night."

"You mean the wound he said he got but you couldn't find?" Cael asked.

Eoghan ran a hand over his jaw. "Aye."

"Lena has gotten strong enough to enter someone's mind in their sleep. It's feasible that she could have hit Balladyn with magic." Erith grabbed Balladyn's shirt at the collar and ripped it in half. She examined his chest with her fingers. "Where exactly did he say he got hit?"

Eoghan squatted down and pointed to the middle of Balladyn's chest. "There."

"There's nothing," Erith said. Her lips were tight as she gained her feet. Her head swung to Aisling. "Do you think he heard you when you spoke?"

Aisling shrugged. "I can't be sure."

"I might be able to help."

Eoghan's gaze landed on Phelan. The Warrior whose god favored gold skin had his long, dark hair pulled back in a queue at the base of his neck, and his blue-gray eyes were locked on Erith.

Phelan shrugged. "I am half-Fae, and my blood heals anything."

Balladyn tried to move. Even when he had been locked in Taraeth's dungeon with the Chains of Mordare, he had at least been able to see and hear. Move. This was unbearable.

Worse, he kept thinking about Rhona. His mind created scenario after scenario of her in danger or hurt. He had promised to remain by her side. He had vowed to keep her safe.

Balladyn tried to yell, but it stuck in his throat. The pain had moved outward. It now covered his entire chest and ran up his neck and down both arms. Whatever it was prevented him from using his eyes, ears, or mouth. A spell, maybe?

Then he remembered the magic strike at the standing stones.

There hadn't been a wound. While Reapers healed quickly, there should have been something that proved he had been pummeled with Dark magic. There hadn't even been a hole in his shirt. He had almost convinced himself that he had imagined it.

Now, he knew differently.

Something had hit him. Had it been meant for him or for Rhona? No one was supposed to have been in the standing stones with her, so there was an argument that she had been the target. On the other hand, Lena might have sensed Reaper magic with Rhona's and lashed out, hoping to land a blow. Which she had.

Where were his brethren? Aisling had been at his side. Why

weren't they helping? But he knew. They weren't with him because they were either in the middle of battle with the soldiers or…they were dead. He didn't even want to contemplate the latter.

He had to regain control of his body. He had an obligation to the Reapers—and Rhona. Balladyn might not be able to explain why he was compelled to protect the Druid leader, but it was there, deeply rooted within him. Almost as if it had been there for an eternity, waiting for the right time to manifest itself.

Rhona. The beautiful Druid with the fiery hair and beguiling eyes. He had irrationally denied the hold she had over him. He would do anything for her. Anything. He might not want to admit how deeply his feelings for her ran, but there was no denying it.

"Balladyn."

His thoughts came to a halt at the feminine voice that reached him. He recognized it. As he searched his mind, trying to put a face to the voice, that uneasy feeling filled him again. He couldn't hear anything else, but he heard the woman.

"It's rude not to answer."

It was the tone that brought Lena's face into his mind's eye. "What do you want?"

"You've had an impressive life. You should be part of the Six. I'd be happy to remove one of the Dark for you to take their place."

"Fek off."

She laughed. "Have you really become so self-righteous since joining the Reapers?"

"Just tell me what you want."

"You."

"Too bad."

Once more, she laughed, the sound grating on his nerves. "Don't be so hasty in your reply until you hear what I have to say."

"Then spit it out."

There was a slight pause. When she spoke again, her voice had an edge to it, letting him know that she was angry. "If you want to be freed from your current predicament, you should be nicer to me."

So, *she* had struck him down. Bloody hell.

"The Reapers will be wiped out, but you don't have to die with them."

"You forget. I know your end goal. You're going to take over by yourself. You'll consume the magic of the other Six. Why would anyone partner with you after such a display? You killed your family, after all."

She clicked her tongue. "I didn't take you for a quitter. You slew Taraeth and became King of the Dark. You should've been the one to kill Usaeil. We both know you could've taken both the Light and Dark thrones if you had really wanted them."

"What's your point?"

"I need someone like you to lead my army. Everyone knows how much you despise the Dragon Kings. I'm giving you the opportunity to be my general when we go after the Kings."

She was daft. Absolutely insane. No one could defeat the Dragon Kings. And he *had* hated them, but he had released that emotion as well as whatever he'd held onto regarding his feelings for Rhi.

"Think on it," Lena said. "But I'll want an answer soon."

The instant her voice faded, the tension in his body eased. Balladyn took a deep breath and blinked open his eyes to find himself staring at the top of the cave. Sound rushed through his ears. Then he saw Phelan standing over him with his wrist held out as if he were about to cut it.

"Welcome back." Phelan moved out of the way.

"Don't do that again."

He turned his head to the side and looked at Aisling, who stood glaring at him. "What happened?"

"We were hoping you could tell us."

At the sound of Erith's voice, he sat up. One by one, he stretched and loosened his muscles as he looked around the cave. "Where's Rhona?"

"At the school. She's safe," Eoghan said as he held out his hand.

Balladyn took it and was pulled to his feet. He dusted himself off, trying not to notice that everyone was looking at him as if he had returned from the dead. He cleared his throat. "I was hit with magic the other night. And it was Lena who did it. She took control of me just now."

"I'm getting really tired of this bitch," Bradach said.

Dubhan popped his knuckles. "Get in line, brother."

"Did she speak to you?" Erith asked.

Balladyn nodded and filled everyone in.

"We had her," Aisling said through clenched teeth. "We had her, and she slipped through our fingers."

Cael grunted as he crossed his arms over his chest. "She won't do it a second time."

"We were hoping to fight the Six on Skye with the help of the Druids as well as everyone from MacLeod Castle," Eoghan said.

Erith blew out a breath. "I think that's exactly what Lena wants."

"I need to get to Rhona," Balladyn said.

Eoghan swung his head to him. "She's safe. We need to talk about this."

"We need everyone," Aisling said. Then she looked pointedly at Erith. "Including Xaneth."

Balladyn suddenly grinned. "That's easily solved. Xaneth always shows up when we're fighting the soldiers. If they come here, so will he."

"First, we need to deduce if a Skye Druid betrayed Rhona," Bradach said.

Eoghan raised his brows. "Let's get that sorted then because we have planning to do."

"I'm going to get Rhona," Balladyn said and teleported out before anyone could stop him.

CHAPTER THIRTY-ONE

Rhona paced her cottage, trying her best not to lose the last bit of her cool as she waited for someone, anyone, to tell her where Balladyn was. She didn't know when he had left. During her questioning of those who hadn't come to the meeting and the lie spell, she'd found herself searching for him—and discovered he wasn't there.

"Rhona," Sorcha started.

She whirled on her cousin. "So help me God, if you tell me to calm down, I'm going to lose it."

"If something had happened, I would know," Cathal told her.

Rhona could feel the eyes of Galen, Reaghan, Larena, and the other Reapers on her, but she didn't care. She glared at Cathal. "Find. Him."

"He isn't the only one missing," Torin said.

A you've-got-to-be-kidding-me look passed over Cathal's face as he slowly closed his eyes. Rhona spun around to Torin. "Who else?"

She had assumed that the others were veiled and outside her cottage as they usually were. Since the only one she could sense was Balladyn, it'd never even entered her mind that more Reapers might have left.

"Way to add more stress," Rordan mumbled as he rolled his eyes.

Torin shot him a dark look. "Wouldn't you want to know?"

"Everyone wants to know," Larena stated. "It might help if you quit being so cryptic and tell Rhona what she needs to know so she can relax."

Rhona smiled gratefully at the Warrior. "Exactly."

"That's the problem," Ruarc spoke. "We don't know."

Sorcha crossed her arms and looked at her mate. "But you do know something."

Cathal sighed loudly and glanced at the ceiling. "Eoghan, Aisling, Bradach, and Dubhan took Balladyn."

"Took?" Rhona couldn't have heard that right. "Took him where?"

Ruarc shrugged. "We don't know. We've not seen them since."

"They'll come when they can," Torin said.

Rhona hadn't realized how much she counted on Balladyn until that moment. How had she gone through years—decades—just fine, and then not be able to function without the sexy Reaper after just a few days? She knew part of it was because he had saved her— twice!—but it didn't explain the fear that wrapped its cold hand around her heart.

Suddenly, she jerked, then instantly relaxed when she felt Balladyn's presence. She turned as he emerged from her bedroom.

"You knew he was here," Rordan stated with a frown.

Torin shook his head. "That isn't possible."

Rhona ignored them as she walked to Balladyn and searched his face. He looked unhurt, but there was something in his eyes as he glanced away. "Are you all right?"

"It's fine now."

"Now?" she asked, her brows raised. "When wasn't it fine?"

Someone cleared their throat behind her. Rhona looked over her shoulder to find Eoghan.

The Reaper leader nodded at her. "It would be better if we continued this conversation in the caves."

Rhona's stomach dropped to her feet. Something bad had happened. Her head swung back to Balladyn. "Tell me."

"I will." He took her hand, his long fingers warm and reassuring as they twined with hers.

She should've been comforted. She wasn't. Deep in her bones, she knew that whatever had them going back to the caves was bad. Very bad.

The next time she blinked, she stood in the caves. The fire still blazed, and she welcomed the heat. Despite the warmth, she couldn't seem to shake off the chill. She moved closer to the blaze, hoping it would help. But she feared that nothing would ever remove the fear icing her heart.

"Before we get into why some of us left, Rhona, did you find the culprit?" Eoghan asked.

She shook her head and met Balladyn's gaze. "Everyone is telling the truth."

"Unless they aren't," Reaghan said.

Rhona was so tired. She wanted to curl up on one of the sofas and bury herself beneath a mound of blankets with a mug of tea. "The spell doesn't allow them to lie."

"They may not know they're lying."

Rhona faced Reaghan, dread filling her.

"Is that possible?" Aisling asked.

Sorcha shoved her auburn curls out of her face. "It shouldn't be. Like Rhona said earlier, we tend to keep such spells to those in Skye. Granted, it doesn't mean others won't share, but it's an unspoken rule."

"Times are changing," Ruarc stated.

Rhona walked woodenly to one of the chairs and sank onto the cushion. "All of this was a waste of time. It could be anyone on Skye. It could be all of them."

"It wasn't a waste. We have more information," Galen said.

Rhona felt a headache starting. She had thought this was the answer. That at the end of it all, she would know who had betrayed her and why. It was too much to think about right now. She looked at Balladyn. "What happened with you?"

For the next twenty minutes, she listened as he and the Reapers who had taken him out of the school explained what'd happened. It was when Erith and Cael were mentioned that Rhona searched the room. She found the couple standing off to the side, watching her. Rhona knew of the goddess and her consort because of Sorcha. She'd never thought to meet them herself, yet there they stood.

Erith was a petite beauty with blue-black hair and the most stunning lavender eyes. Her outfit of black leather and chainmail gave her a badass warrior queen vibe that Rhona wished she could pull off. As for Cael, the former Reaper-turned-god had the Fae good looks. He was tall and muscular with black hair pulled away from his face and gathered at his nape. What set him apart from the other Reapers was his purple eyes. That wasn't the only thing that announced he and Erith were together. Cael also wore a black shirt and black pants paired with black boots.

It was something for Fae to be back on Skye to begin with. Now, to have Death herself and the Reapers, it would rock every Druid who discovered it. *If* they discovered it.

"I still want to know how Rhona knew when Balladyn arrived at her cottage," Rordan said into the silence.

Rhona tried not to fidget under Erith's and Cael's gazes, but she didn't quite manage it.

Erith raised a perfectly arched black brow, a silent question hanging in the air.

Rhona licked her lips, her mouth suddenly dry. "I-I don't know. I can just tell where he is. I always could."

"In any room?" Cael asked.

She nodded.

Erith's gaze moved over Rhona in the direction Balladyn stood. The goddess nodded. Her lavender eyes slid back to Rhona. "Where is Balladyn now?"

A shiver ran down Rhona's back. She didn't know if this was a good thing or not. She might be the leader of the Skye Druids, but a goddess with immeasurable power was demanding an answer. Rhona motioned to the other side of the cave. "There."

"And now?" Cael asked.

Rhona felt like an amusement to them. She lifted her chin. "Beside you."

"You can see him veiled?" Erith asked.

She clasped her hands together to keep them from shaking. "No. I just sense where he is."

"Interesting," Erith replied.

The goddess motioned with her hand, and Balladyn dropped his veil. Rhona smiled when she found him staring at her. He gave her a small nod and a wink that made her want to grin like a schoolgirl.

"What's the next step?" Fallon asked. "Do we wait for the Six to attack?"

Rhona leapt to her feet. "We need the Skye Druids if our original plan is to work. I have to figure out who deceived me."

"How do you want to do that?" Cael asked.

Rhona turned to Galen and Reaghan. "Neither of you were there when I questioned the deputies. I'd like to talk to them again with both of you there."

"Anything we can do," Reaghan said as Galen nodded.

Eoghan asked, "When?"

"Now. I'll call them to the cottage," Rhona replied.

Erith took a step forward. "Do I have your permission to watch?"

Rhona knew Death could do whatever she wanted, but she appreciated Erith's request. "Of course. Any Reaper who wants to remain veiled can watch. Same goes for Larena."

"I'm getting tired of waiting for the battle," Hayden murmured.

Quinn chuckled. "It'll come soon enough."

"Maybe tonight," Balladyn replied.

Eoghan clapped his hands together. "Let's get moving on this, then."

"If I had a bigger house, we wouldn't need to keep going back and forth to the caves," Rhona said when she was back at her cottage.

Balladyn's lips curved into a smile. "I like jumping you."

"It's quite convenient, I must say."

As much as she wanted to continue their banter, more important matters were at hand. She sent her five deputies a text, requesting that they come to her. They replied quickly. Rhona nodded to the group around her as the Reapers, Cael, and Erith veiled themselves along with Galen and Reaghan. Larena's body shimmered for an instant as she released her god, and then she was no longer visible either.

To anyone looking in, Rhona appeared alone. Only she knew otherwise.

As she waited for her deputies to arrive, she heated some water to make tea. She wasn't surprised that Violet and Lyra arrived together.

"I hope our returning means good news," Violet said.

Lyra hurried inside and took off her coat. "We were headed to dinner. There's snow falling."

Rhona glanced outside before shutting the door. "Please, have a seat."

The two Druids talked amicably while Rhona poured the water into mugs and set them on a tray as another knock sounded.

"I've got it," Lyra said as she jumped up.

Rhona heard Evan's voice as he entered her home. She nodded at him as he removed his coat. Rhona's stomach was in knots. She wished with everything she had that the lie spell had worked. It was imperative that they learn the identity of who'd tried to kill her. Because if this plan didn't work, then she wasn't sure what to do.

She began to worry that she had been wrong about it being a Skye Druid. There was a good chance it was some other Druid, or even the Fae Others.

Rhona took a deep breath and lifted the tray as someone pounded on her door. Lyra answered it again while Rhona carried the tray into the living room. The six of them had gathered together several times since she had taken over for Corann, which meant that nobody had trouble making themselves at home and reaching for tea to add milk or honey or both to their cups.

She watched each of them carefully.

Evan was abrasive. He had a knack for rubbing people the wrong way simply by being straightforward about whatever was bothering him. Yet she knew from experience that he was loyal. Evan's goal was to keep the Druids relevant. He wanted to make sure they had a purpose and didn't wither away. He saw them having their group of Druid Others as a way to remind other Druids around the world that the Skye Druids were powerful and important.

Violet had been a staple in their community for years. Rhona used to tease her that she was the Zen among all of them. Violet reminded Rhona of a calm, wise person more than happy to share her wisdom with those who sought it. Many believed she should've taken Corann's position, but Violet had confided in Rhona that she was glad he hadn't chosen her.

Then there was Kerry. She had a kindly face and always had some sweets on her that she handed out to the children. Her cheeks were perpetually rosy, and she always had a smile. Everyone loved Kerry. Rhona had never heard her say a harsh word about anyone, nor had Rhona ever heard anyone say anything bad about Kerry. Beloved, that's what Rhona thought when she considered the Druid.

As for Lyra, she might be the youngest of the deputies, but she had settled into her role eagerly. Lyra was like a sponge, soaking up everything she could as quickly as she could. Her magic continued to grow as she mastered spells. Lyra's magic came from the water, so she was never far from it. Rhona had always felt certain that the Druids on Skye were in good hands with Lyra. Though Lyra wasn't a pushover. She stood her ground when she needed to, but Rhona imagined her as a new soul, eager for life and what came next.

Last was Roy. He was more of a hermit. He didn't particularly like people, but he was a powerful Druid and took the role that Corann had tasked him with without complaint. Corann had made a good decision. Some might consider Roy a curmudgeon, but he was always fair. And despite liking his solitude, he was often immersed in his group of Druids, making sure all was well.

How could any of them have been the one to betray her? Rhona knew all of them intimately. If it were one of them, she would have to do some hard thinking because she had clearly missed something along the way.

"Did you find out who it was?" Evan asked.

Rhona looked at him and grimaced. "Actually, no. That's why I called you all here. I need to ask you the questions again."

CHAPTER THIRTY-TWO

Ireland

The night air was cool and damp, the promise of rain so strong the air fairly dripped with it. Thick clouds shrouded the moon where only a faint glow was visible every now and again. Xaneth prepared to jump from the roof behind the two soldiers of the Six. He was eager for a fight, as it always was when he smelled their evil stench. The number of soldiers and Fae Others he had found the past few days made him wonder how many more he had to kill before they were gone.

Xaneth didn't use orbs of magic when he attacked evil. He liked to be up close and personal with them, so they knew precisely who was sending them to their deaths.

To his surprise, his mind drifted to Aisling. She was in his thoughts more and more. Since she had stopped following him, he should be rejoicing that he didn't have to take the extra steps to avoid her. Yet, now, all he could think about was her. He had gotten so used to seeing her that he still searched for her.

But she was gone. She was back with the Reapers where she

belonged. She never should've tried to come after him to begin with. This was how things were meant to be.

Is it?

Slowly, his head turned to the side once more, looking to the east toward Scotland. Xaneth inwardly berated himself and shook Aisling from his thoughts. Then he focused on the soldiers. He might be a monster, but he was one that killed other monsters.

And he did it better when he was on his own.

Xaneth landed quietly behind the four soldiers. There was a smile on his face as he pulled back his arm to deliver a blow, but he paused when their words reached him.

"It's finally time. The battle we've been waiting for."

"I've dreamed of this day."

"The Reapers won't know what hit them."

"Once the Reapers are gone, nothing will stop us."

"Don't forget the Dragon Kings."

A loud snort. "I'm not afraid of them."

"Don't be a fool. They've dominated this realm for a reason."

"Aye. And now it's our time."

"We're just the soldiers. We won't get the glory. That's for the Six."

"We're still a part of things. That counts."

"Does it?"

"Stop arguing. When do we leave?"

"Soon. Just waiting to get word from the Six."

"Who is taking care of the Druids?"

"There's only a few of them. Who cares?"

"They're Skye Druids, you idiot."

A long sigh. "Don't worry about them. The Six have that covered."

Every muscle in Xaneth's body was tense, urging him to attack, but the soldiers' words struck him. There was going to be a battle with the Reapers? On Skye? Is that why he kept looking toward Scotland?

Then his next thought went to Aisling.

Fury roared through him. Xaneth growled and stepped from the shadows. The four whirled around to him. Before they knew what had happened, Xaneth had beheaded one and knocked another to the ground. The other two attacked at once. Xaneth's rage only doubled as he thought about these soldiers—any soldiers—going after Aisling.

A memory of her fighting them in the alley and one blinding her made Xaneth see red. He released a battle yell, wanting to kill —*end*—every soldier and Fae Other. Everything went out of focus. He had but one thought: End them all.

Xaneth had no idea how much time had passed when he blinked and returned to himself. His breath billowed from him in huffs. The chilly night was silent and still. He scanned the area for his next opponent, but none came. He lowered his eyes and found that the four were nothing but scattered ash on the concrete. Blood dripped from his fingers to splash on the wet pavement. He looked down at himself. There wasn't just blood but also bits of the soldiers on him.

He enjoyed wiping out evil. It was an infection that ran rampant, and someone had to stop it. He was more than happy to assume that role. Besides, it seemed to be what he needed.

But he had never blacked out during a fight.

Xaneth barely noticed when it began to drizzle. He backed away from the piles of ash. At least there would be four fewer soldiers.

He looked toward Skye. The Reapers were there, which meant *she* was on the isle. The thought of her being hurt had caused an all-consuming frenzy and unquenchable wrath to rise. It should give him pause. If nothing else, it was a warning that he should keep far away from Aisling.

Even as that thought went through his mind, he jumped to Skye.

Xaneth didn't know where the Reapers were. He had no idea where the battle would be held. But there was one thing he was good at—finding evil.

He closed his eyes and drew in a deep breath, letting the scents of Skye envelop him. The salt from the sea, the smoke from fires, wet wool from the rain-soaked sheep, and vehicle exhaust. Then he caught a whiff of evil.

Xaneth's eyes snapped open as he turned toward the scent. "Got you."

~

"You better be right."

Lena barely contained her eyeroll at Barry's words. "It's the perfect time."

"We've already had one chance at them. We won't get another after this," Nola said from her position beside Barry.

Sheila calmly smiled. "Lena has done an excellent job of leading us to this point. I might not agree with every decision she's made, but look where we are. We survived a battle with the Reapers, and we're about to go in for round two."

"The fact that they only killed one of us during our last fight with them says something," Enya agreed.

Lena scarcely noticed that Nola and Barry glared at her. She was thinking about her recent clash with the Reapers that the other five didn't know about. The Reapers had nearly had her. Even Chevonne had almost gotten a kill shot. But the one that worried Lena the most was the Light Fae that had come out of nowhere.

He hadn't acted as if he were part of the Reapers. No, he had come at her as if his very life depended upon her death. Lena shivered, thinking of the strength of his magic. She needed to find out who he was. He had to be a Reaper. How else would he have found them?

She thought back to the battle and tried to recall it frame by frame in her mind. Reliving the moment she'd taken her family's magic was one of her favorite things to do, but this time, she looked beyond them to the Reapers, Chevonne, and the male. The Light had only taken his gaze from her once, and he had looked at the long-haired Dark female, who had been staring at him.

Hmm. There was something there. Lena would need to look deeper. All she had to do was get her hands on the female to learn who the male was. Then she could take him out so he was no longer a threat.

Satisfied with her plan, Lena blinked and returned her attention to the room. She glanced around when she detected the silence.

"Nice of you to return to us," Barry said with a smirk.

Lena quirked a brow. "I was going over my plans. What were you doing? Whining about not being in charge?"

Barry's face mottled red with fury. Oona halted whatever remark started to fall from his lips by speaking up.

"We're going to Scotland. Dragon King territory. What we're planning will bring attention to us. I have reservations about that. We won't be ready to fight the Kings until after the Reapers are gone."

"No one will bother us," Lena said.

Enya frowned. "How can you assure that?"

"We're going to take a page from the Kings themselves. We're going to encase the entire island in a magical bubble. No one will be able to get in or out until we're finished with the Reapers. We've been trading punches, and it's time for it all to end," Lena declared.

Sheila made a sound in the back of her throat. "I like it, but it's also going to trap us."

"Are you afraid to die?" Lena snapped.

Sheila's silver eyes narrowed. "Are you?"

"I'm not going to die. None of us is."

Barry snorted derisively. "You can't promise that."

Lena was fast losing patience. "I brought us here. I will take us the rest of the way." At least as far as she needed them. She would take their magic, along with their lives, which, when added to the power she would take from the Reapers, would make her invincible.

"*We* got us here," Nola corrected. "The six of us. Our combined magic. Your position in this group has gone to your head."

Lena nearly laughed out loud. They had no idea.

Sheila nodded. "Nola's right. It was all of us. No one person gets the credit. Just as we make sure there isn't only one of us taking the power. That's why this works."

"Does it?" Barry asked softly, his gaze locked on Lena.

Had she underestimated him? Was he onto her? It wouldn't be hard to take his life during the upcoming battle. The last thing she wanted was for him to ruin all her carefully laid plans. Too much had already been foiled with Chevonne still living, and Ruarc becoming a Reaper—both of which she planned to target.

"It has to," Oona said into the silence. "Otherwise, we disband now. We have followers because of what we've promised our people. The Fae council is hanging on by the skin of its teeth. If we falter now, it'll strengthen. Everything we've been fighting for will have been for nothing. If the Fae council takes over, we will still be hidden citizens of this realm, bowing to the wishes of the Dragon Kings. I, for one, won't do that. We're all different with varying agendas, but the one thing we can agree on is the future of the Fae. We're so close to everything. Put aside petty differences. We are the Six. We make decisions together. We carry out those decisions together." Oona turned her head to look at Lena. "Going forward, this is how it has to be, or we choose another to take over as our leader."

Lena lifted a brow at the Light's pluck. "That was quite a speech."

"Someone needed to say it. Do you agree with everything I said?"

Lena made sure her face was serene. "We are the Six. That's how the Others work, and it's how we'll defeat the Reapers."

"And the Dragon Kings," Nola said with an eager grin.

Barry chuckled as he glanced at Nola. "One step at a time. First, it's the Reapers and Death."

Enya rubbed her hands together. "Are we done talking? I'm ready to kick some Reaper arse."

CHAPTER THIRTY-THREE

Balladyn moved his gaze between Rhona and each of the five deputies as she spoke. To her credit, Rhona didn't give anything away. Not whether the Druids answered with lies or truths, nothing. Her face remained neutral, her tone even. To the point where not even he could determine what she was thinking.

Out of the corner of his eye, Balladyn saw Cathal shift his feet in annoyance. Rhona was taking her time questioning the deputies this second go-round. Everyone was on edge, including Rhona. Balladyn didn't blame her for carefully asking each question. Still, as the minutes stretched into an hour and then started in on two, Balladyn began to worry that she had yet to figure out who it was.

It wasn't until Galen physically jerked as if struck that they got anywhere. Balladyn looked at the Warrior, who gave a nod, his face pale. Balladyn then knelt behind Rhona, and careful not to touch her or the chair, whispered, "We found something."

When Roy finished answering the question, Rhona released a big breath and smiled as she got to her feet. "Thank you all for going through that a second time."

"I can no' believe you actually thought it was one of us," Evan stated.

Rhona shrugged. "I had to be certain."

"You know we will do anything to help sort this out," Kerry said.

Lyra flashed a bright smile. "Go rest, Rhona. Especially after everything you've been through."

Balladyn got to his feet and remained beside Rhona as she exchanged a few other bits of small talk with the Druids as they put on their coats and walked out into the night. No one moved for a few moments in case any of them returned.

"They're gone," Ruarc said as he, Dubhan, and Aisling jumped into the cottage.

Eoghan, Bradach, and Cathal lowered their veils, revealing them as well as Galen and Reaghan. A heartbeat later, there was an iridescent shimmer in the air before Larena tamped down her god and became visible.

Rhona whirled around to face Balladyn. "What happened?"

He looked at Galen, who was still pale. "He found something."

"What?" Rhona urged. "Who?"

Galen moved to a chair and sank onto it. He bent over, resting his elbows on his knees as he dropped his head into his hands. "Bloody hell. I doona ever want to experience that again."

Reaghan rushed to his side and put one hand on his back, the other clutching his arm. "Give him a moment. Rhona? Did your spell work this time?"

"No," Rhona said, irritation coloring her voice. "I don't know why."

"Because they believe they're speaking the truth," Galen answered. He slowly lifted his head and looked at Rhona. "No spell would've worked."

Balladyn frowned at the news. "So, it's Roy, I assume, since you reacted while Rhona was talking to him."

"Nay." Galen drew in a long breath and slowly released it as he sat up. "At first, I paid particular attention to each of them as Rhona spoke and they answered. Then I began to search their minds when they weren't being questioned. That's when I found it."

Rhona wrung her hands. "Found what?"

"It was as if someone got into their mind and locked away a

small portion. As if it never existed. I'm surprised I even found it. It was just a brush, but there was no mistaking the feel of evil."

Balladyn fisted his hands. "It's time you told us who it is."

Galen's eyes moved from him to Rhona. "Kerry."

Balladyn grabbed Rhona when her knees buckled. She quickly got her legs back under her, but he still didn't release her.

"No," Rhona said. "It can't be. Kerry is beloved by everyone. I've known her my entire life. She's the one person everybody can count on. She's always been there for the Skye Druids, but especially me. She's the last person I'd consider turning against me."

Eoghan shrugged. "It's what makes her so perfect."

"I could've sworn it was Evan," Balladyn replied.

Dubhan snorted as he nodded. "Me, too."

"Hold up," Aisling said, her brows drawn together. "Are you sure, Galen? All five of the deputies got the emails about the Druid Other group. They admitted that. If I were going to use someone, I'd have gone after Lyra. She's younger, stronger."

Galen ran a hand down his face. "I know what I felt."

"We need to search Kerry's computer," Reaghan interjected as she rubbed her hand up and down Galen's back. "She claims not to have replied, but we can discover if she did simply enough."

Balladyn glanced at Rhona when she gripped his hand tightly. She was shaken by this news. She might have expected one of them, but the fact that it was Kerry took her aback.

"Galen, thank you," Rhona said. "I appreciate the help you and Reaghan offered. I'm not discounting what you felt, but I need proof."

The Warrior nodded, understanding in his eyes. "I would demand the same. No matter how many times you use the lie spell, she'll answer the same because she believes what she says to her verra core. To find the answers, we need to break through what's being withheld from her."

"Will she even be able to handle the truth?" Reaghan asked with a frown.

Torin grunted. "If someone fekked with my mind like that, I'm not sure what I'd do."

"Oh, I know what I'd do to the bastards," Rordan mumbled.

Bradach nodded. "Exactly."

"Whatever we're doing, we need to move quickly," Eoghan said.

Larena lifted a hand. "I can get into her house and check the emails."

"I'll follow Kerry," Aisling offered.

Balladyn looked at Rhona. "You need to start thinking about how you're going to handle this."

"She's a link to the Fae Others," Ruarc said. "We can't have that."

Rhona lifted her chin. "I'm not taking anyone's life until I have facts and details. I want to hear from Kerry."

"Are we sure the other four didn't have their minds messed with?" Dubhan asked. He wrinkled his nose at Galen. "No offense, mate, but it took you a while to sense it in Kerry."

Galen waved away his words. "None taken. I can no' say for certain without touching each of them. My skills have grown considerably enough that I can use my power without touch now, but it's better if I have that connection. I know what to search for now."

"Then do it," Rhona urged. "I have to know."

Eoghan caught Galen's eye. "I can take you around to them. It'll be tricky because they're going to see you since you have to touch them, and I can't veil you to do that."

"I only need a moment of contact," the Warrior said.

Rhona swallowed loudly. "Lyra and Violet are going to eat. Evan will be at a pub, but Roy will head home."

"We'll do the best we can," Eoghan promised.

Galen kissed Reaghan before standing and turning to Eoghan.

"I'll let you know Kerry's movements," Aisling said before teleporting after Eoghan and Galen.

Larena shrugged. "One of you want to take me to Kerry's so I can search her computer?"

"I will," Bradach said.

After the two of them left, the room grew quiet. Balladyn knew that Rhona wasn't prepared for the next steps, but she would have to be in case the worst happened.

"I thought I was prepared for this," Rhona whispered.

Balladyn glanced at his brethren before they took up their spots outside to guard the cottage. Balladyn swung his head to Rhona as she made her way to the sink and turned on the water to wash the dishes. He almost reminded her that magic could do that for her, but then he realized that she needed a menial task.

"How did I miss it?" she finally asked.

"You heard Galen. It wasn't meant to be found."

She stopped washing and looked at him. "By a Druid."

"Look at the powers the Reapers have. We weren't able to determine it either."

Rhona shook her head and returned to washing. She was silent for several minutes before saying, "I can't order her death. I don't care that I'm in this position and am supposed to do what's right for our people. I can't do it."

"No one is asking you to." At least, not now. A lot could change between now and then, especially if Larena found anything on the computer, but Balladyn kept that to himself.

Rhona rinsed the last of the cups and set them aside to dry before she wiped her hands on a towel. Then she turned to face him. "Whatever the outcome, this will destroy us."

He walked to her and gently grasped her shoulders. "No, it won't. Because you won't allow it."

"How can you be so sure?"

"Because I have faith in you. You're special, Rhona. Corann chose you because he saw what I do. A powerful Druid with a good heart and the ability to stand against whatever comes her way."

She leaned against him, her arms wrapping around him. Balladyn closed his eyes and enfolded her in his embrace. He loved that she leaned on him. Though she had no idea that it served him more than it did her. He hadn't realized how much love he had to give until Rhona, or that he wanted to give it to someone.

His throat clogged with emotion. Regardless of whether she didn't care about his past or didn't understand what he had done, she was there with him when no one else ever had been. She was strong enough to handle all of this herself but had turned to him. She'd let him see her fears, her vulnerabilities, her doubts.

And he wanted her to know that all he saw in return was a resilient, beautiful, determined, capable Druid. She was like a giant oak, rooted deep in her culture and home. One that could withstand the greatest of storms.

Everyone had turned to Corann before. Soon, they would look to Rhona in the same manner.

"Trust yourself," he continued. "You'll know what to do when the time comes."

CHAPTER THIRTY-FOUR

Aisling found Kerry easily enough. The older Druid hummed as she pulled herself out of her tiny vehicle and made her way into the noisy pub. The tavern was crowded and loud. Aisling didn't want to be jostled and have someone notice her, so she watched where Kerry went and then teleported, veiled, to that location. Even then it was too much. Aisling ended up squishing herself into a corner.

She ran her gaze over the occupants of the pub. Everyone spoke as if they knew each other. Aisling shuddered, thinking of her past. She didn't know how everyone handled everyone else being in their business.

Several people called out greetings to Kerry, who quickly waved and shouted a hello before taking her seat. Aisling stood right beside the Druid. If any of them had thought to use magic, they probably would have discovered her. That was the problem with the Skye Druids. They had been the strongest of their kind for so long that they assumed no one would mess with them.

Unfortunately, they were dead wrong.

Rhona had nearly lost her life because of that belief.

"Your usual?" a woman with dyed blond hair and flashing blue eyes asked.

Kerry nodded. "Thanks, love."

The Druid then began humming again as she took out her mobile phone and started playing solitaire. A few minutes later, the woman brought over a tumbler of whisky. Kerry grinned her thanks but kept her attention on her phone. Aisling inwardly groaned at the many mistakes the Druid made in her game. It became so painful to watch that Aisling turned her attention to the others in the pub.

The pub had low ceilings and several small rooms. Yet even she had to agree that it had an atmosphere she would've enjoyed. Whether it was the smell of old alcohol, the shine of the highly polished wooden bar, the pictures of the various places on Skye, or just the people, the pub attracted all kinds.

"Hey," a teenager with bad acne and dark hair that kept falling in his eyes said as he walked up.

Kerry's head lifted from her phone. "John. How are you, lad?" she asked with a smile.

"I took your advice and talked to Mum. We sorted our problems," he said shyly.

The Druid reached over and patted his hand. "I told you your mum wasn't as bad as you thought."

"It was a miscommunication." He shrugged. "Just like you said."

"I'm glad you spoke with her. Things have been hard for her since the divorce, pet. She's doing the best she can."

John nodded, biting his lip as he glanced away. "I made things worse by acting like a wanker."

Kerry threw back her head and laughed, her ample curves moving with her merriment. "Well, let's not act like that anymore." Her laughter died as she caught his eye. "You're becoming a man, my lad. I'm proud of you."

Aisling watched the teenager walk away with pep in his step and a smile. Her gaze lowered to Kerry, who watched John. No wonder Rhona had been so surprised by Galen's declaration that Kerry was her betrayer. Then again, Aisling knew firsthand that well-intended people often mucked up others' lives.

Before Kerry's food arrived, a pretty, black-haired woman made her way over. Kerry caught sight of her and motioned the woman to a chair with a smile. "Sit, Margot, sit. How are you?" Kerry asked.

Margot grinned, though it didn't quite reach her eyes, and then folded her hands together before shoving them between her thighs. She glanced around the pub. "I'm good. Just wanted to thank you for the basket of jams you dropped by. It was very kind of you."

"You let me know if you need anything. You or your sister."

"She has her husband. She'll be fine."

Kerry raised a brow, her look conveying that she wasn't convinced. "And you?"

"I've got friends."

"You just lost your mother, pet. Lean on people when you need to. You don't have to go around doing everything yourself."

Margot's smile was easier. "It's good to have a friend like you."

Aisling shook her head. Either Kerry had no idea what she had done, or she was the vilest, most malevolent person Aisling had ever been around.

Margot left as Kerry's food came. The deputy went back to her game and happily munched on her dinner while also taking down two glasses of whisky before paying her tab and making her way back to her car. Aisling teleported into the backseat so she knew where the Druid was headed.

Fifteen minutes later, they pulled up to a white cottage with an impressive view of the mountains on one side and the sea on the other. Aisling didn't pay any of it any attention. She jumped into the house to warn Larena, but the laptop didn't look as if it had been touched. Then she turned her head and spotted Bradach and the Warrior.

"We just finished," Bradach said.

Larena's lips twisted. "I got what we need."

Aisling glanced at the door. "I'm going to stay a little longer and see what happens."

"Be careful," Bradach cautioned before teleporting himself and the Warrior out.

The key turned in the door, and Kerry hurried in, humming once more.

Xaneth jumped behind a building and bent over as the smell of evil grew so thick that he was sick with it. The Fae Others were on Skye. A great number of them, and from what he could tell, the Druids had no idea. He had looked around but had yet to find the Reapers. Where were they?

Where was Aisling?

He straightened and breathed through his mouth. The only way to make this sickness go away was to kill the evil. It would be easy. They were close, but Xaneth hesitated. He didn't want to alert the Fae Others that they had been spotted. It might screw up any plans the Reapers had. Also, he hoped Lena would show for the battle. He was going to finish what they had started.

Xaneth almost said Aisling's name. He knew the Reaper would come. At least, he thought she would. After ignoring her for so long, she might have turned her back on him completely. But he needed information.

For the moment, however, he had to put some distance between himself and the evil before his base need to eradicate them overshadowed everything else.

"What are you thinking?"

Erith stood with her arms crossed over her chest as she stared into the shadows on the dark wall. She swung her gaze to Cael as they remained in the caves with the Warriors and Druids. "There have been leaders who clung to a single belief so long that they didn't realize when it was time to let it go and find something else."

"That's true," Cael said with a nod. He glanced behind him to the fire, where the others sat talking. "What's your point?"

"Does that apply to me?"

He frowned and blinked, his confusion evident. "Where did you get that?"

"How long have the Reapers been in place? Is it too long?"

"Nay," he answered immediately.

She flattened her lips. "You say that because we're together."

"I say it because it's true. You help maintain the balance."

"Who's to say that it isn't time for me to hand the reins to someone else?"

Cael gaped at her. "Who else would do it? There isn't another you."

"Oh, my love. If you think I'm the only goddess in the universe, you are sadly mistaken."

"You never speak of them."

"I've not met any, but I've been around long enough to know there is so much out there we don't know and can't explain. If there is one of me, there are more. That is fact."

He blew out a breath. "Do you want to find one to take your place?"

"No."

"Does one of them want to take your place?"

"I don't know."

His face went hard. He lowered his voice into a tone that softened his anger. "Sweetheart, then what is it you want?"

"I don't know. I'm just talking."

Cael raked a hand through his hair. "Bloody hell."

Erith took pity on him and dropped her arms to her sides as she took his hands in hers. "I'm trying to look at every angle of the Fae Others to see if there's something we aren't seeing."

"They're killing Fae. That's pretty fekking clear to me."

She wrinkled her nose. "Yes, of course. But we've long talked about the changes that need to happen for the Fae. Nothing we're hearing about the Council has been good. If that folds, we're right back to the way things were."

"I know. We've always stayed out of Fae business. Do you want that to change?"

"I'm not sure. It's just that I've held true to my original proclamation when I formed the Reapers. All these millennia later, and nothing has changed."

His wide lips curved into a sexy smile as he bent and gently kissed her. "I wouldn't say that. Some major things changed."

Erith grinned. Cael always knew what to say. "I might have been a little selfish in my decision."

"I don't care about the reason. Only that it happened, sweetheart," he murmured.

Try as she might, she couldn't hold on to the happiness his words had brought. "How would I know I was wrong? How would I know I've clung to things too long?"

"I would tell you. And if I didn't do it, one of the Reapers would."

Erith licked her lips as she turned her head to the Warriors and Druids. "I don't feel good about this upcoming battle."

"Anything in particular?"

"Too many others are involved. We know what we're going into."

Cael gently turned her head back to him. "So do they."

"Not really."

"They've fought many battles."

Erith jerked her head toward the fire. "Them. What of the Skye Druids?"

"You know the answer to that."

"Just because they're the strongest Druids doesn't mean they're infallible."

Cael pulled her closer. "They went up against Moreann."

"That's right. Moreann. Another Druid. Not the Fae, not soldiers, and certainly not the Six."

His brow puckered. "You think they're going to die."

"Do you think we'll all come out of this alive?"

Cael held her gaze for a long moment. "No."

"Knowing that, can you welcome everyone to join us?"

He glanced away.

Erith nodded. "Exactly. We need their numbers, but they'll be going to their deaths."

"Not all of them."

"Enough," she countered. "I know you've gone over the plan meticulously, as only you can."

He sighed. "Aye. I have, and some will die."

Erith leaned her head against his chest. "It's going to happen soon. I can feel it."

"All of us can. The very air on Skye has shifted. It's time the rest of the Reapers came."

"Is it?"

He pulled back to look at her, his frown deepening. "We need them to win."

"If we lose this, there needs to be others who can stand against the Six."

"You know I can see all the outcomes. I'm telling you we need the rest of the Reapers."

Erith heard his words, but she knew in her gut what had to happen. "They'll be needed later."

"It will have to be the Kings if we don't succeed. Leaving the Reapers out is wrong. We're strongest together."

Erith had always sought Cael's counsel on things. She knew he was right, but something told her that bringing the rest of the Reapers here was a mistake. If all the Reapers joined with the Warriors and Druids from MacLeod Castle and Skye, then they could end the Fae Others. They had a real chance. The allies standing with them were powerful beings.

And all of them united could be decisive on the outcome.

Still, something warned her that there was also a chance things could go pear-shaped. Someone had to be around to warn the Kings and take a stand with them. That couldn't happen if the Reapers, Warriors, and Druids were dead.

"I should've stopped by Dreagan and spoken with Con," Erith mumbled.

Cael asked, "Is he back from Zora?"

"I don't know. It doesn't matter. The fact is, the Kings should know what's happening in case…" Damn, she couldn't even finish. All the time wasted in not going to Con made her anxious. "I need to go. Right now."

"Nay," Cael snapped loud enough to draw the eyes of those around the fire. His gaze held hers. "I'll go. You stay and prepare with everyone here. They need you. I'll be back with the other Reapers. Who knows, maybe the Kings will come."

Erith stopped him. "Not the other Reapers."

"Er—"

"I mean it," she said over him. "You can't."

He searched her face. After a moment, he reluctantly nodded. "What of the Kings? They won't be happy that the Fae are on Skye."

"Let them come if they want to. Just not the Reapers."

Cael searched her face. "Can you tell me what's driving this decision?"

"I don't know."

He nodded and pressed his lips to hers. "See you shortly."

"I love you," Erith said as she gripped his hand.

His face softened. "I love you."

She had to make herself release him. When he vanished, she doubled over, fighting not to give in to a cry at the desolation that unexpectedly opened like a maw within her. She had to get him back. Immediately.

"Cael," she called and waited for him to return. "Cael!"

He still didn't materialize in front of her.

Erith dropped to her knees. Something was wrong. Dreadfully wrong.

"Breathe. You need to breathe," Isla said.

Erith glanced at the Druid, wondering when she had approached. And she wasn't the only one. The Warriors and Druids surrounded her.

"What is it?" Fallon asked.

If she fell apart now, it would ripple through everyone. That wasn't a way to start a battle. But how could she go on with the emptiness that stretched within her like a great yawning pit? And she knew who was responsible—the Six. All she wanted to do was cry and scream because she couldn't get the thought out of her head that she would never see Cael again.

Erith blinked back tears as she looked at the faces around her. The Warriors and Druids had willingly come to Skye to help. Did she tell them that decision likely meant they had forfeited their lives? She had believed that with Cael and the Reapers, she could handle the Six. That thinking had prevented her from alerting the Dragon Kings about a battle on their soil. Of all the foolish decisions she had made, Erith regretted this one the most.

Somehow, she pulled herself together and got to her feet. Emotion clogged her throat, but she swallowed it down. Everything in the universe eventually died. If this was her time, she wasn't going out on her knees. "Get ready. The battle is about to start."

CHAPTER THIRTY-FIVE

Rhona tried to hang onto the words Balladyn had given her when Bradach and Larena returned.

"I'm sorry," Larena said.

It had been foolish to hope that, somehow, Galen had been wrong about Kerry—about any of the Druids wanting to hurt her. But it had been wishful thinking. Rhona straightened her spine. "What did you find?"

"The email Kerry received is almost word for word what Lyra said was in hers," Bradach explained.

Larena nodded. "Kerry responded by telling them she wanted no part in it. Then she went on a lengthy diatribe of why the Skye Druids were as commanding as they were and why they didn't need to create such a group."

"A very lengthy post," Bradach said with a wrinkle of his nose.

Rhona frowned. "You're telling me that Kerry took up for us?"

"That wasn't the only email," Larena replied. "For the past month, Kerry has been trading emails with whoever sent the first one."

Balladyn crossed his arms over his chest and frowned. "You don't know the sender?"

"I'm not a hacker," the Warrior answered.

Bradach shrugged. "It's not something we've ever had to do. I wouldn't know where to begin."

"What were the other emails?" Rhona was barely hanging on. She needed to know everything, as difficult as it would be to hear. And she suspected it was going to be a doozy.

Larena paused as her gaze shifted to Rhona. "Whoever the sender is, they knew what they were doing. I think they identified how Kerry would respond and used that. They were subtle in their slow and methodical manipulation of her to eventually change her views to theirs."

"You've got to be kidding me," Rhona murmured.

Bradach blew out a breath. "Whoever this is, is good. They didn't verbally attack her. They didn't force their views on her. It was a discussion. A debate."

"But, ultimately, one where Kerry changed her mind about the Druid Others," Larena added.

Rhona was going to be sick. How had this happened? And was it happening to more Druids on Skye? Is that how it all began? "Kerry never said anything. I saw no change in her whatsoever. How could a spell have been used via the internet to make her forget those emails?"

"She met with them," Balladyn guessed.

Larena's lips twisted ruefully. "Aye."

"Of course," Rhona said as she shook her head. "Kerry went to see her sister in Glasgow a few weeks ago."

Balladyn's face hardened. "An easy journey for someone from Ireland to make."

"The emails stopped after that," Larena said.

Rhona turned against the counter and put her hands on the edge of the sink as she looked out the window to see the beginning snow flurries. "That's when she began plotting to take my life."

"Did anyone else from Skye go to Glasgow with her?" Bradach asked.

Rhona shook her head. "Not that I'm aware of, but it could've happened."

"What did you find out?" Balladyn asked.

Rhona looked over her shoulder to find that Eoghan and Galen had returned. She faced them, unsure how much more she could take.

"None of them had the same feel about them as Kerry," Galen confirmed.

She should be relieved, but she wasn't. "It was just Kerry who betrayed me then?"

Larena and Bradach filled Galen and Eoghan in on what they'd discovered.

"Where's Aisling?" Eoghan asked.

Bradach answered, "She said she was going to stay behind and watch Kerry for a bit."

"If the Druids learn that Reapers got into their homes and spied, it's going to get ugly," Larena warned.

Rhona grunted as she wrapped her hands around her waist. "Things got ugly when I was nearly killed. These are the steps that had to be taken. If there's a backlash, I'll take it."

"I doubt anyone would've made different decisions if they were in your place," Galen replied.

Eoghan blew out a breath. "We know who turned against you, Rhona. It'll be easy to contain Kerry so we can gather the rest of the Druids for the battle."

"We don't know when that'll be," Bradach said.

Balladyn rubbed his chest. "It's going to be soon."

"I agree," Eoghan said.

Rhona pushed away from the counter. "Let's do this now, then."

"You aren't coming," Balladyn stated.

She swung her head to him and raised a brow. "If you think to keep me away, think again. Kerry is a Druid and one of my deputies. I need to be there to tell her what's happening and why."

"And if she attacks you?" Larena asked.

Rhona shrugged. "Then she attacks."

"Let's all go," Galen said. "We can watch Rhona's back, and if Kerry willna come quietly, then we doona give her a choice."

Balladyn's nostrils flared. "I'd feel better if you weren't involved."

"Tough," she answered.

He sighed loudly but didn't say more.

Rhona looked at Eoghan and nodded. If the Reapers really wanted to, they could leave without her, but she knew they wouldn't.

"You'll need your coat," Balladyn said. "Since I gather we won't arrive inside her home."

Rhona thought about that for a moment. "Actually, I think everyone but me should be inside the cottage. Aisling is already there. I don't want Kerry to know about any of you unless it's absolutely necessary."

"What do you want to do with her?" Bradach asked.

With her stomach clenching in trepidation, Rhona said, "There is a place on Skye where Druids are taken in such situations."

"You have a Druid prison?" The surprise on Eoghan's face mirrored everyone else's.

Rhona wished her stomach would settle. "It's not widely known, and it's only used for emergencies."

"Where is it?" Balladyn asked.

"Beneath the Red Hills," she replied.

Galen's gaze widened. "The Red Cuillins?"

"Aye."

Balladyn shrugged. "If Kerry doesn't agree to go herself, we'll step in."

"Agreed," Rhona said.

She walked to where her coat hung and shrugged into it. When she turned around, Balladyn was beside her.

"Ready?" he asked.

She glanced at Eoghan, Galen, Bradach, Larena, and then at Balladyn. "Not in the least. Let's go."

One second, Rhona was in her cottage. The next, frigid air blasted her as she stood outside Kerry's door. She shivered and hurriedly rapped her knuckles on the wood. Rhona felt Balladyn's presence beside her. She liked that he stayed with her. Rhona was about to knock a second time when she heard the bolt turning.

Kerry peered around the corner of the door, surprise flashing on her face. "Come inside. It's freezing."

Rhona quickly entered the house and was greeted with warmth that made her sigh. Then she remembered why she'd come. She rubbed her hands together and faced Kerry as the woman turned to her.

"Is everything all right?" the Druid asked with a worried frown.

Rhona smiled sadly and shook her head. "It isn't. I discovered who betrayed me."

"Thank goodness. Who was it? Did they admit to why?" Kerry asked in rapid succession.

Rhona took a deep breath. She didn't want to do this. She didn't want to be here or have this responsibility, but she was, and she did. No matter how difficult this was, she had to see it through. For her sake. For Kerry's.

And for every Druid on Skye.

Kerry's forehead furrowed. "It isn't Lyra, is it?"

"Why would you ask if it was her?"

"She's the youngest. I know Evan runs his mouth, but I've learned in my years that it's the quiet ones you need to worry about. Lyra is sweet, but that doesn't mean she isn't up to something."

Rhona's heart ached. "It isn't Lyra. It's you, Kerry."

The Druid stumbled backwards as if Rhona's words had physically struck her. Kerry put her hand on her chest, her mouth going slack as shock visibly rippled through her body. "Why would you make such an accusation? You know that isn't true."

"It is." *Fek. Why does this have to be so awkward?*

Kerry shook her head. "I would never turn against you or our people."

"There's proof."

"Then show me," Kerry demanded. Bright splotches of red covered her face as she fisted her hands. "I don't appreciate you pointing the finger at me. Not after everything I've done for our community."

Rhona felt Balladyn's presence behind her, which helped her

continue. "I understand your anger, but once I show you, you'll understand."

"I'm waiting," Kerry snapped.

Rhona had never seen the Druid angry, at least not like this. "Check your emails. Look in the trash."

"You hacked my system? No doubt you planted things," Kerry stated as she strode past Rhona, bumping into her.

Rhona didn't react to Kerry's rage. As she had said, it was understandable and expected. She stood calmly to the side as Kerry opened the laptop and signed into her emails. Kerry took a moment to look through her current messages before going to the trash folder.

"The first email arrived on the eleventh of last month," Rhona said.

Kerry said nothing as she searched for the email. It didn't take her long to find it. She made a noise as she opened and read it. Rhona watched the Druid's face as the ire melted away and bewilderment took its place.

"Who would send this?" Kerry slowly pulled out the desk chair and sank into it as she read through the email chain.

Rhona counted on Kerry willingly going to the Red Hills. She didn't want the Druid seized, but at the same time, Rhona knew that the lives of many hung on the upcoming battle. If the Reapers had to take Kerry, then that's what would happen.

But Rhona really hoped that wouldn't be the case.

"This is a mistake," Kerry said in a calmer voice when she finished reading. She kept staring at the emails on the screen. "I would remember if I wrote these."

Rhona called to her magic and felt it rush through her, at the ready if she needed it. "You went to Glasgow."

"To see my sister."

"I think that's where you met the person who wrote those emails. I think it's also the person who used magic to make you forget about the correspondence, them, and setting me up to die."

Kerry spun in her chair. "Rhona, I would never!"

"You did."

"Read the emails," she argued. "I stood up for our way of life and the decision you made about the Druid Others."

Rhona swallowed, wondering if Corann had ever faced a situation like this. It would've been nice to know how he'd handled it so she could follow his lead. Instead, she was muddling her way through it all on her own—well, not totally on her own.

"The sender manipulated you," Rhona replied. "You read your replies. You begin to agree with them."

Kerry glanced at the screen and shrugged helplessly. "So what if I agree with some of what is said? That doesn't mean I was responsible for your attack."

"You went to Glasgow."

"You have no proof that I met anyone."

Rhona would've given the same argument. "Kerry, I'd like for you to agree to come with me to the Red Hills."

The Druid's face drained of color. "You want to imprison me?"

"I want to make sure you're in a place where you can't hurt anyone or yourself. I also want to make sure that no one can hurt you."

Kerry placed her hands on her knees and lowered her gaze to the floor. "You think I would turn against you."

"You already have." The words hurt to say. Mainly because Rhona had known and liked Kerry. If the Fae Others could get to someone like Kerry, then they could get to anyone.

"Are you going to tell everyone before I have a chance to defend myself?"

"No. Someone used magic on you, and we're going to find a way to reverse it."

"You or the Reapers?" Kerry asked as she lifted her head to pin Rhona with a look.

"I'm not above asking anyone who might be capable of helping. I've known you for my whole life. You wouldn't do this without being controlled somehow." At least that's what Rhona prayed had happened, even though she wasn't positive. The more she spoke with Kerry, the more she doubted.

Everything.

Kerry let out a long breath and got to her feet. "It's been a long time since we brought anyone to the Red Hills. I don't want to die there."

"I'll fight to make sure that doesn't happen," Rhona promised.

"I want a fair trial."

"You'll have it. I give you my word as head of our order."

Kerry nodded. "Then I'll go."

"Balladyn," Rhona said.

He lowered his veil and bowed his head to Kerry.

Rhona smiled sadly as she reached out her hand to the Druid. "It'll be a quicker journey this way."

"I can't believe this is happening," Kerry mumbled.

Rhona's heart was heavy. "This isn't a sentencing. This is only for a time while we sort out a few things."

Kerry reluctantly took her hand.

Balladyn asked, "Where exactly am I going?"

"North side of the Red Cuillins. The entrance is on the northeast," Rhona explained.

Balladyn nodded. "I'll get us as close as I can."

Then he took her arm. Rhona sucked in a breath when the wind slammed into her. She blinked open her eyes as snowflakes peppered her face, whipped by the furious wind. Rhona had to shield her eyes to get her bearings. She found the entrance and pointed to it. Just as she was about to tell Balladyn, he jumped them there.

She went into the tunnel first with Kerry following and Balladyn bringing up the rear. Rhona was glad to be out of the storm, but it was still freezing in the mountain. The tunnel went on for some time, winding this way and that, the ground dipping and rising until she reached a low-ceilinged cavern and the six smaller ones that formed a semicircle at the far end of the cave.

Rhona stood aside and let Kerry pick which of the smaller cavities she wanted. After she chose one of the middle two, Rhona whispered the words that'd suddenly come to her the moment Corann announced she would lead their people. The spell locked

Kerry inside and prevented her from doing magic. Rhona then created a fire to heat the area.

"Our community means everything to me," Kerry said solemnly. "I don't want to be remembered for something I wasn't even aware I did."

Rhona put her hands in her coat pockets to warm them. "We'll figure this out. I promise."

CHAPTER THIRTY-SIX

The sound of Erith's voice cutting off as she called to him left Cael reeling. He repeatedly attempted to return to her but couldn't reach her, which shouldn't be possible. He raked a hand through his hair and released a shout of frustration. One by one, he called for the other Reapers.

Baylon, Kyran, Talin, Neve, Fintan, and Daire from the original Reapers, as well as mates Maeve, Kyra, Breda, Fianna, and Chevonne. Cael didn't want to tell any of them that he couldn't get to Skye, but he certainly didn't want to share the news with the women about where their mates were.

"Is it time?" Kyran asked.

Cael fisted his hands. His blood ran like ice, his heart thumping heavily as his fear intensified. "I left to tell the Kings what was happening. Erith…she…she called for me, but my name was cut off."

"Like she stopped it?" Neve asked.

Why couldn't they understand? He didn't have time to tell them every detail. "It just stopped! Now, I can't get to her or the others on Skye."

"Fek me. I can't either," Baylon said with a frown.

Breda shook her head of black and silver hair. "I just tried, too. Something is blocking us."

The last time Cael had felt like everything was unraveling had been when Bran had tried to kill Erith. "I can't lose her."

Maeve walked up to him and gave him a shake. "You won't, but we need to come up with a plan."

"The Kings," Cael said. "I need to alert them."

Fintan cracked his knuckles. "Go. We'll continue working on why we can't get to Skye."

"It might be like the shield Bran used to keep me away from Ettie. We got into that. We can get into this one," Daire said.

Talin grunted. "If that's what this is."

"We need to get closer to Skye," Chevonne suggested. "Just because we can't teleport there doesn't mean we can't see the isle."

Cael nodded, thankful that they were able to think clearly. "I'll be back as soon as I can."

He jumped inside the manor at Dreagan near the front door. It was rude not to knock, but time was of the essence. Cael didn't bother to shout. The Dragon Kings had known he entered their domain the instant he crossed the invisible shield around their land.

"Cael?" Hal called as he walked from the kitchen.

"I need all of you. Now," Cael stated harshly.

Hal nodded. "I just sent a message to everyone."

Within seconds, Kings filled the area. Cael swiftly recounted everything that had occurred since Rhona was attacked until he came to Dreagan.

"Why did you no' contact us sooner?" Warrick demanded furiously.

Dmitri crossed his arms over his chest. "Skye is part of Scotland. We doona take kindly to Fae, especially Fae Others, coming on to our lands."

"I know!" Cael drew in a breath and fought for calm as he briefly closed his eyes. "We hoped to contain it ourselves."

Cain stepped forward. "Are you sure this isna something Erith did to keep you out? She did say no' to bring the other Reapers."

"She called to me," Cael replied. "She wouldn't do that and then not allow me to return to her."

Ulrik nodded. "I agree. Of course, we'll help. What do you need?"

Cael looked around at the faces staring back at him. "Where's Con?"

"He and Rhi are still on Zora. There have been some developments there," Ulrik explained.

Cael waved away his words. "Never mind. You have the bracelet that lets you teleport. See if you can get to Skye."

Ulrik touched the silver cuff on his wrist, but he didn't vanish. A frown marred his features as he tried two more times. "I'm no' able."

"Fek!" Cael shouted as he whirled around, his panic doubling. "This is the Fae Others. I know it." He turned back to the Kings. "The Reapers are teleporting as close to Skye as they can and then finding another way to get there. I need to do the same."

Thorn grinned as he looked at Ulrik. "I know how we can get there."

"There's a chance we'll be seen," Guy warned.

Rhys shrugged. "These are extenuating circumstances. I say we go."

"I can hide us with a storm," Arian offered.

Ulrik nodded and headed toward the conservatory, which led to a hidden entrance to Dreagan Mountain. "Then we go."

"I'll meet you there," Cael called before teleporting to his Reapers.

Xaneth had to get as far away as the top of a Red Cuillin before he could control his need to kill the soldiers. The storm that raged almost matched what he felt inside. He stood in the elements, gladly taking everything Mother Nature threw his way.

He was content to have his face lifted toward the sky. However, something told him to look down. He caught a glimpse of Balladyn and two Druids before they disappeared into the mountain. Xaneth wondered what they were doing, but he didn't follow. The only Reaper he was interested in was Aisling.

"Stop," he growled at himself.

But it was too late. She had wormed her way into his mind. It seemed the harder he fought to remove her, the more she was there.

It didn't matter though. Soon, he wouldn't exist.

He was counting on that.

Xaneth threw out his arms and hollered his rage at being tortured by Usaeil, for having his life taken from him, and for turning into a monster that had no future.

For not knowing Aisling.

Balladyn followed Rhona as she retraced her steps through the tunnel. After several minutes, she stopped and turned to him. "What aren't you telling me."

"What do you mean?"

"You know what I mean."

Balladyn created a light so she could see him. "I don't."

"Do you have any idea how many times you rub your chest?" she asked pointedly.

He glanced down to see that he was doing it. Balladyn dropped his arm. "It's nothing."

"Has Lena contacted you again?"

"Nay."

"She gave you an ultimatum."

He flattened his lips. "I'm not siding with her."

"Maybe you should."

He pulled back in shock. "Absolutely, not."

"No, listen. If they win, you align with her and betray her from within."

Balladyn shook his head before she even finished speaking. "She'll expect that. I know I would. Besides, she isn't going to win."

"There should be a plan B in case the Six are victorious."

"They won't be."

"She got into my head. She reached you when the other Reapers were near. I think it's something we need to consider."

Balladyn parted his lips to answer when he heard Eoghan shout his name. "We have to go." He grabbed Rhona and jumped them to her caves at the pools where Eoghan and the others waited.

"Is Kerry secure?" Sorcha asked.

Rhona nodded as she looked around. "What's going on?"

"It's time," Erith said as she walked toward them. "Broc found soldiers on Skye."

"We need the Druids," Rhona said.

Lucan said, "Fallon and Broc are taking Cara and Sonya to the deputies so they can spread the word."

"We need Kerry's division," Rhona stated and turned to Balladyn.

Before he could reply, Lucan said, "They're having the other four get that group."

Balladyn turned to Rhona. "This is your home. Where do you want the battle to happen?"

Everyone stilled, waiting to hear what she had to say.

Rhona shifted nervously. "I-I don't know. We didn't talk about this."

"That's our fault," Erith said. "We should have. Right now, you need to decide on a location so we can know how to set up."

Balladyn wished he could take this fight anywhere else, but the Six wanted it here on Skye. They had set everything up so it would be on this island. He took Rhona's hands in his and nodded. "You know this land better than any of us."

"Here," she said. "At the pools."

Bradach grunted. "Fitting, I suppose. This is where the Fae and Druids first met."

"And it'll be where all of us will end the Fae Others," Isla said.

Eoghan motioned everyone near the fire. "We don't know if the Six will be here, but we're hoping they will. The Reapers will be grouped together. Let the soldiers attack us. Make them think we're the only ones here."

"Are the other Reapers coming?" Rordan asked.

Erith shook her head. "No."

"What?" Cathal asked with frown.

Eoghan shot him a glare before looking at the Warriors. "Then all of you come in to flank them."

"How many soldiers are we talking?" Quinn asked.

Balladyn shrugged. "It could be twenty or two hundred or two thousand."

"Which is why all of us should be here," Rordan said.

Erith's lavender eyes speared him. "It's my call. If the Six win, I want there to be someone to fight them."

Rordan was silent for a moment, and then he nodded.

"Where's Cael?" Bradach asked.

Balladyn caught Erith's slight jerk at the mention of Cael. He glanced at Eoghan and saw that he, too, had noticed it.

"He went to tell the Kings what is going on," Erith replied.

Eoghan waited for a heartbeat, then two before he continued. "After the Warriors, the Druids should take their places."

"We work best in a circle so our magic flows. We'll be sure to surround the area with as many rings of Druids as we can," Rhona said.

Erith rested her hand on the black sword at her hip. "Anything can happen. Be prepared. We have the advantage, but we can't underestimate our enemies."

As if on cue, couples turned to each other to say their farewells.

Balladyn squeezed Rhona's hand as they shared a look. This might be the last time he saw her. His chest grew tight at the thought. It was on the tip of his tongue to tell Rhona…what? What did he want to tell her? That he had feelings for her. That he was falling for her. That in all the years he'd lived, he'd never met anyone like her—and never would again?

Instead, he wrapped an arm around her and kissed her as if it were their last time. He poured his feelings and the words he couldn't get past his lips into the kiss, showing her how he felt if he couldn't tell her. Her arms wrapped around his neck as she held him tightly. There was desperation and fear in her kiss, as there was in his.

Reluctantly, he ended the embrace and gazed down at her, committing her face to memory.

"Don't you dare die," she told him.

He tucked a strand of red hair behind her ear. "Ditto."

CHAPTER THIRTY-SEVEN

It was really happening. Rhona couldn't believe it. She had been so focused on uncovering the traitor that she had put the battle out of her mind. It had been a foolish thing to do because her head buzzed with all the different outcomes as she and the Warriors and Druids waited in the caves.

This wasn't her first battle. But that didn't make it any easier.

She had friends who'd died when they fought Moreann, but none of them had held her heart as Balladyn did.

Rhona gasped and doubled over, placing her hands on her knees as she fought against a wave of dread and heart-gripping anxiety. She loved Balladyn. She *loved* him. Why hadn't she told him? Before they said goodbye might have been her one chance to tell him how she felt. Her heart and mind rebelled at the thought of Balladyn not surviving the battle.

Tears pricked her eyes. Rhona hadn't thought she would be so fortunate to find a man who saw her, understood her and was willing to stand beside her. But Balladyn was all those things and so much more. He had given her strength when hers faltered.

He bolstered her courage when hers deserted her.

He trusted her when she didn't trust herself.

"Oh, gods," Rhona whispered as the tears fell freely. There was no holding them back, no stopping the onslaught of regret that enveloped her like a suffocating scourge.

She squeezed her eyes closed as his handsome face filled her mind. The way he had held her, looked at her, kissed her. She had waited her entire life to have something so special. She wouldn't let it be taken from her. But she knew firsthand that Fate could be a brutal bitch.

Rhona tried to stanch the tears, but once they started flowing, there was no stopping them. She dropped to her knees and wrapped her arms around herself as she bent forward so her forehead rested against the cold ground. The tears loosened the wall she had created to contain everything she'd felt after her two attacks. Suddenly, she was drowning in emotions.

A soft hand came to rest on her back and gently moved in calming circles. "I can take away the pain."

Rhona sniffed and turned her head to the side to see Marcail. Rhona knew everything about the MacLeod Druids since Corann made her study them. The dark-haired Druid who was wife to Quinn MacLeod had the ability to take someone's emotions. It was such a tempting offer that Rhona nearly took it. But as difficult as all of it was to process—especially now—she couldn't do it. "No, thank you."

"Then don't stop the tears. Whatever is bubbling forth is doing so for a reason. Better now than on the battlefield."

Rhona sat up and wiped at the wet tracks on her face. She glanced toward the fire where the others were. No one else had noticed her breakdown, and she was thankful for that. "I don't know what I'm going to do if I don't see him again."

"I remember that feeling well," Marcail said as she sat beside her. "There was a time I fought against the love that'd developed between Quinn and me, but in the end, I knew I was meant to be with him. We were battling Deirdre then, and I wasn't sure if either of us would make it. That kind of fear is debilitating. It robbed me of thought."

"Yes," Rhona said with a nod.

Marcail's turquoise eyes held hers. "I imagine what happened to you in Ireland still weighs upon you, as well."

"It does."

"I'd like to tell you that everything will be okay, but I can't. When we've won the battle, then you can sort through the layers of emotions you feel over your attack."

Rhona nodded in understanding. "But now I need my head in the game."

"I hate to be blunt."

"It's the truth. I won't do anyone any good like this." Rhona got to her feet and dusted herself off. "Corann spoke about Deirdre a few times. How powerful the *drough* was, and that she could've taken over if none of you had fought her."

Marcail shrugged and stood. "She came close to defeating us many times. It felt like we fought against her for decades. We vanquished her because we worked together. Because we trusted each other. We could've remained at MacLeod Castle and said this wasn't our fight, but that isn't who we are. Our Druid culture is fading, as is our magic. One day, it may be gone for good. But I'm not going to sit by and let anyone hasten that along. Especially not some Fae Others."

"I'm glad all of you are here."

"Don't mistake my words, Rhona," Marcail said with a smile. "You and your Skye Druids could probably handle things yourselves. And never forget that Corann chose you to take his place for a reason."

Rhona still wasn't sure why he had.

Marcail's brows drew together. "What is it?"

"I don't have any special magic like you and most of the other Druids on Skye."

"So?" Marcail replied with a shrug.

"It means I'm not that powerful."

A small laugh escaped Marcail. "You underestimate yourself."

Rhona watched the Druid walk away while Marcail's words reverberated in her head. If there was ever a time for her to cut out her fear and fully embrace her role, it was now. The fate of the Reapers and those battling the Fae Others rested on that.

The ground suddenly shook. Rhona looked up as debris fell from the ceiling. The battle had begun.

~

The last time Balladyn had been so eager for battle was when he had been after Usaeil. Before that was when he'd led the Light against the Dark army. He was a warrior, a Fae born for battle, for blood.

For vengeance.

And today, he unleashed his warrior on the soldiers who surrounded him and his brethren.

Today, he would remind anyone who had forgotten who he was.

Balladyn pulled back his lips as he threw an orb of magic and spun to dodge a blow. He called his sword to him, the pommel fitting his hand like a glove. He wielded the blade with precision, slicing the head from a soldier with one blow.

His sword had been formed in the Fires of Erwar and would kill any Fae the instant the weapon scored their skin. It had been a gift from Usaeil when he had become captain of her Queen's Guard. He'd meant to use it to end her life. Now, he wielded it to cut a swath through the rush of soldiers that poured across Skye like a swarm.

The sheer size of the army surprised him. This battle was the one to end them all.

This battle would determine if the Reapers lived or died.

~

"Nothing is working!" Talin yelled.

Cael stared in disbelief at the dome that encompassed Skye. "Keep at it," he ordered the Reapers, who had been using magic to break through it.

They concentrated their efforts on one spot, believing they

could weaken it enough to break it completely—or at least open it enough for them to get through. Yet each orb that connected with the shield sent a blast of red light out before disintegrating. Cael was in shock. Erith's magic was the most formidable he had ever seen. When she gave some of it to each of the Reapers, it made them stronger, faster, and more powerful than any other Fae. Yet the Six had seemed to exceed Erith's power. If they couldn't break through the dome and get to Erith and the rest of the Reapers, then...

"Cael!"

He jerked his head to the side at the sound of Neve's voice. Cael's gaze followed her hand to see the Dragon Kings high in the night sky as clouds blew around them. The wind masked the Kings' arrival. Cael didn't stop lobbing magic at the barrier as the clouds seemed to stop and hover over them.

The Kings began diving from their lofty height and blasting the dome with magic and dragon fire. The fire covered the entire barrier, lighting everything into a reddish-orange hue. Cael thought that might be enough to take it down since nothing survived dragon fire. But it merely shrank the dome.

"Fek me," Cael murmured.

It would take days for the barrier to fall at this rate. What were the Six using to keep it from breaking?

The dragons' angry roars confirmed that they had already seen what little headway they had made.

"Don't stop!" Cael bellowed.

Xaneth's entire body buzzed with the reek of evil that covered Skye. He paused and watched as soldiers poured out to encircle the Reapers. There were so many of the Fae Others. Even after all those he had taken out, Xaneth couldn't believe the number of soldiers he saw now. There were thousands.

The Reapers were far outnumbered. They fought valiantly; their skill showcased in how they worked together. But despite the

Reapers' abilities, the soldiers held their own. Which meant, it was only a matter of time before the soldiers won.

Likely the point of their numbers.

And it infuriated Xaneth.

It was time he joined the Reapers and showed the soldiers—and the Six—that they wouldn't win so easily. Just as Xaneth was about to jump into the fray, the sight of a maroon-skinned man with lightning shooting from his hands and into the soldiers nearest him caught his attention. The soldiers fell, and more men, their skins various colors, joined the battle. Xaneth grinned as he remembered hearing talk of the Warriors. He was finally getting to see them in action.

Xaneth teleported into the melee near Aisling and let out a shout as he threw a blast of magic that killed four soldiers near him.

"About fekking time," she told him.

Xaneth glanced at her, but she didn't look his way. He went back to doing what he did best—killing evil.

CHAPTER THIRTY-EIGHT

Rhona's heart pounded against her ribs in an erratic rhythm. She couldn't stop thinking about Balladyn as he waged war on the Fae Others. Was he injured? Was he still standing? Was he even alive?

Her gaze shifted to the Druids from MacLeod Castle. They stood together stoically after their husbands had gone into battle. Rhona didn't know how they hadn't broken down. She was barely holding it together.

She didn't just worry about Balladyn. It was her Druids, her land.

They were all at Fate's mercy.

Which she didn't like. Why had Skye been chosen? It had to be more than just Sorcha being mated to Cathal. As Balladyn had said, the Fae knew of the Skye Druids, but they essentially ignored them since they couldn't compare to the strength of the Fae.

So, what was it?

Her thoughts turned to Balladyn and how he had heard something across the realms and then found her on the rainy streets in Belfast. And when he braced himself over her in the standing stones and somehow gave her his magic. He was so much more than just a Fae.

Rhona grasped the wall to keep herself standing as it hit her. "It's *him*."

"Who?" Sonya asked, turning her way.

Rhona tried to calm her breathing, but she couldn't quite manage it. Her entire body shook as she faced the Druids. "Balladyn. He's the key."

"To what?" Marcail asked.

Rhona's throat tightened. Her blood ran like ice in her veins. "Everything."

Gwynn frowned as she shook her head. "I don't understand. What are you talking about?"

"This place," Rhona said, waving her arms. "The Fairy Pools. I forgot the story Corann told me a long, long time ago. I forgot it."

The ground shook again. They didn't have time for this, but Rhona had to share what she knew. "I thought it was just a song. Corann used to sing it when he brought Sorcha and me to the pools. It was about a special Fae who was neither Light nor Dark. A Fae the Ancients spoke to. A Fae the Ancients chose as Warden of the Druids."

Marcail and the other Druids stared back at her with a mixture of shock, surprise, and even some doubt.

"He knew where to find me. He shared his magic with me. Inside *me*." Rhona tried to take a breath, but her chest felt as if something were constricting it. "Lena spoke to him. She gave him an ultimatum. Why him? Why has he been able to do everything he's done? Because there is something special about him."

Gwynn raised a dark brow. "With both of you."

"I agree," Marcail, said. "They went to great lengths to remove you. The more you talk, the more I think it's so you and Balladyn couldn't strengthen what's between you. Was there more to the song?"

Rhona closed her eyes and tried to recall it. Corann had sung it so much that she and Sorcha began picking it up. But the harder she tried to remember, the more the words faded. Then her eyes snapped open as Sorcha started to sing.

"Wolves watching amongst the trees
Our enemy surrounds us, silent as a breeze
But one lies in wait, both Dark and Light
A being of two worlds, gifted with might.
The Warden hears from all realms
For Skye's fiery prize is love's helm."

There was silence in the cave before someone murmured, "Bloody hell."

"How did we forget?" Sorcha asked Rhona.

Rhona shrugged. "I don't know."

"It's all there. Everything," Sorcha said.

Marcail asked, "What's the rest of the song? Are there more answers there?"

Sorcha turned to Rhona. "She and Balladyn are the answer."

"I don't understand," Gwynn said.

Rhona licked her lips. "The song is about a union between a Druid from Skye and a powerful being of two worlds."

"Balladyn," Sorcha said. "And Rhona. How else do you explain their connection?"

Isla blew out a breath. "I agree. Rhona, you have to get to Balladyn. He needs to know about this."

Rhona didn't need to be told twice. She ran through the tunnel and up to the hidden entrance behind the waterfall. The sting of the frigid water against her skin was nothing compared to the wind that sucked the air from her lungs. When she emerged, the stench of burnt flesh and the deafening sounds of combat assaulted her.

Above her, snow fell in lazy flurries as if people weren't dying. A flash of light caught her attention. When she looked up, it appeared as if the sky were on fire along the horizon before fading away. A few minutes later, it happened again. She didn't know why the fire hadn't reached them, and she could only hope that it was an ally coming to help and not more enemies.

Rhona rushed past the Warriors and spotted the Skye Druids

coming in droves to circle the battle. Rhona searched the melee for some sign of Balladyn, but she couldn't find him.

"Go!" Marcail yelled from behind her. "Find Balladyn!"

"I should be here!" Rhona said, her ears ringing from the noise. All the Druids were joining together.

Marcail gave her a push. "It's you and Balladyn. Your magic combined and shared."

Rhona's head turned to Sorcha. Her cousin nodded as they gathered in the circle and grabbed the hands of the Druids next to them. Rhona's eyes scanned the many faces of the Skye Druids she had known her entire life. She'd sworn to Corann that she wouldn't let the Druids falter.

She took off running through the solid black throng of soldiers and amongst Warriors and Reapers.

Xaneth knew he was injured, but he didn't feel any of the wounds. Soldier after soldier fell to ash before him. He was determined to kill them all. Then he heard Aisling grunt. His head whipped to the side to see her drop to one knee as three soldiers attacked.

With a growl, he turned toward them and ran the short distance to Aisling. He rammed an orb of magic through one soldier so hard that it passed through him and into the one beside him. Ash filled the air as he turned to the third. He and Aisling delivered simultaneous blows of magic. Their eyes met.

Her gaze shifted over his shoulder as she shoved him out of the way and somersaulted over him. Xaneth fell to the ground and turned to watch as a spike came from the heel of her combat boot and sank into the top of a soldier's head.

Xaneth jumped up and grabbed her as orbs came flying. They landed on the ground, rolling twice before he landed over her, both of them breathing hard. He couldn't believe how close she had come to being killed.

She smiled before darting her eyes to the side. "Xaneth."

In a blink, they were both on their feet, fighting the next wave.

Balladyn had never felt such pain. All he wanted to do was lay down and let himself mend. So many wounds dotted his body that none of them were healing. Worse than that, he hadn't seen the Six.

Something bumped into his back as he pulled his sword from a soldier. Balladyn glanced over his shoulder to see Eoghan, who looked as bad as he felt. A quick scan of the rest of the Reapers showed they were just as battered.

"Where is Cael?" Eoghan shouted.

Balladyn shrugged and pushed off him to swing his sword through the air, cutting a ball of magic in half so it fell harmlessly to the ground. He spun and flung two orbs at a soldier who rushed him. Balladyn dropped to one knee and thrust his sword, the soldier crumbling into ash.

There wasn't time to see to his newest wound as Balladyn got to his feet and met his next opponent. Ruarc shouted his name. Balladyn turned toward the Reaper and caught sight of someone running through the battle. Then he saw red hair.

"Nay," he murmured when he realized that it was Rhona.

Balladyn ran to her, fighting soldiers along the way and praying he got to her before one of them did. His thoughts halted as someone tackled him to the ground. Balladyn yanked his gaze from Rhona as the soldier pushed a ball of magic into his chest.

"Have you made your decision?" the soldier asked.

Balladyn stared into silver eyes and shoved his magic into the soldier's groin. The Fae bellowed in agony as he rolled away. Balladyn vaulted to his feet and drove his sword into the soldier's chest before turning back to the last place he'd seen Rhona.

But she was no longer there.

He hurriedly scanned the battleground, his gaze searching for flaming hair. His chest tightened. She had to be there.

"Rhona!"

Rhona struggled to catch her breath as the soldier slowly walked to her. She had been thrown backward; the air knocked from her lungs. The soldier stood over her, an orb of magic in his hand as his red eyes glittered with excitement. She called to her power. It coursed through her in a rush. She waited until it pooled in her hands. Just as he reared back his arm, she let it fly. Someone came from the side and knocked the soldier to the ground as he had done with her.

She turned her head in time to see Balladyn break the soldier's neck with his bare hands.

Balladyn turned to her. Then, he was beside her, checking her. "Are you injured?"

Rhona shook her head. "I'm fine."

"You shouldn't be here."

"I came to tell you something," she said as he got to his feet and pulled her up with him. "There's a song that C—"

"Now isn't the time," he spoke over her.

Rhona jerked at his arm. He pulled away and faced a soldier. Rhona saw movement out of the corner of her eye and turned to see another coming at her. She shoved her magic at him. The soldier gaped in astonishment before she sent another round, taking his life.

Lightning suddenly struck near her, taking nearly a dozen soldiers at once. She turned to see Malcolm. Lucan was near him, using darkness and shadows to disorient the soldiers before killing them.

Balladyn grabbed her arm and turned her to him. "You need to get with the other Druids."

"I need to be with you."

"It's too dangerous."

She put her hand on his chest. "Lena wants you. You are more than just a Reaper, Balladyn. And she knows it."

His brows snapped together. "What?"

"You giving me your magic? Lena is afraid of that."

Balladyn blinked. "You want me to give you my magic again?"

"I think we're meant to fight her and all of the Fae Others as one. You and me."

He glanced to the side.

Rhona spotted the soldiers coming for them. "Corann used to sing a song to me when I was little. It was you he was singing about. You need to believe me. I know how to defeat the Six."

Balladyn took her hand. "Tell me what to do."

CHAPTER THIRTY-NINE

The relief that went through Rhona was so swift, she swayed. She couldn't help but notice Balladyn's many injuries. She didn't know how he was still standing, but if he could do it, then she would, too. "It's us. Together. Sharing our magic."

"Like at the standing stones."

She nodded.

"I don't know what I did or how I did it," he murmured as his attention turned to the approaching soldiers.

Ice spears from Arran flew from the sky and impaled another group of soldiers.

Rhona was thankful the Warrior had bought them a little more time to talk. "We'll figure it out. Lena wanted me dead. Not to get to the Druids, but to make sure you and I couldn't discover this connection. We're the answer."

"The Six aren't here."

"Oh, they're here," she said with a certainty she couldn't explain.

Balladyn rubbed his chest, a pained look crossing his face. "Aye. You may be right."

A shudder, like fingers from a ghost, scurried down her spine.

She might have figured out what Lena and the Six intended, but Rhona wasn't ready for what came next. The air was pungent with death. And there was no guarantee she would come out the other side of the battle.

Balladyn's expression hardened as he looked over her. "It's time to see if you're right."

Rhona glanced over her shoulder, her stomach dropping to her feet like a stone when she spied six Fae in white robes, standing in a circle. She couldn't see their magic flowing from them, but by their raised hands, she imagined that was exactly what was happening.

"It's the Six," Balladyn said as he moved in front of her, his stance wide as he lifted his sword in his right hand and formed an orb of magic in his left.

How many times could Rhona skirt death? She might have used up all her chances. The fear inside her urged her to run to safety, to get as far from the battle as she could. How would she ever look any of her people in the eye again if she ran from her destiny? She didn't want to die, but this was bigger than her. This was bigger than Balladyn, bigger than the Reapers.

Rhona called to her magic, letting it root her to the isle she loved.

Balladyn looked at her and nodded. "Stay with me."

She had no time to ask what was next when he started toward the Six.

Erith couldn't remember the last time fury had consumed her so completely.

But her anger wasn't alone. Fear nestled securely within her chest, as well.

Cael had yet to answer her calls. The only reason for that was if something prevented him or…if something had happened to him. She refused to believe that she had lost him after all this time.

The fire above continued to engulf the sky but never reached them. It made her wonder if Cael had gotten to the Kings. If that was dragon fire, why weren't they all at the battle? The fact that they weren't could only mean that the Six had made it so no one could get there to help. Erith had tried to teleport out once more but couldn't. And if she couldn't get out, then Cael couldn't get in. No one was going to keep her from her mate.

Erith pulled back her lips as she impaled two soldiers upon her sword. She turned to face her next opponent when she spotted the Six.

They were the ones who wanted her and the Reapers dead. They were the ones who had destroyed countless Fae, upending the careful balance that Erith maintained. It was the Six who had to be stopped. Now. For so long, Erith had sent her Reapers to battle such villains. The Six knew that she was strong, but the Reapers made her stronger. Because they were a team, a family.

One that threatened everything the Six wanted.

Erith should've gone after them herself from the very beginning. She should've known what the Fae Others were about. The Reapers were powerful, quick, and more than experienced. She had taken them for granted.

But if she lost even one of them, she would never forgive herself.

She twisted her wrist as she swung her sword around her. Once, she had been the Mistress of War and had killed indiscriminately. She used to fear that part of herself, dread how out of control she was when she became that person. Cael had told her that she could be both Death *and* the Mistress of War. And she had been with great success.

But the controlled, moralistic goddess of Death had no place on this battlefield.

Lena's gaze found Erith. In the Sixes' eyes, Erith saw the exhilaration for their upcoming clash. Erith felt it, as well. One of them would die tonight.

Erith took a breath as the power of her black sword filled her palm and then rushed through her body. The weapon had taken many lives.

It had one more to claim.

Aisling saw the Six before Xaneth did. She couldn't believe that they were actually there. It was time for the Reapers to take them out. With the Warriors, Druids, and Xaneth joining in, there was no reason they shouldn't be triumphant.

"No," Xaneth bellowed as he grabbed Aisling's hand and yanked her back when she would've teleported to the Six.

She spun to him. "Let me go."

"They'll kill you if you go."

"As long as I take at least one of them with me, that's fine."

A muscle in his jaw tensed. He said nothing as he moved around her to face the soldiers who had come up behind her. Aisling debated leaving Xaneth with them while she went after the Six. But she couldn't do it.

"Fek!" she yelled and threw a ball of magic into the back of a soldier's head.

She spun to face her next foe when something knocked her breath from her. Aisling glanced down to see the wound in her chest. At first, she felt nothing. It was like she was looking at someone else. In the next second, agony swallowed her.

Her knees gave out as Dark magic sizzled through her flesh and muscle to finally sink through her ribcage. She landed hard on her back. Her heart struggled to continue beating, her lungs fought for air.

She looked around at her fellow Reapers. They were all covered in dirt and blood. Each of them had copious wounds, but they kept fighting. Aisling spotted Erith as the goddess stalked toward the Six. It would be an epic fight, and she wished she could take part or even see it.

Aisling wanted to tell Erith how much being a Reaper meant to her. She wanted to let her brethren know how much she loved them. Unfortunately, she had wasted every chance she had.

Xaneth. She tried to locate him with her eyes, but she couldn't find him. She wouldn't know what to say to him if she did.

She turned her eyes to the sky, wanting to see the stars one last time. Instead, she saw fire spreading across it. She gasped for breath. Her body wasn't healing. The magic she'd been struck with was different. She needed to tell the Reapers and Erith what to expect.

Aisling used every bit of energy to part her lips. She tried to scream a warning, but her voice only made a scratching noise that no one would hear over the battle. A tear escaped. She had always known that she would die in battle. Alone.

The edges of her vision started to blur. Her eyes wanted to close, but she forced them to remain open as if that would somehow help her transition into death.

Someone stood over her. It took effort to focus on their face. They were yelling at her angrily. Try as she might, she couldn't understand their words. Her lids closed, no longer able to remain open.

"Aisling!"

Was that Xaneth? Or was she hearing what she wanted to hear?

That had been her life from the very beginning. She always seemed one step behind in everything.

She was drifting into the darkness. It wasn't as cold as she'd thought it would be. Maybe she had no reason to fear it. Perhaps she would finally find the peace she never thought she deserved.

"Nayyyyy!" Xaneth shouted as he straddled Aisling.

Everything he did to wake her failed. The wound was horrible. He glanced at Lena. The bitch had delivered the blow to Aisling. He wanted to make Lena pay for that and all that she stood for.

If he did, it meant that Aisling would die.

He was meant to take out evil, and there was nothing more wicked than the Six and their soldiers that surrounded him right then. The monster inside demanded he soak himself in blood, insisted that he end the vile Fae Others.

A tiny part of the old him that remained pleaded for him to get Aisling to safety and heal her. Xaneth knew that Aisling wouldn't leave him if the situation were reversed. She would protect him, shield him.

That was when he realized why he didn't want her around. She made him remember the Fae he'd once been. Did he end the Six and lose Aisling? Or did he save her and find the Six later?

Xaneth threw back his head and roared his frustration. Then he gathered Aisling's limp body in his arms and teleported to a nearby mountain.

Lena smiled in glee. Everything was going just as she wanted. The other Six had been shocked and concerned to see the Warriors on Skye, but they didn't bother her. At least they wouldn't once she completed her final act as leader of the Six and became the empress of the Fae Others, and then the Fae.

She wished her ancestors were there to see that she was the one who'd achieved what they couldn't. She was the one the rest of her family had overlooked, the one they considered odd and different. The one they had urged to be more like them.

Lena was tired of being what everyone else wanted. She had never belonged in her family, and she hadn't understood why until she discovered her lineage. It appalled her to see how far her family had gone to erase the past and their relatives. Once she embraced the truth of what she felt within her, she had found her way.

And that way was taking her to a place where no one would be able to topple her.

Not even a goddess.

Misery and panic thudded along with Cael's heart. The Reapers and Dragon Kings should've been able to break through the dome by now.

"Nothing is working."

He glanced over his shoulder to see Ulrik. Cael thought of Erith, of the Reapers within. "We're not giving up."

"I didna say we were," Ulrik snapped. "I'm stating a fact. We need to come up with something else."

Cael spun on him. "What else?" he yelled. "All the Skye Druids are trapped in there. The Warriors and Druids of MacLeod Castle. The Reapers. Erith. If we don't get to them, they'll die."

"We're doing this wrong," Fintan said as he teleported to them.

Ulrik turned his head to him. "What do you mean?"

"We're using our magic but not together. The Six are combining theirs. So should we," Fintan explained.

Cael should've thought of that sooner, but he'd been too consumed with getting back to Erith.

"I've got an idea," Ulrik said with a smile right before touching the silver cuff at his wrist and teleporting out.

Cael turned to Fintan. "Good thinking."

No sooner had he finished talking than Ulrik returned with his mate, Eilish. Beside the powerful Druid was Darcy, Faith, Devon, Esther, Gemma, Claire, and Bernadette. All Dragon King mates who were either Druids or had a connection to Druids.

"What the hell?" Darcy asked as she looked around.

Cael called to the rest of the Reapers just as the Dragon Kings landed and began shifting into human form. "As long as this barrier is up, no one can get through it or out of it."

"The battle is raging," Ulrik stated. "We need to get to them to help."

Eilish flicked back her long, dark hair. "Oh, we're about to."

"If the Others could combine Fae and Druid magic, I can no' wait to see what Reaper, Druid, and Dragon King magic can do together," Ulrik said with a smirk.

Cael nodded as he thought of Erith. "Let's find out, shall we?"

CHAPTER FORTY

Balladyn's head snapped to the side when he heard the roar of anger. He spotted Xaneth just before the Fae teleported away with Aisling. Balladyn hoped that Aisling was all right, but he couldn't think about that now. He had to keep Rhona safe.

And alive.

What she had told him had left him cold. He had known there was something about Skye and the Druids that the Fae Others wanted. Now, he knew. That didn't make things any easier, though. He had no idea how he would transfer his magic to Rhona. He wasn't sure how he had done it the first time. Then there was the ache in his chest that was intensifying rapidly.

Reaching the Six wasn't quick. Opposition met him and Rhona every few steps. Though he had been worried about her, she stood her ground against the soldiers. Still, Balladyn made sure he kept her within view.

The Reapers might be injured, but they were all still on their feet. Barely. Balladyn remained standing by sheer will alone. The Warriors made an impact with the soldiers, but even they sported wounds. Balladyn couldn't wait until the Druids joined in. Then, the Six would really get to see a show.

"Balladyn," Rhona called.

He turned his head to look in the direction she pointed. Erith stalked toward the Six while Lena watched her with a smile.

Balladyn opened his mouth to alert the other Reapers when the Six turned their power on Erith. The goddess lifted her sword as the magic slammed into her. She leaned into it as it pushed her back, her feet sliding on the ground. An eerie, red light shimmered around the area where the Sixes' magic clashed with Erith's sword.

The Six then sent blasts at each of the Reapers. Balladyn saw it coming and tried to prepare. He reached for Rhona, but she was too far away. Balladyn raised his magic as a shield, but the Six tore through it easily, sending him sprawling backward, his head banging against a rock.

The sight of so many Reapers knocked to the ground at once shook Rhona. She glanced at Balladyn, fully expecting him to still be standing. Instead, she found him lying still with his eyes closed.

The moment she took her eyes off the soldier she had been fighting, he used the distraction to his advantage and struck her with several orbs. The first hit was at her knees, knocking her legs out from under her. The second came at her face, but she turned away so that it smashed into her shoulder instead, the force of it sending her onto her back.

The pain was unimaginable.

Her muscles seized, and her lungs battled for breath. Her heart raced. Her brain wanted to focus on the anguish of her wounds, but she called to her magic to calm and steady herself. She was dying. Nothing could save her now, but she could help Balladyn.

Tears from the pain fell freely as she turned her head to look at the man who had her heart. She was surprised to find that he was close enough to touch. All she had to do was reach out her hand a little more. When she tried, more pain radiated from her injuries. She cried out, unable to stop herself.

"Balladyn," she said as she blinked through her tears and focused on his face. "Come back. I need you."

Rhona was glad that no soldiers came to finish her. Maybe they didn't think she was worth it. Hopefully, this time would be the downfall of them all.

"Balladyn," she called louder. "Open your eyes for me now." When he didn't, she squeezed hers closed as a fresh wave of tears came. "I love you. I should've told you so many times. I need you now."

When she opened her eyes, he was staring at her.

～

"I love you."

Rhona's voice pulled Balladyn to consciousness. His eyes jerked open to find her lying near him, crying. Then she looked at him.

She smiled through her tears. "I knew you'd hear me. Reach out to me."

He winced at the pain in the back of his head as he rose on an elbow. That's when he saw the wound on her shoulder. Worry shot through him. Balladyn scooted closer to her in a panic. He held his hands over her injury, trying to think of a spell that would stop the pain and allow her to heal. But his mind was blank.

"It's okay," she said.

Balladyn lifted his gaze to hers. "How can you say that?"

"Because I know what to do."

Her face was so very pale. He wanted to get her somewhere safe and find Druids who could save her. Balladyn looked around, but he didn't see the other Reapers. Erith still battled against the Sixes' magic. The Warriors were in serious trouble, with several lying still on the ground. The Druids had taken their places, encircling the battle, standing three-deep. Yet it didn't look as if their magic affected the Six at all. Even he couldn't feel it.

"Balladyn."

Rhona sounded so calm. He lowered his gaze to her. She was

dying. After saving her twice, he wasn't about to lose her now. "You need to help."

"I need you. Take my hands."

"We don't have time for this." But he still did as she asked.

Rhona's lips lifted in a grin. "Trust me."

He stared into her beautiful green eyes. She had told him that she loved him. Of all the people she could have given her heart to, she had chosen him. "I do."

"I know," she whispered.

"I saved you before. I can do it again."

"This time, I'm saving you."

He didn't know what she meant until he felt something move from her hands into him. Her Druid magic. He gaped at her. "Rhona, no."

"Lena feared exactly this. Show her why."

Balladyn closed his eyes as her unique magic swam through him, touching and twining with his. It was exhilarating. And terrifying. He'd only ever known his magic, but now he knew what Rhona's felt like. His tired, bruised, and broken body was suddenly hale and hearty, feeling as if he had rested for a week. Balladyn glanced down to see his wounds healing faster than ever.

"Go rid the world of the Six," Rhona said.

Balladyn looked at her and shook his head. "We do it together."

As he said the words, he pushed his magic into her. Rhona gasped, first in shock and then in pain. Her body stiffened before her muscles softened to relax. Her shoulder wound began mending, as did the one on her knee. His gaze skidded back to her face as the color returned rapidly.

He waited until her injuries had mended before holding out his hand. "Ready?"

"Oh, yes."

Balladyn got to his feet and pulled Rhona up with him. The soldiers were intent on the Warriors, who were doing their best to keep them away from the Druids. The Six put everything they had into fighting Erith, which meant no one paid attention to either of them or the Reapers.

He and Rhona walked together, hand-in-hand toward the Six. Balladyn paused along the way to squat next to Cathal, who was beginning to stir. When his fellow Reaper opened his eyes, Balladyn said, "Be ready."

He nodded before teleporting to Bradach. Balladyn straightened. The Six and their soldiers had thought that one blast of magic could keep a Reaper down. They'd underestimated the Reapers, and that would be their downfall.

He didn't understand how his and Rhona's magic passed through each of them freely, but it did. Not only that, he felt even stronger, as well. Who would've thought that a Druid's magic could strengthen his? Certainly not him. He glanced at Rhona.

"I feel it, too." She looked at him before returning her gaze to the Six. "I don't know what to do, but I know we have to go to them."

He nodded. "Aye."

~

The sight of her Reapers going down enraged Erith. Her sword blocked the magic of the Six, but she couldn't make any headway. At this rate, there would be a stalemate unless someone could get in a hit.

And she really wanted it to be her.

Movement caught Erith's attention. She looked to the side and saw Balladyn and Rhona. The two looked different. There was a faint, shimmery glow around them. Balladyn's clothes were singed, but he was healed. Same with Rhona. Erith swung her gaze to the Druids and wondered if they had something to do with it. She then looked at the Six. They didn't seem fazed by the Druids standing against them.

A curious look came over Lena's face before she took a step back from the circle of the Six. Erith watched as Lena killed the rest of the Six with a snap of her fingers, their magic flying toward her with gale-force speed. Lena spread her arms and welcomed the magic as it slammed into her.

Erith caught herself before she fell forward as the magic that had been trained on her vanished. She adjusted her grip on her sword and started toward Lena again but halted at the sight of Balladyn and Rhona.

This was it. What she was meant to do. Rhona's body vibrated with energy and power. She was here but not. The intensity of Balladyn's magic was more intoxicating than she remembered. The pain that had consumed her was a distant memory.

A calm had come over her ever since Balladyn had shared his magic. It was almost as if an invisible gateway existed between the two of them that allowed their magic to pass easily and freely from one to the other. This was something more, something entirely different and unexpected.

Something formidable.

Yet she wasn't afraid. Not of the power, not of Balladyn or facing Lena. She had always thought herself inferior to other Druids because she had no special ability. But she did. And it was one that no one else had ever brandished before.

The sight of Lena taking the lives and magic of her counterparts didn't surprise Rhona. Lena would be incredibly strong. Violently so. As if reading her mind, Balladyn's hand tightened around hers.

"What is this?" Lena demanded as she faced them.

Rhona met the Fae's gaze. "What you feared."

"If you knew the power racing through me right now, you'd know I'm frightened of nothing."

Rhona shrugged one shoulder. "That's why you went to such lengths to have me killed."

Lena rolled her red eyes. "It would've made things simpler."

The Druids' chants grew louder, swirling all around Rhona and Balladyn, wrapping them in the special magic that had always existed on Skye.

"Don't fight it," Rhona whispered to Balladyn.

Balladyn was startled at the rush of Druid magic that came up from the ground. More came from the sky and every direction. With each surge, his Reaper magic answered. Rising, expanding. Intensifying. The air hummed with it. He could hear the Druids' chants, the spell forming in his mind before they even spoke it.

"Enough of this," Lena said and struck out.

Balladyn casually lifted a hand and stopped Lena's orb in midair.

The Fae's eyes narrowed as she glared at them. "Looks like I need to take your magic as I've done with the others. I warned you, Balladyn. You chose the wrong side."

"I chose the only side," he replied.

He began forming an orb, and Rhona joined him.

Lena lifted her hand to snap her fingers. As one, Balladyn and Rhona threw the ball of magic. It sailed through the air and hit Lena on her left hand. The skin immediately turned black. She howled in agony and rage as the hand withered and turned to dust. She stopped it from going further with magic.

"No," Lena murmured. Panic slid over her face as she looked at her missing hand. "It's not possible." Lena looked at them and screamed, "You'll pay for that."

Rhona raised a brow. "You wanted this fight. We're going to finish it."

Balladyn motioned for Lena to come at them. "What are you waiting for?"

The Druids' chants grew louder as the wind lashed angrily over the land. A clap of thunder filled the air, followed by dragon roars. Erith and the Reapers came to stand on either side of Balladyn and Rhona.

It was as if all the magic of Skye and the Druids flowed through Balladyn, into Rhona, and then back again on an endless loop. Everything became clear. His journey as a captain of the Queen's Guard for the Light, as King of the Dark, and then as a Reaper. He had been meant to experience all of it, each part of the voyage building and bringing him to this moment.

He had been searching to find himself, to discover where he belonged. When, all along, he had been becoming…*this*. He wasn't quite sure what this was yet, but he knew it was where he belonged. On Skye.

With Rhona.

Balladyn felt her gaze on him. He turned to her as her red hair billowed gently around her. No words passed between them, but he didn't need them. He knew what she was thinking, just as she knew his mind. She began to form a ball of magic that hovered between them. He grew it with her, and for the first time, he really looked at it. It wasn't iridescent as all Fae orbs were. This one swirled green and white. As different as he was.

Balladyn reared back his hands and hurled the ball toward Lena. She raised a shield of magic, just in time. It managed to slow the orb. Balladyn watched as his and Rhona's magic gradually slid through Lena's defenses. Lena screeched in fury.

Rhona smiled at her. "Ready for more?"

Lena shot them a lingering glare as Erith threw her sword at her. The Dragon Kings were headed toward her. Balladyn smiled as he saw the demise of the Fae. He didn't care who delivered the killing blow as long as it was done.

Lena had one more surprise up her sleeve, though, as she managed to teleport away.

CHAPTER FORTY-ONE

The power was heady as it flowed through Rhona. But more than that, she felt as if she were one with Skye. The only thing that marred the moment was that Lena had gotten away, living to fight another day.

Her skin heated at the touch of Balladyn's gaze. Rhona slid her attention to him. She gaped at the sight of his silver eyes ringed in dark crimson. "What happened?"

"I was hoping you'd tell me."

They reached for each other at the same time, their hands joining. When her feet left the ground, she gripped his fingers tighter.

"Are you doing this?" she asked.

Balladyn nodded toward the Druids as their ascent continued. "I think it's them."

Tears stung her eyes when she heard the drums of the Ancients. They were thunderous, but Rhona didn't care. She basked in the sound. Then she realized that Balladyn could hear them, too.

"We've been waiting for this day," the voices of the Ancients said. *"The battle is far from over."*

"We'll be ready," Balladyn replied.

Rhona looked over the isle of Skye from her vantage point. She no longer felt the cold or the wind. She was exhilarated. She took in the ground littered with ash and corpses. What soldiers remained had left with Lena. Rhona's smile faded when she saw the wounds on the Reapers, Warriors, and even some Druids. Balladyn's attention remained skyward. Rhona looked up to see the Dragon Kings circling and weaving through the night sky.

The drums began to fade, and with them, she and Balladyn floated back to the ground. The wind died, and everything returned to normal. Almost immediately, each of the Dragon Kings shifted and landed around them.

Rhona parted her lips to speak. There was so much she wanted to say to Balladyn.

"I love you," he said before she could. "I think I've always loved you. I just didn't know where to find you."

She laughed softly. "I love you so much I'm bursting with it."

His lips curved into a smile as he caressed his fingers down the side of her face. "There's so much I want to say."

"Me, too." Rhona saw others approaching out of the corner of her eye. "Everyone is going to have questions."

Amusement filled Balladyn's red-ringed, silver eyes. "I confess, I do, too."

"Someone want to tell me what I just witnessed?" Rordan asked.

Rhona glanced at the Reaper, but Erith snagged her attention. The goddess and Cael stood, embracing each other in solitude.

"We couldn't get in," Daire explained. "Our magic couldn't touch whatever barrier Lena erected."

Rhys grunted as he crossed his arms over his chest. "Nor ours."

"It took all of us together," Eilish said with a grin. "We took a page from the Others and combined our magic."

Anson looked around and shrugged. "It appears as if the Kings were no' needed."

"You were," Sorcha said as she finally walked up, holding Cathal's hand. She gazed at Rhona. "I…"

Rhona nodded, understanding her cousin's shock. "Me, too."

"There are a lot of people wanting an explanation," Ruarc said as he leaned heavily on his mate, Chevonne, as his wounds healed.

Rhona slid her gaze to Balladyn. He gave her a nod as Erith and Cael finally broke apart and joined them. The Druids moved closer, as well.

Erith's lavender gaze came to rest on Rhona. She cleared her throat and released one of Balladyn's hands to face the crowd before her. "Corann used to sing a song to Sorcha and me. I had forgotten it, but there was a reason he sang it to us. Because it involved a special Fae." She looked at Balladyn. "One who isn't only Fae. One of the Light and the Dark. One who is something much more."

"I'll be damned," Cael murmured.

Rhona smiled as she stared into Balladyn's eyes. The connection between them was so new that she was still getting used to the sensations—but loving every moment of it.

"I was only part of it," Balladyn said. "Rhona was the other. It's why Lena wanted her dead. Without her, none of what you saw could've happened."

Fintan smoothed his white hair away from his face. "For those of us who missed it, what happened?"

"When Balladyn shared his magic with me in the standing stones, it showed us what was possible. And what we had to do to fight Lena," Rhona explained.

Eoghan blinked. "That's what we saw? You combining your magic?"

"Not combining. Sharing," Balladyn corrected.

Rhona nodded. "Mine flows into him, and his into me."

"Even now?" Erith asked.

Balladyn bowed his head. "Even now."

"He's the Warden," a Druid in the back shouted.

Marcail smiled. "From the song you sang us earlier. It was a prophecy."

"Interesting," Ulrik said as he exchanged a look with the other Dragon Kings. "Rhi is going to be sad that she missed all of this."

Cathal grunted. "I hate to piss on things, but we didn't win."

"Nay, but Lena was terrified of what she saw with these two," Eoghan said as he nodded at Balladyn and Rhona.

"Aisling," Balladyn suddenly said.

The Reapers frowned, looking for her.

"I saw Xaneth leave with her. She was badly injured," Torin said.

Erith nodded. "We'll find her."

"Thank you," Rhona said as she let her gaze move over the Druids, Warriors, Reapers, and Dragon Kings. "The Six brought this fight to Skye, and with everyone's help, we held them back."

Eoghan's lips twisted. "And delivered a vicious wound to her."

"We might not have won, but there are two things she's scared of," Ruarc said. He looked at Rhona and Balladyn. "These two and Xaneth."

Erith lifted her chin. "The next battle will be on our terms."

Rhona suddenly feared that Erith would call Balladyn and the Reapers away. She tightened her fingers around his, causing his gaze to swing to her.

"I know," he said in a low voice.

It felt as if everyone were staring at her. Rhona wanted to get far from everyone so she could talk to Balladyn. She had no idea what would happen going forward. She knew what she wanted, but that didn't mean it would happen. Balladyn was the Warden, but he was also a Reaper. She didn't imagine that Erith would release him from his obligation simply because of what had happened on Skye.

"We can help clean up," one of the Dragon Kings offered.

Fallon said, "I'll start returning the Skye Druids to their homes."

Rhona's heart began to thump in her chest. Balladyn's thumb caressed the back of her hand, but it didn't calm her. She knew what was coming, and she wasn't sure she could handle it.

"Take Rhona home," Cael told Balladyn. "I'm sure the two of you would like to be alone."

Thankfully, Balladyn didn't wait. They were at the pools one moment, and the next, they stood in Rhona's cottage. Balladyn yanked her against him, his arms wrapping securely around her. She closed her eyes and savored the feel of him.

"I'm ashamed to say I used to discount Druid magic," he said after a short time. "The feel of it tonight was something I can't put into words. Strong and yet soft. Resilient but tranquil."

She nodded in agreement. "The first time I felt your Fae magic, it made me feel as if every nerve ending was crackling with power."

"Aye. Exactly."

Rhona leaned back to look at him. "Your eyes have changed."

"What?" He frowned. "How?"

"They're silver and ringed with red now."

He thought about that for a moment and then shrugged. "It makes sense. I feel different."

"So do I," she said with a grin.

"I'm glad you remembered Corann's song."

She ran her hands over his upper chest. "Me, too. Though I'm sure we would've figured it out without that. Once I saw Lena, and the Druids started chanting, it was like I knew exactly what to do."

"I wish we would've been able to end Lena's reign tonight."

"We'll get another chance."

He quirked a black brow. "Will we?"

"Hmm," she said, wrinkling her nose. "Perhaps we only work on Skye."

"What is a Warden supposed to do?"

She shrugged and rose to press her lips to his. "I don't know exactly. The song doesn't go into it. Maybe be more of a guardian?"

"You and the Druids do that just fine."

"It could be because these were special circumstances."

He glanced away. "Perhaps."

Silence filled the cottage. Neither of them wanted to bring up the one thing that both wanted to know—how they were going to be together.

It wasn't in Rhona's nature to ignore something, and while it was nice to pretend that she could have her happily ever after, the truth would find her eventually. It was better to meet it head-on. "What happens now? Will you return to wherever it is the Reapers go?"

"I gave Erith my vow. I'm a Reaper until I die."

Even though she had known that would be his answer, hearing the words made her throat clog with hurt, anger, and soul-crushing desolation.

"And you?" he asked. "Will you stay here?"

She blinked to hold back her tears. "Corann trusted me to lead my people."

"Which leaves us nowhere."

Rhona swiped at a tear that escaped. Balladyn pulled her back into his arms. The minute her cheek met his chest, she began to cry silently. How could she have found someone so perfect, only to lose him?

"I'll return often," Balladyn whispered against her hair. "I'll hear your call no matter where I am. Fate has deemed that connection."

It was a far cry from what she wanted but something was better than nothing. She sniffed. "We'll make it work."

They clung to each other for long minutes. Only the knock on her door roused them.

"Ignore it," Rhona murmured. "I don't want to be bothered."

Balladyn sighed. "It's Erith and Cael."

Perfect. So, they were calling him away already. Couldn't they at least give them the rest of the night? Resentment flooded Rhona as she released Balladyn and stalked to the door. She yanked it open to find the couple before her. They were in clean clothes, all signs of battle erased.

"May we come in?" Erith asked.

Rhona wanted to slam the door in their faces, but that would be childish and petulant. Besides, they could've teleported inside her home. They had been courteous enough to knock. She forced herself to step aside and allow them to enter.

The heaviness in Rhona's chest made her want to double over and scream at the unfairness of Balladyn being taken from her. But how could she put all the blame on him? Was he asking why she couldn't hand things over to someone else and go with him?

Nothing about this was just or right.

The only way she would get through this was by detaching

herself. Because she refused to fall apart until she was alone. Rhona found a spot on the rug and stared at it, concentrating on holding back her tears.

"We wanted to give both of you more time, but we thought it would be better to talk to you sooner rather than later," Cael said.

Rhona crossed her arms over her chest. Her anger spilled over, and before she could stop herself, she said, "You just had to come get him now."

"Is that what you think?" Erith asked softly.

Rhona didn't bother to look at the goddess. Hadn't her words and tone said it all?

"I can see that you do." Erith let out a long breath. "I thought I had lost Cael when he wouldn't answer my call. I was…beside myself."

Cael wrapped an arm around her shoulders and kissed her temple. "I was a crazy man. Unable to think straight or make a coherent decision when I couldn't get to Erith. All I wanted was her."

"Sorcha sang me the entire song. It's about both of you. There's no doubt in our minds," Erith said.

Cael made a sound in the back of his throat. "Not that we doubted it after seeing the two of you fighting Lena."

"That orb." Erith shook her head, her brows raised. "It was a mix of Reaper and Druid magic. I've always known you were something more, Balladyn. This showed everyone."

Rhona tried to ignore the hope that rose inside her. She looked at Balladyn to find him staring at her. The love shining in his eyes made tears overflow her lashes and drop onto her cheeks.

"You are my Reaper," Erith continued. "But you are also part of the Skye Druids."

Balladyn yanked his gaze from Rhona to look at the goddess. "What are you saying?"

"Your place is on Skye for as long as you want it to be." Erith turned her head to Rhona and smiled before looking at Balladyn again. "There will be times I'll call on you."

Balladyn nodded quickly. "You know I'll answer. I gave you my vow."

"Of course, Rhona will be allowed on our realm," Erith added.

Rhona was floored. She raced to him as they happily held each other.

"How could we break this apart?" Cael asked.

Rhona hoped he didn't want an answer because Balladyn had lowered his lips to hers, and all she wanted was to feel him inside her.

"I think it's time we go," Erith said.

Balladyn didn't wait for them to leave as he jumped them into Rhona's bathroom. He removed their clothes with magic and jumped them beneath already hot, running water. He pushed her against the wall and pressed his body against hers.

Rhona moaned at the feel of his arousal between them. She looped a leg around his hip to bring him closer. His mouth found hers again, the kiss passionate and scorching. She was on fire with need, a hunger he had awoken inside her.

Balladyn lifted her, holding her above his erection. He ended the kiss and looked into her eyes as he slowly lowered her. Rhona sighed in ecstasy. He felt so good, so right.

"I love you," Balladyn said as he began to move.

She touched his face, her heart full. "I love you."

EPILOGUE

Balladyn stood outside to greet the morning sun. After hours of lovemaking, Rhona was sleeping soundly. He breathed in the crisp winter air. So many had no idea how close they had come to death last night. If he hadn't answered the pull and found Rhona on the streets of Belfast, if he hadn't remembered the spell to slow her bleeding, if he hadn't gone to her in the standing stones, then Lena would've won.

Lena's magic had been strong before she'd taken the rest of the Sixes'. After consuming their power, she would likely be difficult to kill. He and Rhona might have struck her, but she was still alive. Which meant she remained a threat. At least, Rhona and Skye were safe.

And would remain that way for as long as he lived.

He heard the door open and glanced over his shoulder to see Rhona with a blanket wrapped around her. She opened her arms as she came up behind him and wound them around his waist, enfolding him in the cover with her.

"I wondered where you'd gone," she murmured sleepily.

"I didn't want to wake you."

She rested her cheek against his back. "I'd rather wake up beside you."

Balladyn grinned as he covered her hands with his. "I agree."

"I can't believe you get to stay."

He felt her smile against him. "Happy?"

"Deliriously so. You?"

"Undeniably." He turned to face her.

Rhona's green eyes crinkled with her smile. "You being here could facilitate the Druids' renewed friendship with the Fae."

"You want that?" he asked in surprise.

She twisted her lips. "It's something to think about."

"Aye." Just as soon as they took care of Lena.

"For now, I'd like you to come back to bed."

Balladyn chuckled as he touched his nose to her cold one. "You are chilly."

He jumped them to bed, burying them beneath the covers. Rhona curled against him and was asleep again within seconds. Balladyn drew in a deep breath and slowly released it. So, this was what happiness felt like. He could definitely get used to it.

Xaneth tried again and again to wake Aisling. Her wound wasn't healing. He began to wonder if he'd made the right decision in taking her from the Reapers. It might have been better to turn her over to Erith. The goddess would've known what to do.

"You're a fighter," he told Aisling as he carefully moved one of her long braids away from her face. "So, fight."

He'd never felt so helpless, so powerless. Why had he thought that he could help Aisling? Lena's magic was something else entirely now. If she could do this to Aisling, what would Lena do to others?

But Xaneth knew the answer.

He studied Aisling's chest. It wasn't moving. He shook his head. She couldn't be gone. She just couldn't be. She was evocative and vigorous, fierce and remarkable. There should be more like Aisling in the world. It wasn't fair that Lena had extinguished her flame.

Xaneth stumbled to his feet. He knew what he was. He had accepted it and taken to his path eagerly. Aisling had brought back a fleck of light to his life once more. Now that, too, was gone.

"Nay!" he shouted and slammed his fist against the side of the cave.

He didn't stop the magic that shot through him and spread through the space. His attention was on his quarry. Only one person would pay for taking Aisling from him—Lena.

Xaneth was about to teleport out when he heard Aisling draw in a breath.

~

Aisling gasped as air filled her lungs. Her eyes snapped open only to find herself staring up at the curved ceiling of a dark cave. For a moment, she'd thought someone had been with her, but she heard nothing but her breathing.

She tentatively touched her chest to find her injury healing. Aisling tried to remember what had happened after she'd fallen unconscious on the battlefield, but she had no memories. She had no idea where she was or how she had gotten there.

Her mind raced as her body finished mending. She climbed to her feet and glanced down at her chest. The hole in her clothes was massive. The hit she had taken had been lethal. Of that, she was sure. So, how was she alive?

Aisling?

Eoghan's voice in her head startled her. She replaced her clothing with a thought then looked around the cave. She wasn't alone. She could send out magic and make whoever it was reveal themselves, but she didn't feel they were a threat. Though she wished they would make themselves known. Why did they want to remain secret?

She wanted to stay and find out, but the need to discover what had happened during the battle—especially to Xaneth—made her decision for her.

"Xaneth?" she said, wondering if he was there.

She shook her head as soon as she said his name. Of course, it wasn't him. He would be long gone and as far from her as possible. He would only associate with her during battle. Aisling frowned, once again wondering how she had ended up wherever this was. What about her family? Were they safe? Was the threat of the Six gone?

With one last look at the cave, she teleported to Eoghan.

Kerry looked at Rhona and Balladyn as they stood before her cell. She had felt the tremors of the battle. Though she was in the Red Hills because of her actions, she was angry that she hadn't been allowed to fight next to her people. It was a vicious slight. Everyone would've noticed her absence.

"I love Skye. I love my people," she said. "I've only ever wanted what was best for us."

Rhona's lips flattened. "I know."

"You're worried I'll turn on you again." Kerry should've known that Rhona would think that.

Rhona didn't pull any punches as she nodded. "It has crossed my mind."

"Lena used me," Kerry argued. "You read my emails. I defended us. I defended *you*."

"Until you didn't. However, Lena went to great lengths to kill me."

Kerry held her breath. She couldn't lose her place on Skye. She wouldn't know what to do with herself if she did. "Rhona, I'm loyal to you and the Skye Druids."

"I'm going to release you and allow you to remain on Skye."

"Thank you. Thank you so much." The relief made her lightheaded. She had thought Rhona would say something else. Kerry tried to walk out of her cell, but the magic kept her in place. She frowned as she looked at Rhona. "What is it?"

"There's a condition."

Kerry steeled herself. "And that is?"

"You'll step down as deputy. Someone else will take your place."

Arguments rushed to Kerry's lips. How would it look that she was no longer there for her people to turn to? On the other hand, Rhona was allowing her to stay on Skye—her home. As much as it hurt her pride, Kerry nodded. "Fair enough."

Rhona reached up and dropped her hand straight down while chanting two words. Kerry felt the air shift, and this time when she tried to walk out of the cavern, she was able.

She went to stand before Rhona. "I'll never do anything to harm anyone again. You have my word as a Druid."

"I'll hold you to that," Rhona said.

Kerry glanced at Balladyn, who hadn't uttered a word the entire time. Then she started toward the tunnel. She didn't get two steps before she found herself back in her cottage. Kerry looked around, but she was alone. At least she thought she was. She shivered. The Fae were on Skye once more. It didn't matter that they were Reapers. They were still Fae.

She went to her bedroom and changed. Tomorrow was the beginning of a new era for her. How would she ever face the others? There would be so many questions. She didn't want to lie, but she couldn't tell anyone the truth.

"This isn't fair," Kerry murmured.

She hadn't done anything wrong. She had stood up for Rhona, and for Skye. They should be praising her, not taking away her role as a deputy.

"I was used."

Anger bubbled the more she thought about it. The Fae Others had manipulated her. She was a victim. Why wasn't Rhona comforting her instead of censuring her? No, it wasn't fair. Not after everything Kerry had done for Skye and every Druid on the island. How dare they do this to her?

The room thudded with the sound of drums before a multitude of Ancient voices sounded. Kerry jerked back with her hands over her ears, terror holding her firmly in its grip. She squeezed her eyes closed as she began to shake. Try as she might, she couldn't make out what the Ancients were saying.

Suddenly, the many voices halted until there was only one.

"You were used. What kind of Druid are you?"

Kerry's hands fell away as she blinked at the clear, concise voice. "I'm a Skye Druid." She used the wall to get to her feet. "And I'm never going to forget that again."

~

Thank you for reading **DARK ALPHA'S COMMAND**! I hope you loved Balladyn and Rhona's story as much as I loved writing it. Next up in the Dark World is the first in the new Skye Druids series, IRON EMBER.

Magic reigns and danger abounds.

Buy IRON EMBER now at
https://donnagrant.com/books/iron-ember/

~

If you love the Reaper series, you are in for the exciting series finale, DARK ALPHA'S FURY…

Buy DARK ALPHA'S FURY today at
https://donnagrant.com/books/dark-alphas-fury/

To find out when new books release
SIGN UP FOR MY NEWSLETTER today at
http://www.tinyurl.com/DonnaGrantNews.

Join my Facebook group, Donna Grant Groupies, for exclusive
giveaways and sneak peeks of future books.

Keep reading for an excerpt from IRON EMBER, a sneak peek of
DRAGON LOVER, and a glimpse at DARK ALPHA'S FURY…

EXCERPT OF IRON EMBER
SKYE DRUIDS SERIES, BOOK 1

Delve into the thrilling first installment of the all-new Skye Druids series by *New York Times* bestselling author Donna Grant, where magic reigns and danger abounds.

Skye isn't just an island. It's a home. A refuge. But not to Elodie MacLean. Not anymore. Tragedy tore her world apart and then took the one thing she felt made her whole. She vowed she'd never return, but that's exactly where she ends up. Now, surrounded by the ghosts of her past, Elodie must navigate her version of Hell and try to make peace with herself and her family. But someone or something doesn't want her on Skye, and she finds herself attacked —and this time not by her personal demons.

Scott Ryan has a mission: uncover who has been killing Druids and why. When his quest takes him to the beautiful Isle of Skye, he doesn't think anything could captivate him more than the land itself —until he lays eyes on the breathtaking and confident beauty his leader sent him to find. However, it's clear that she has trust issues, and he can't reveal his plans—at least, not yet. But he's always been sure of his ability to sway a person, and she's a challenge he's more than happy to accept, especially when he finds he will do anything to protect her.

With so much history and so many secrets, victory is anything but guaranteed for the couple and their allies. And the forces at work, those who wish to rule the Scottish isle and all those who reside there, have a plan that nobody will see coming.

~

Chapter One

She was back.

It was the last place she wanted to be but the only place she had to run to.

Elodie threw open the curtains. Dust danced in the air, the sunlight catching it. She stared out the dirty window to the sea beyond. Skye. The home she'd proclaimed she would never leave because she loved it so fiercely.

It was also the place she had sworn to never return to.

And yet, here she was.

"Bloody hell," she murmured as she turned her back to the window and looked over what remained of the furniture from her parents' cottage.

Her gaze slid to the hearth where echoes of children's laughter clung to the stones. Her mother had made the best hot cocoa. After playing for hours outside in the winter, Elodie, her elder sister, Edie, and her brother, Elias, would sit before the fire with steaming cups of cocoa and her grandmother's strawberry scones.

Elodie squeezed her eyes shut. She wanted to hold onto the lighthearted memories, but the other ones were always on their heels—the ones that had altered all their lives, throwing them into chaos.

She blew out a breath and focused on the clutter and mess before her. The dust was so thick that she knew she would end up with respiratory problems for days if she didn't take precautions. And it wasn't as if she could use magic to prevent it.

Returning to Skye was like walking through one of Dante's nine circles of Hell. Elodie didn't know how she would survive being back on the island. If only she'd had somewhere else to go. *Anywhere* else. If she still believed, she would think Skye had interfered and brought her back.

"If that's the case, then my magic wouldn't be gone, now would it?"

It was hard not to be bitter and angry about her life. She owned her decisions, but she had been on a different path. Then, everything had imploded with the force of a nuclear explosion.

When she looked around after, everyone just went about their lives as if her family hadn't been rocked to its core. As if she and her siblings hadn't had their blinders ripped off with such force that it'd changed all three of them in one heartbeat—their innocence gone in the blink of an eye.

Corann had tried to help, but the old Druid hadn't been able to reach any of them. And Elias had left. Elodie still hadn't forgiven him for leaving her and Edie to navigate the churning waters of their society. Elodie might have been the youngest, but she was the one who'd ended up taking care of Edie. Her sister had the kind, gentle spirit of their mother. Elodie had lashed out and turned to drinking and drugs, but Edie had gone into herself.

Elodie walked through the main area of the cottage and past the kitchen to the hallway. Pictures of their family still hung on the walls. Snapshots of a happy life that had hidden the rot beneath. She stopped at one where Edie smiled brightly with a cake and lit candles before her. Maybe Elodie hadn't been the one to take care of Edie. They had leaned on each other, clinging to one another and struggling to keep their heads above water. It was only because of her sister that Elodie hadn't sunk too deeply into the hard life.

She'd known she had to be there for Edie. And in the end, they'd kept each other afloat.

Until Elodie hadn't been able to stay another minute on Skye.

Fifteen years. It seemed like a lifetime, but it was much too soon to be back. Nothing would keep her on Skye longer than necessary this time. Not her sister. Nothing. Skye had annihilated her family. It had destroyed her. How Edie could remain on the isle was a mystery. And Elias? All Elodie could hope for was that her brother had found some semblance of happiness. They all deserved it.

Elodie forced herself to walk to each room, but she couldn't manage to go inside her parents'. She stood before the closed door as screams and shouts from that horrible day filled her head. Elodie backed away and turned on her heel. How in the world would she stay in the cottage? Sleep just feet from where it'd all happened.

"I can't," she stated with a shake of her head.

Elodie grabbed her purse and the single bag that held her measly belongings and started for the door. Then she remembered *why* she was on Skye.

"Fuck!" she yelled and fought the sudden urge to release the scream of frustration that welled up.

She wasn't a crier, but everyone had their breaking point. She forced the tears back and dropped her bags. The only way to get on with her life was to take her sister's offer. All Elodie had to do was clean up the cottage so they could sell it. It was a good deal. Elodie had the place to herself instead of sleeping on the sofa at Edie's crowded house with her sister's kids and husband. And all without having to pay any sort of rent.

Since Elodie was homeless and jobless and had less than two hundred pounds to her name, it really was a blessing. At least she'd thought that until she arrived on Skye. Even driving around the island had made her chest constrict. Her anxiety rose with every mile. Then she'd arrived at the cottage. It had taken Elodie half an hour to work up the courage to actually walk inside.

"Maybe I deserve this torture," she said aloud. "I didn't exactly live a good life."

This was supposed to be her chance to start over. To travel the path she'd been on before she got derailed.

"Fine. Let's do this."

She opened the door, then went to all the windows and opened them despite the frigid temperatures and the threat of rain. The dust had to go somewhere, and the sooner she got it out of the house, the better. Elodie started in the bedroom she had once shared with her sister. She carefully folded the bed linens from each twin bed and dumped them outside. Thankfully, Edie had given her fresh sheets, pillows, and blankets.

Next, she found an old towel and used some cleaner to wipe down the walls and window, sweeping the cobwebs from the corners before vacuuming the carpet. Only then did she bring in her bag and purse.

Elodie wiped her face with her arm and made her way to the main area. Someone had placed sheets over the furniture. She slowly and carefully folded them, but there was so much dust that some still escaped. The pile joined the bed linens outside. On her way back inside, she smiled as she saw the dust wafting out the windows. Hopefully, most of it would land outside instead of back in the house.

The smallish living area didn't take long to wipe down. The windows would take more than one cleaning. She didn't want to touch the outside yet. That was a whole other matter entirely. Her first priority was to get the inside clean enough that she could locate any repairs that needed to be addressed. Only after she did that would she tackle the outside.

The old cottage was too quiet. Elodie pulled out her phone and put on her favorite playlist as she went back to cleaning. She kept moving, which helped to keep her warm. There was a brief shower, but she didn't bother closing the windows. The house needed to be aired out to get rid of the musty smell. She suddenly froze, the hairs on the back of her neck lifting. Slowly, she straightened from scrubbing the bathroom counter and looked at the doorway. No one was there. At least no one she could see.

A chill raced down her spine. With the sponge still in her gloved hands, she walked into the hallway. She glanced at her parents' room, then looked the other way. Elodie slowly made her way to the kitchen. Her gaze landed on a tall, gorgeous man with black and silver hair, standing next to a pretty female with red hair.

The man was a Fae. It seemed there was no escaping them anywhere, but they hadn't been allowed on Skye in decades. At least as far as she knew. What was he doing back?

"Hi," the woman said.

Elodie swung her gaze to the female. She looked close to Elodie's age, and something about her seemed familiar.

"You don't remember me, do you?" the woman asked with a smile.

Elodie shook her head. It was unnerving that people already knew she was on the isle. Worse that they remembered her when she had done everything to forget Skye and everyone on it. "I don't."

"You've been gone awhile. I'm Rhona."

In an instant, Elodie remembered Rhona and her cousin, Sorcha. They used to come over occasionally. She had always liked both girls. Elodie glanced at the floor, slightly embarrassed for the harsh welcome she had given them. "Of course."

Rhona looked at the man beside her, love shining in her eyes. "This is Balladyn."

"A Fae," Elodie said before she could stop herself.

Balladyn inclined his head of long hair. His eyes were silver, but she saw a ring of red around them. "Reaper, actually." His voice had an Irish lilt.

Reaper. Elodie wasn't sure what that meant.

"We wanted to welcome you back and see if you needed anything," Rhona said.

Elodie shifted her feet nervously. Did they know she'd lost her magic? "That wasn't necessary."

"You're one of us," Rhona said with a soft look. "We look after our own."

Resentment threatened to choke Elodie, and she had to remind herself that she shouldn't direct her anger at Rhona. She hadn't been any older than Elodie back then. Corann was a different matter. "Corann sent you?"

A frown moved over Rhona's face so quickly that Elodie almost missed it. "We lost Corann. I've taken his place."

"Oh." Damn. She should've had Edie bring her up to date on things. Then again, Elodie hadn't wanted to talk to any Druids, so she had made sure not to take an interest in anything. "Honestly, I won't be here long. As soon as I get the place fixed up and sold, I'm leaving."

Rhona's green eyes narrowed slightly. "That's a pity. We could use you."

No one ever had use for her. Elodie glanced at Balladyn to see that the Reaper's gaze hadn't moved from her. It was unnerving to have him watch her in such a way, and yet she didn't feel threatened. "It's for the best."

"Why don't you come for tea later this week? We can catch up," Rhona said.

Elodie's plan to keep to herself was rapidly disintegrating. She liked Rhona—or at least the person she had once been. It wasn't in Elodie's nature to be outright rude, but Rhona would likely ask questions that Elodie wasn't prepared to answer. And she was tired of lying. "I'm no–"

"Please don't decline. Think it over." Rhona smiled. "Please."

Well, bugger it. "I'll consider it."

Rhona's smile was huge. "Great. And if you need any help, we can get this place together quickly."

The offer was so tempting that Elodie nearly took it. If they did, she could leave Skye that much quicker. However, if she agreed to Rhona's offer, it would inevitably lead to those pesky questions she was intent on dodging. "Thanks, but I've already made good headway today."

"At the very least, let me fix the leaking roof," Balladyn said.

Her gaze snapped to him. The roof was leaking? She glanced around but didn't hear any dripping. Then a drop landed on top of her head. This might be a bigger project than she'd thought. She faced him and forced her tight lips into a smile as her stomach churned with anxiety. "I would appreciate that."

"It's done," he said with a bow of his head.

"Thank you."

Rhona flashed another smile. "It's good to have you back. I hope you'll consider the tea."

Elodie held her smile until the two of them suddenly disappeared. She blinked and frowned. Balladyn must have teleported them out. At least the leak was fixed. She looked up at the ceiling and spotted the water damage.

"I'm going to be here forever," she grumbled.

~

Buy IRON EMBER now at
https://donnagrant.com/books/iron-ember/

GLIMPSE AT THE NEXT REAPERS BOOK

DARK ALPHA'S FURY, REAPERS SERIES, BOOK 16

Xaneth and Aisling's story is coming soon!

Buy DARK ALPHA'S FURY today at https://donnagrant.com/books/dark-alphas-fury/

ABOUT THE AUTHOR

New York Times and *USA Today* bestselling author Donna Grant has been praised for her "totally addictive" and "unique and sensual" stories. She's written more than one hundred novels spanning multiple genres of romance including the bestselling Dark King series that features a thrilling combination of Dragon Kings, Druids, Fae, and immortal Highlanders who are dark, dangerous, and irresistible. She lives in Texas with her dog and a cat.

www.DonnaGrant.com
www.MotherofDragonsBooks.com

facebook.com/AuthorDonnaGrant

instagram.com/dgauthor

bookbub.com/authors/donna-grant

amazon.com/Donna-Grant/e/B00279DJGE

pinterest.com/donnagrant1